CW01461137

SECRETS IN THE SNOW
& OTHER CHRISTMAS CRIME STORIES

More short stories available
from Macmillan Collector's Library

SECRETS IN THE SNOW

& OTHER CHRISTMAS CRIME STORIES

Selection and introduction by
MATTHEW BOOTH

MACMILLAN COLLECTOR'S LIBRARY

This collection first published 2025 by Macmillan Collector's Library
an imprint of Pan Macmillan
The Smithson, 6 Briset Street, London EC1M 5NR
EU representative: Macmillan Publishers Ireland Ltd,
1st Floor, The Liffey Trust Centre, 117–126 Sheriff Street Upper,
Dublin 1, DO1 YC43
Associated companies throughout the world
www.panmacmillan.com

ISBN 978-1-0350-5146-5

Selection copyright © Macmillan Publishers International Ltd. 2025
Introduction copyright © Matthew Booth 2025

The permissions acknowledgements on p. 327 constitute an extension of this copyright page.

1 3 5 7 9 8 6 4 2

A CIP catalogue record for this book is available from the British Library.

Endpaper pattern by Andrew Davidson
Typeset in Plantin by Jouve (UK), Milton Keynes
Printed and bound in China by Imago

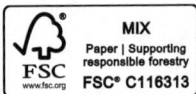

MIX
Paper | Supporting
responsible forestry
FSC
www.fsc.org
FSC® C116313

Visit **www.panmacmillan.com** to read more
about all our books and to buy them.

Contents

Introduction

MATTHEW BOOTH

There is something cosy about the image of a typical Christmas celebration: a family sitting round the dinner table, a decorated tree in the corner of the room with the selection of gifts underneath, and snow on the window pane. But dark deeds can intrude into these jovial settings, and in this collection of Christmas crime stories you will find brilliant examples of mysterious thefts, family secrets and baffling murders disrupting the customary festive cheer.

It is fitting that so many of the stories you are about to read take place in country houses. Christmas is a time for the family home and the country manor house is the archetypal location for a classic murder mystery: the guests are assembled in the library, the logs are burning in the fire, whilst elsewhere in the house a dead body lies waiting to be discovered. At this time of year, the murder mystery and its traditional domestic setting are perfectly in tune. If some of the stories do not take place within those twelve days sung about in the famous carol, it does not mean that they do not belong in a collection such as this. It is the overall impression of Christmas that matters: the long, dark evenings, a bitter chill in the air, and a white blanket of freshly fallen snow. We are concerned as much with mystery at midwinter as with crime at Christmas.

Snow is prominent in the opening story, 'The Adventure of the Beryl Coronet'. Arguably, no crime fiction anthology is truly complete without Sherlock Holmes. In this neat mystery, a lesser-known Holmes tale by Arthur Conan Doyle (1859–1930), the detective is on the trail of some missing gems, and Holmes is at his best: reading clues not only in people's characters and behaviour, but also in footprints in the heavy, midwinter snow.

Footprints in the snow also feature in 'Blind Man's Hood', but it is their absence which matters rather than their presence. How has a killer managed to commit murder in a locked house without leaving any footprints in the surrounding snow? Locked-room mysteries are a noted sub-genre of the detective story, and the master of them was John Dickson Carr (1906–1977), writing here under his pseudonym, Carter Dickson. It is not only a fine mystery, but something which touches on another genre of story popular at this time of year – the ghost story.

Edmund Crispin (1921–1978), creator of amateur

sleuth and Oxford don Gervase Fen, also liked to sprinkle his crime fiction with ghostly seasoning. In 'The Name on the Window', Crispin gives us a baffling murder and the suggestion that the scene of the crime is haunted. Fen is at his quirky best here, and the story highlights Crispin's talent for plotting and his natural flair for comedy, qualities which make reading his detective stories such a joy.

Ghostly possibilities also haunt 'The Mystery of the Felwyn Tunnel' by L. T. Meade (1844–1914) and Robert Eustace (1869–1943), which concerns a number of inexplicable deaths in a railway tunnel whose explanation may (or may not) be the work of some supernatural agency. There is an overtly supernatural element to 'The Ghost's Touch' by Fergus Hume (1859–1932), which is an entertaining mystery about family inheritance, with a Christmas ghost thrown in for flavour.

Ethel Lina White's 'Waxworks' might also suggest horror, with its story of a man who dies from fright and its titular connection with films such as *Mystery of the Wax Museum* (1933), starring Lionel Atwill, and Vincent Price's *House of Wax* (1953). However, the story is in fact one of suspense, and the skill with which White builds tension comes as no surprise, given that she also wrote the novel *The Wheel*

Spins, the inspiration for Hitchcock's classic movie *The Lady Vanishes* (1938).

Mistaken identity often surfaces in crime fiction, and this collection showcases this theme with 'The Chinese Apple', written by Marjorie Bowen (1885–1952) under her pen-name Joseph Shearing. It is a dark, suitably macabre Christmas story, involving not only characters who may not be who they claim, but also a cunning theft. It is neatly plotted and deeply atmospheric, with a chilling ending which will leave your spine frozen long after you have turned its final page.

False identities and disguises play a part in 'The Hole in the Wall' by the inimitable G. K. Chesterton (1874–1936), a story which sees murder at a Christmas fancy-dress party and in which a dark secret lying under a frozen pond in the grounds is uncovered. Secrets frozen under a winter's frost also feature in the excellent 'Secrets in the Snow' by J. Jefferson Farjeon (1883–1955), which concerns a young woman seeking shelter from the harsh winter snow, only to find herself on the trail of some missing jewellery.

We encounter more stolen gems in 'The Necklace of Pearls' by Dorothy L. Sayers (1893–1957), whose amateur sleuth, Lord Peter Wimsey, remains, like Holmes, one of the giants of detective fiction. Here, we see Wimsey at a Christmas party, the host of which gives his daughter a valuable necklace that's promptly pilfered. The story is whimsical (pun intended!), but its seasonal flavour is evident from its opening paragraph, and its solution relies entirely on a particular festive tradition. Not only that, when Wimsey reveals the solution, you'll kick yourself for not solving the mystery before he does.

But it is not all murder and mayhem. Every crime story has a dash of romance to it, and for us, it is courtesy of E. W. Hornung (1866–1921), who was not only Arthur Conan Doyle's brother-in-law, but also the creator of gentleman thief A. J. Raffles. In 'The Christmas Story', we find a struggling journalist finding love amongst a series of apparently criminal acts.

There is little more for me to say. So, I shall simply recommend that you take a seat by the fire, pour yourself a glass of something festive and embark on a trip down the dark, snow-covered streets of murder, mystery, intrigue and horror which these stories have to offer.

SECRETS IN THE SNOW
& OTHER CHRISTMAS CRIME STORIES

ARTHUR CONAN DOYLE

The Adventure of the Beryl Coronet

"Holmes," said I, as I stood one morning in our bow-window looking down the street, "here is a madman coming along. It seems rather sad that his relatives should allow him to come out alone."

My friend rose lazily from his arm-chair and stood with his hands in the pockets of his dressing-gown, looking over my shoulder. It was a bright, crisp February morning, and the snow of the day before still lay deep upon the ground, shimmering brightly in the wintry sun. Down the centre of Baker Street it had been ploughed into a brown crumbly band by the traffic, but at either side and on the heaped-up edges of the foot-paths it still lay as white as when it fell. The gray pavement had been cleaned and scraped, but was still dangerously slippery, so that there were fewer passengers than usual. Indeed, from the direction of the Metropolitan Station no one was coming save the single gentleman whose eccentric conduct had drawn my attention.

He was a man of about fifty, tall, portly, and imposing, with a massive, strongly marked face and a commanding figure. He was dressed in a sombre yet rich style, in black frock-coat, shining hat, neat brown gaiters, and well-cut pearl-gray trousers. Yet his actions were in absurd contrast to the dignity of his dress and features, for he was running hard, with occasional little springs, such as a weary man gives who is little accustomed to set any tax upon his legs. As he ran he jerked his hands up and down, waggled his head, and writhed his face into the most extraordinary contortions.

"What on earth can be the matter with him?" I asked. "He is looking up at the numbers of the houses."

"I believe that he is coming here," said Holmes, rubbing his hands.

"Here?"

"Yes; I rather think he is coming to consult me professionally. I think that I recognize the symptoms. Ha! did I not tell you?" As he spoke, the man, puffing and blowing, rushed at our door and pulled at our bell until the whole house resounded with the clanging.

A few moments later he was in our room, still puffing, still gesticulating, but with so fixed a look of grief and despair in his eyes that our smiles were turned in an instant to horror and pity. For a while he could not get his words out, but swayed his body and plucked at his hair like one who has been driven to the extreme limits of his reason. Then, suddenly springing to his feet, he beat his head against the wall with such force that we both rushed upon him and tore him away to the centre of the room. Sherlock Holmes pushed him down into the easy-chair, and, sitting beside him, patted his hand, and chatted with him in the easy, soothing tones which he knew so well how to employ.

"You have come to me to tell your story, have you not?" said he. "You are fatigued with your haste. Pray wait until you have recovered yourself, and then I shall be most happy to look into any little problem which you may submit to me."

The man sat for a minute or more with a heaving chest, fighting against his emotion. Then he passed his handkerchief over his brow, set his lips tight, and turned his face towards us.

"No doubt you think me mad?" said he.

"I see that you have had some great trouble," responded Holmes.

"God knows I have !—a trouble which is enough to unseat my reason, so sudden and so terrible is it. Public disgrace I might have faced, although I am a man whose character has never yet borne a stain. Private affliction also is the lot of every man; but the two coming together, and in so frightful a form, have been enough to shake my very soul. Besides, it is not I alone. The very noblest in the land may suffer, unless some way be found out of this horrible affair."

"Pray compose yourself, sir," said Holmes, "and let me have a clear account of who you are, and what it is that has befallen you."

"My name," answered our visitor, "is probably familiar to your ears. I am Alexander Holder, of the banking firm of Holder & Stevenson, of Threadneedle Street."

The name was indeed well known to us as belonging to the senior partner in the second largest private banking concern in the City of London. What could have happened, then, to bring one of the foremost citizens of London to this most pitiable pass? We waited, all curiosity, until with another effort he braced himself to tell his story.

"I feel that time is of value," said he; "that is why I hastened here when the police inspector suggested that I should secure your co-operation. I came to Baker Street by the Underground, and hurried from there on foot, for the cabs go slowly through this snow. That is why I was so out of breath, for I am a man who takes very little exercise. I feel better now, and I will put the facts before you as shortly and yet as clearly as I can.

"It is, of course, well known to you that in a successful banking business as much depends upon our being able to find remunerative investments for our funds as upon our increasing our connection and the number of our depositors. One of our most lucrative means of laying out money is in the shape of loans, where the security is unimpeachable. We have done a good deal in this direction during the last few years, and there are many noble families to whom we have advanced large sums upon the security of their pictures, libraries, or plate.

"Yesterday morning I was seated in my office at the bank when a card was brought in to me by one of the clerks. I started when I saw the name, for it was that of none other than—well, perhaps even to you I had better say no more than that it was a name which is a household word all over the earth—one of the highest, noblest, most exalted names in England. I was overwhelmed by the honor, and attempted, when he entered, to say so, but he plunged at once into business with the air of a man who wishes to hurry quickly through a disagreeable task.

"'Mr. Holder,' said he, 'I have been informed that you are in the habit of advancing money.'

"'The firm do so when the security is good,' I answered.

"'It is absolutely essential to me,' said he, 'that

5

I should have £ 50,000 at once. I could of course borrow so trifling a sum ten times over from my friends, but I much prefer to make it a matter of business, and to carry out that business myself. In my position you can readily understand that it is unwise to place one's self under obligations.'

"'For how long, may I ask, do you want this sum?' I asked.

"'Next Monday I have a large sum due to me, and I shall then most certainly repay what you advance, with whatever interest you think it right to charge. But it is very essential to me that the money should be paid at once.'

"'I should be happy to advance it without further parley from my own private purse,' said I, 'were it not that the strain would be rather more than it could bear. If, on the other hand, I am to do it in the name of the firm, then in justice to my partner I must insist that, even in your case, every business-like precaution should be taken.'

"'I should much prefer to have it so,' said he, raising up a square, black morocco case which he had laid beside his chair. 'You have doubtless heard of the Beryl Coronet?'

"'One of the most precious public possessions of the empire,' said I.

"'Precisely.' He opened the case, and there,

imbedded in soft, flesh-colored velvet, lay the magnificent piece of jewelry which he had named. 'There are thirty-nine enormous beryls,' said he, 'and the price of the gold chasing is incalculable. The lowest estimate would put the worth of the coronet at double the sum which I have asked. I am prepared to leave it with you as my security.'

"I took the precious case into my hands and looked in some perplexity from it to my illustrious client.

"'You doubt its value?' he asked.

"'Not at all. I only doubt—'

"'The propriety of my leaving it. You may set your mind at rest about that. I should not dream of doing so were it not absolutely certain that I should be able in four days to reclaim it. It is a pure matter of form. Is the security sufficient?'

"'Ample.'

"'You understand, Mr. Holder, that I am giving you a strong proof of the confidence which I have in you, founded upon all that I have heard of you. I rely upon you not only to be discreet and to refrain from all gossip upon the matter, but, above all, to preserve this coronet with every possible precaution, because I need not say that a great public scandal would be caused if any harm were to befall it. Any injury to it would be almost as serious as its complete loss, for there are no beryls in the world to match these, and it would be impossible to replace them. I leave it with you, however, with every confidence, and I shall call for it in person on Monday morning.'

"Seeing that my client was anxious to leave, I said no more; but, calling for my cashier, I ordered him to pay over fifty £ 1000 notes. When I was alone once more, however, with the precious case lying upon the table in front of me, I could not but think with some misgivings of the immense responsibility which it entailed upon me. There could be no doubt that, as it was a national possession, a horrible scandal would ensue if any misfortune should occur to it. I already regretted having ever consented to take charge of it. However, it was too late to alter the matter now, so I locked it up in my private safe, and turned once more to my work.

"When evening came I felt that it would be an imprudence to leave so precious a thing in the office behind me. Bankers' safes had been forced before now, and why should not mine be? If so, how terrible would be the position in which I should find myself! I determined, therefore, that for the next few days I would always carry the case backward and forward with me, so that it might never be really out of my reach. With this intention, I called a cab, and drove out to my house at Streatham, carrying the jewel with me. I did not breathe freely until I had taken it up-stairs and locked it in the bureau of my dressing-room.

"And now a word as to my household, Mr. Holmes, for I wish you to thoroughly understand the situation. My groom and my page sleep out of the house, and may be set aside altogether. I have three maid-servants who have been with me a number of years, and whose absolute reliability is quite above suspicion. Another, Lucy Parr, the second waiting-maid, has only been in my service a few months. She came with an excellent character, however, and has always given me satisfaction. She is a very pretty girl, and has attracted admirers who have occasionally hung about the place. That is the only drawback which we have found to her, but we believe her to be a thoroughly good girl in every way.

"So much for the servants. My family itself is so small that it will not take me long to describe it. I am a widower, and have an only son, Arthur. He has been a disappointment to me, Mr. Holmes—a grievous disappointment. I have no doubt that I am myself to blame. People tell me that I have spoiled him. Very likely I have. When my dear wife died I felt that he was all I had to love. I could not bear to see the smile fade even for a moment from his face. I have never denied him a wish. Perhaps it would have been better for both of us had I been sterner, but I meant it for the best.

"It was naturally my intention that he should succeed me in my business, but he was not of a business turn. He was wild, wayward, and, to speak the truth, I could not trust him in the handling of large sums of money. When he was young he became a member of an aristocratic club, and there, having charming manners, he was soon the intimate of a number of men with long purses and expensive habits. He learned to play heavily at cards and to squander money on the turf, until he had again and again to come to me and implore me to give him an advance upon his allowance, that he might settle his debts of honor. He tried more than once to break away from the dangerous company which he was keeping, but each time the influence of his friend Sir George Burnwell was enough to draw him back again.

"And, indeed, I could not wonder that such a man as Sir George Burnwell should gain an influence over him, for he has frequently brought him to my house, and I have found myself that I could hardly resist the fascination of his manner. He is older than Arthur, a man of the world to his fingertips, one who had been everywhere, seen everything, a brilliant talker, and a man of great personal beauty.

Yet when I think of him in cold blood, far away from the glamour of his presence, I am convinced from his cynical speech, and the look which I have caught in his eyes, that he is one who should be deeply distrusted. So I think, and so, too, thinks my little Mary, who has a woman's quick insight into character.

"And now there is only she to be described. She is my niece; but when my brother died five years ago and left her alone in the world I adopted her, and have looked upon her ever since as my daughter. She is a sunbeam in my house—sweet, loving, beautiful, a wonderful manager and housekeeper, yet as tender and quiet and gentle as a woman could be. She is my right hand. I do not know what I could do without her. In only one matter has she ever gone against my wishes. Twice my boy has asked her to marry him, for he loves her devotedly, but each time she has refused him. I think that if any one could have drawn him into the right path it would have been she, and that his marriage might have changed his whole life; but now, alas! it is too late—for ever too late!

"Now, Mr. Holmes, you know the people who live under my roof, and I shall continue with my miserable story.

"When we were taking coffee in the drawing-room

that night, after dinner, I told Arthur and Mary my experience and of the precious treasure which we had under our roof, suppressing only the name of my client. Lucy Parr, who had brought in the coffee, had, I am sure, left the room; but I cannot swear that the door was closed. Mary and Arthur were much interested, and wished to see the famous coronet, but I thought it better not to disturb it.

"'Where have you put it?' asked Arthur.

"'In my own bureau.'

"'Well, I hope to goodness the house won't be burgled during the night,' said he.

"'It is locked up,' I answered.

"'Oh, any old key will fit that bureau. When I was a youngster I have opened it myself with the key of the box-room cupboard.'

"He often had a wild way of talking, so that I thought little of what he said. He followed me to my room, however, that night with a very grave face.

"'Look here, dad,' said he, with his eyes cast down, 'can you let me have £200?'

"'No, I cannot!' I answered, sharply. 'I have been far too generous with you in money matters.'

"'You have been very kind,' said he: 'but I must have this money, or else I can never show my face inside the club again.'

"'And a very good thing, too!' I cried.

12

"'Yes, but you would not have me leave it a dishonored man,' said he. 'I could not bear the disgrace. I must raise the money in some way, and if you will not let me have it, then I must try other means.'

"I was very angry, for this was the third demand during the month. 'You shall not have a farthing from me,' I cried on which he bowed and left the room without another word.

"When he was gone I unlocked my bureau, made sure that my treasure was safe, and locked it again. Then I started to go round the house to see that all was secure—a duty which I usually leave to Mary, but which I thought it well to perform myself that night. As I came down the stairs I saw Mary herself at the side window of the hall, which she closed and fastened as I approached.

"'Tell me, dad,' said she, looking, I thought, a little disturbed, 'did you give Lucy, the maid, leave to go out to-night?'

"'Certainly not.'

"'She came in just now by the back door. I have no doubt that she has only been to the side gate to see some one; but I think that it is hardly safe, and should be stopped.'

"'You must speak to her in the morning, or I will, if you prefer it. Are you sure that everything is fastened?'

"'Quite sure, dad.'

"'Then, good-night.' I kissed her, and went up to my bedroom again, where I was soon asleep.

"I am endeavoring to tell you everything, Mr. Holmes, which may have any bearing upon the case, but I beg that you will question me upon any point which I do not make clear."

"On the contrary, your statement is singularly lucid."

"I come to a part of my story now in which I should wish to be particularly so. I am not a very heavy sleeper, and the anxiety in my mind tended, no doubt, to make me even less so than usual. About two in the morning, then, I was awakened by some sound in the house. It had ceased ere I was wide awake, but it had left an impression behind it as though a window had gently closed somewhere. I lay listening with all my ears. Suddenly, to my horror, there was a distinct sound of footsteps moving softly in the next room. I slipped out of bed, all palpitating with fear, and peeped round the corner of my dressing-room door.

"'Arthur!' I screamed, 'you villain! you thief! How dare you touch that coronet?'

"The gas was half up, as I had left it, and my unhappy boy, dressed only in his shirt and trousers, was standing beside the light, holding the coronet

14

in his hands. He appeared to be wrenching at it, or bending it with all his strength. At my cry he dropped it from his grasp, and turned as pale as death. I snatched it up and examined it. One of the gold corners, with three of the beryls in it, was missing.

"'You blackguard!' I shouted, beside myself with rage. 'You have destroyed it! You have dishonored me for ever! Where are the jewels which you have stolen?'

"'Stolen!' he cried.

"'Yes, you thief!' I roared, shaking him by the shoulder.

"'There are none missing. There cannot be any missing,' said he.

"'There are three missing. And you know where they are. Must I call you a liar as well as a thief? Did I not see you trying to tear off another piece?'

"'You have called me names enough,' said he; 'I will not stand it any longer. I shall not say another word about this business since you have chosen to insult me. I will leave your house in the morning and make my own way in the world.'

"'You shall leave it in the hands of the police!' I cried, half-mad with grief and rage. 'I shall have this matter probed to the bottom.'

"'You shall learn nothing from me,' said he, with

a passion such as I should not have thought was in his nature. 'If you choose to call the police, let the police find what they can.'

"By this time the whole house was astir, for I had raised my voice in my anger. Mary was the first to rush into my room, and, at the sight of the coronet and of Arthur's face, she read the whole story, and, with a scream, fell down senseless on the ground. I sent the house-maid for the police, and put the investigation into their hands at once. When the inspector and a constable entered the house, Arthur, who had stood sullenly with his arms folded, asked me whether it was my intention to charge him with theft. I answered that it had ceased to be a private matter, but had become a public one, since the ruined coronet was national property. I was determined that the law should have its way in everything.

"'At least,' said he, 'you will not have me arrested at once. It would be to your advantage as well as mine if I might leave the house for five minutes.'

"'That you may get away, or perhaps that you may conceal what you have stolen,' said I. And then realizing the dreadful position in which I was placed, I implored him to remember that not only my honor, but that of one who was far greater than I was at stake; and that he threatened to raise a scandal which would convulse the nation. He might avert it all if he would but tell me what he had done with the three missing stones.

"'You may as well face the matter,' said I; 'you have been caught in the act, and no confession could make your guilt more heinous. If you but make such reparation as is in your power, by telling us where the beryls are, all shall be forgiven and forgotten.'

"'Keep your forgiveness for those who ask for it,' he answered, turning away from me, with a sneer. I saw that he was too hardened for any words of mine to influence him. There was but one way for it. I called in the inspector, and gave him into custody. A search was made at once, not only of his person, but of his room, and of every portion of the house where he could possibly have concealed the gems; but no trace of them could be found, nor would the wretched boy open his mouth for all our persuasions and our threats. This morning he was removed to a cell, and I, after going through all the police formalities, have hurried round to you, to implore you to use your skill in unravelling the matter. The police have openly confessed that they can at present make nothing of it. You may go to any expense which you think necessary. I have already offered a reward of £ 1000. My God, what shall I do! I have lost my honor, my gems, and my son in one night. Oh, what shall I do!"

He put a hand on either side of his head, and rocked himself to and fro, droning to himself like a child whose grief has got beyond words.

Sherlock Holmes sat silent for some few minutes, with his brows knitted and his eyes fixed upon the fire.

"Do you receive much company?" he asked.

"None, save my partner with his family, and an occasional friend of Arthur's. Sir George Burnwell has been several times lately. No one else, I think."

"Do you go out much in society?"

"Arthur does. Mary and I stay at home. We neither of us care for it."

"That is unusual in a young girl."

"She is of a quiet nature. Besides, she is not so very young. She is four-and-twenty."

"This matter, from what you say, seems to have been a shock to her also."

"Terrible! She is even more affected than I."

"You have neither of you any doubt as to your son's guilt?"

"How can we have, when I saw him with my own eyes with the coronet in his hands."

"I hardly consider that a conclusive proof. Was the remainder of the coronet at all injured?"

"Yes, it was twisted."

"Do you not think, then, that he might have been trying to straighten it?"

"God bless you! You are doing what you can for him and for me. But it is too heavy a task. What was he doing there at all? If his purpose were innocent, why did he not say so?"

"Precisely. And if it were guilty, why did he not invent a lie? His silence appears to me to cut both ways. There are several singular points about the case. What did the police think of the noise which awoke you from your sleep?"

"They considered that it might be caused by Arthur's closing his bedroom door."

"A likely story! As if a man bent on felony would slam his door so as to wake a household. What did they say, then, of the disappearance of these gems?"

"They are still sounding the planking and probing the furniture in the hope of finding them."

"Have they thought of looking outside the house?"

"Yes, they have shown extraordinary energy. The whole garden has already been minutely examined."

"Now, my dear sir." said Holmes, "is it not obvious to you now that this matter really strikes very much deeper than either you or the police were at first inclined to think? It appeared to you to be a simple case; to me it seems exceedingly complex. Consider what is involved by your theory. You suppose that your son came down from his bed, went, at great risk, to your dressing-room, opened your bureau, took out your coronet, broke off by main force a small portion of it, went off to some other place, concealed three gems out of the thirty-nine, with such skill that nobody can find them, and then returned with the other thirty-six into the room in which he exposed himself to the greatest danger of being discovered. I ask you now, is such a theory tenable?"

"But what other is there?" cried the banker, with a gesture of despair. "If his motives were innocent, why does he not explain them?"

"It is our task to find that out," replied Holmes; "so now, if you please, Mr. Holder, we will set off for Streatham together, and devote an hour to glancing a little more closely into details."

My friend insisted upon my accompanying them in their expedition, which I was eager enough to do, for my curiosity and sympathy were deeply stirred by the story to which we had listened. I confess that the guilt of the banker's son appeared to me to be as obvious as it did to his unhappy father, but still I had such faith in Holmes's judgment that I felt that there must be some grounds for hope as long as he was dissatisfied with the accepted explanation. He hardly spoke a word the whole way out to the southern suburb, but sat with his chin upon his breast and his hat drawn over his eyes, sunk in the deepest thought. Our client appeared to have taken fresh heart at the little glimpse of hope which had been presented to him, and he even broke into a desultory chat with me over his business affairs. A short railway journey and a shorter walk brought us to Fairbank, the modest residence of the great financier.

Fairbank was a good-sized square house of white stone standing back a little from the road. A double carriage-sweep with a snow-clad lawn, stretched down in front to two large iron gates which closed the entrance. On the right side was a small wooden thicket, which led into a narrow path between two neat hedges stretching from the road to the kitchen door, and forming the tradesmen's entrance. On the left ran a lane which led to the stables, and was not itself within the grounds at all, being a public, though little used, thoroughfare. Holmes left us standing at the door, and walked slowly all round the house, across the front, down the tradesmen's path, and so round by the garden behind into the stable lane. So long was he that Mr. Holder and I went into the dining-room and waited by the fire until he should return. We were sitting there in silence when the door opened and a young lady came in. She was rather above the middle height, slim, with dark hair and eyes, which seemed the darker against the absolute pallor of her skin. I do not think that I have ever seen such deadly paleness in a woman's face. Her lips, too, were bloodless, but her eyes were flushed with crying. As she swept silently into the room she impressed me with a greater sense of grief than the banker had done in the morning, and it was the more striking in her as she was evidently a woman of strong character, with immense capacity for self-restraint. Disregarding my presence, she went straight to her uncle, and passed her hand over his head with a sweet womanly caress.

"You have given orders that Arthur should be liberated, have you not, dad?" she asked.

"No, no, my girl, the matter must be probed to the bottom."

"But I am so sure that he is innocent. You know what women's instincts are. I know that he has done no harm and that you will be sorry for having acted so harshly."

"Why is he silent, then, if he is innocent?"

"Who knows? Perhaps because he was so angry that you should suspect him."

"How could I help suspecting him, when I actually saw him with the coronet in his hand?"

"Oh, but he had only picked it up to look at it. Oh do, do take my word for it that he is innocent. Let the matter drop and say no more. It is so dreadful to think of our dear Arthur in prison!"

"I shall never let it drop until the gems are found—never, Mary! Your affection for Arthur blinds you as to the awful consequences to me. Far from hushing the thing up, I have brought a gentleman down from London to inquire more deeply into it."

"This gentleman?" she asked, facing round to me.

"No, his friend. He wished us to leave him alone. He is round in the stable lane now."

"The stable lane?" She raised her dark eyebrows. "What can he hope to find there? Ah! this, I suppose, is he. I trust, sir, that you will succeed in proving, what I feel sure is the truth, that my cousin Arthur is innocent of this crime."

"I fully share your opinion, and I trust, with you, that we may prove it," returned Holmes, going back to the mat to knock the snow from his shoes. "I believe I have the honor of addressing Miss Mary Holder. Might I ask you a question or two?"

"Pray do, sir, if it may help to clear this horrible affair up."

"You heard nothing yourself last night?"

"Nothing, until my uncle here began to speak loudly. I heard that, and I came down."

"You shut up the windows and doors the night before. Did you fasten all the windows?"

"Yes."

"Were they all fastened this morning?"

"Yes."

"You have a maid who has a sweetheart? I think that you remarked to your uncle last night that she had been out to see him?"

"Yes, and she was the girl who waited in the drawing-room, and who may have heard uncle's remarks about the coronet."

"I see. You infer that she may have gone out to tell her sweetheart, and that the two may have planned the robbery."

"But what is the good of all these vague theories," cried the banker, impatiently, "when I have told you that I saw Arthur with the coronet in his hands?"

"Wait a little, Mr. Holder. We must come back to that. About this girl, Miss Holder. You saw her return by the kitchen door, I presume?"

"Yes; when I went to see if the door was fastened for the night I met her slipping in. I saw the man, too, in the gloom."

"Do you know him?"

24

"Oh yes; he is the green-grocer who brings our vegetables round. His name is Francis Prosper."

"He stood," said Holmes, "to the left of the door—that is to say, farther up the path than is necessary to reach the door?"

"Yes, he did."

"And he is a man with a wooden leg?"

Something like fear sprang up in the young lady's expressive black eyes. "Why, you are like a magician," said she. "How do you know that?" She smiled, but there was no answering smile in Holmes's thin, eager face.

"I should be very glad now to go up-stairs," said he. "I shall probably wish to go over the outside of the house again. Perhaps I had better take a look at the lower windows before I go up."

He walked swiftly round from one to the other, pausing only at the large one which looked from the hall onto the stable lane. This he opened, and made a very careful examination of the sill with his powerful magnifying lens. "Now we shall go up-stairs," said he, at last.

The banker's dressing-room was a plainly furnished little chamber, with a gray carpet, a large bureau, and a long mirror. Holmes went to the bureau first and looked hard at the lock.

"Which key was used to open it?" he asked.

"That which my son himself indicated—that of the cupboard of the lumber-room."

"Have you it here?"

"That is it on the dressing-table."

Sherlock Holmes took it up and opened the bureau.

"It is a noiseless lock," said he. "It is no wonder that it did not wake you. This case, I presume, contains the coronet. We must have a look at it." He opened the case, and, taking out the diadem, he laid it upon the table. It was a magnificent specimen of the jeweller's art, and the thirty-six stones were the finest that I have ever seen. At one side of the coronet was a cracked edge, where a corner holding three gems had been torn away.

"Now, Mr. Holder," said Holmes, "here is the corner which corresponds to that which has been so unfortunately lost. Might I beg that you will break it off."

The banker recoiled in horror. "I should not dream of trying," said he.

"Then I will." Holmes suddenly bent his strength upon it, but without result. "I feel it give a little," said he; "but, though I am exceptionally strong in the fingers, it would take me all my time to break it. An ordinary man could not do it. Now, what do you think would happen if I did break it, Mr. Holder?

26

There would be a noise like a pistol shot. Do you tell me that all this happened within a few yards of your bed, and that you heard nothing of it?"

"I do not know what to think. It is all dark to me."

"But perhaps it may grow lighter as we go. What do you think, Miss Holder?"

"I confess that I still share my uncle's perplexity."

"Your son had no shoes or slippers on when you saw him?"

"He had nothing on save only his trousers and shirt."

"Thank you. We have certainly been favored with extraordinary luck during this inquiry, and it will be entirely our own fault if we do not succeed in clearing the matter up. With your permission, Mr. Holder, I shall now continue my investigations outside."

He went alone, at his own request, for he explained that any unnecessary footmarks might make his task more difficult. For an hour or more he was at work, returning at last with his feet heavy with snow and his features as inscrutable as ever.

"I think that I have seen now all that there is to see, Mr. Holder," said he; "I can serve you best by returning to my rooms."

"But the gems, Mr. Holmes. Where are they?"

"I cannot tell."

The banker wrung his hands. "I shall never see them again!" he cried. "And my son? You give me hopes?"

"My opinion is in no way altered."

"Then, for God's sake, what was this dark business which was acted in my house last night?"

"If you can call upon me at my Baker Street rooms tomorrow morning between nine and ten I shall be happy to do what I can to make it clearer. I understand that you give me *carte blanche* to act for you, provided only that I get back the gems, and that you place no limit on the sum I may draw."

"I would give my fortune to have them back."

"Very good. I shall look into the matter between this and then. Good-bye; it is just possible that I may have to come over here again before evening."

It was obvious to me that my companion's mind was now made up about the case, although what his conclusions were was more than I could even dimly imagine. Several times during our homeward journey I endeavored to sound him upon the point, but he always glided away to some other topic, until at last I gave it over in despair. It was not yet three when we found ourselves in our room once more. He hurried to his chamber, and was down again in a few minutes dressed as a common loafer. With his collar turned up, his shiny, seedy coat, his red cravat, and his worn boots, he was a perfect sample of the class.

"I think that this should do," said he, glancing into the glass above the fireplace. "I only wish that you could come with me, Watson, but I fear that it won't do. I may be on the trail in this matter, or I may be following a will-of-the-wisp, but I shall soon know which it is. I hope that I may be back in a few hours." He cut a slice of beef from the joint upon the sideboard, sandwiched it between two rounds of bread, and, thrusting this rude meal into his pocket, he started off upon his expedition.

I had just finished my tea when he returned, evidently in excellent spirits, swinging an old elastic-sided boot in his hand. He chucked it down into a corner and helped himself to a cup of tea.

"I only looked in as I passed," said he. "I am going right on."

"Where to?"

"Oh, to the other side of the West End. It may be some time before I get back. Don't wait up for me in case I should be late."

"How are you getting on?"

"Oh, so so. Nothing to complain of. I have been out to Streatham since I saw you last, but I did not call at the house. It is a very sweet little problem, and I would not have missed it for a good deal.

29

However, I must not sit gossiping here, but must get these disreputable clothes off and return to my highly respectable self."

I could see by his manner that he had stronger reasons for satisfaction than his words alone would imply. His eyes twinkled, and there was even a touch of color upon his sallow cheeks. He hastened upstairs, and a few minutes later I heard the slam of the hall door, which told me that he was off once more upon his congenial hunt.

I waited until midnight, but there was no sign of his return, so I retired to my room. It was no uncommon thing for him to be away for days and nights on end when he was hot upon a scent, so that his lateness caused me no surprise. I do not know at what hour he came in, but when I came down to breakfast in the morning, there he was with a cup of coffee in one hand and the paper in the other, as fresh and trim as possible.

"You will excuse my beginning without you, Watson," said he; "but you remember that our client has rather an early appointment this morning."

"Why, it is after nine now," I answered. "I should not be surprised if that were he. I thought I heard a ring."

It was, indeed, our friend the financier. I was shocked by the change which had come over him, for his face, which was naturally of a broad and massive mould, was now pinched and fallen in, while his hair seemed to me at least a shade whiter. He entered with a weariness and lethargy which was even more painful than his violence of the morning before, and he dropped heavily into the arm-chair which I pushed forward for him.

"I do not know what I have done to be so severely tried," said he. "Only two days ago I was a happy and prosperous man, without a care in the world. Now I am left to a lonely and dishonored age. One sorrow comes close upon the heels of another. My niece, Mary, has deserted me."

"Deserted you?"

"Yes. Her bed this morning had not been slept in, her room was empty, and a note for me lay upon the hall table. I had said to her last night, in sorrow and not in anger, that if she had married my boy all might have been well with him. Perhaps it was thoughtless of me to say so. It is to that remark that she refers in this note:

"'MY DEAREST UNCLE,—I feel that I have brought trouble upon you, and that if I had acted differently this terrible misfortune might never have occurred. I cannot, with this thought in my mind, ever again be happy under your roof,

31

and I feel that I must leave you for ever. Do not worry about my future, for that is provided for; and, above all, do not search for me, for it will be fruitless labor and an ill-service to me. In life or in death, I am ever your loving

MARY.'

"What could she mean by that note, Mr. Holmes? Do you think it points to suicide?"

"No, no, nothing of the kind. It is perhaps the best possible solution. I trust, Mr. Holder, that you are nearing the end of your troubles."

"Ha! You say so! You have heard something, Mr. Holmes; you have learned something! Where are the gems?"

"You would not think £1000 apiece an excessive sum for them?"

"I would pay ten."

"That would be unnecessary. Three thousand will cover the matter. And there is a little reward, I fancy. Have you your check-book? Here is a pen. Better make it out for £4000 pounds."

With a dazed face the banker made out the required check. Holmes walked over to his desk, took out a little triangular piece of gold with three gems in it, and threw it down upon the table.

With a shriek of joy our client clutched it up.

"You have it!" he gasped. "I am saved! I am saved!"

The reaction of joy was as passionate as his grief had been, and he hugged his recovered gems to his bosom.

"There is one other thing you owe, Mr. Holder," said Sherlock Holmes, rather sternly.

"Owe!" He caught up a pen. "Name the sum, and I will pay it."

"No, the debt is not to me. You owe a very humble apology to that noble lad, your son, who has carried himself in this matter as I should be proud to see my own son do, should I ever chance to have one."

"Then it was not Arthur who took them?"

"I told you yesterday, and I repeat to-day, that it was not."

"You are sure of it! Then let us hurry to him at once, to let him know that the truth is known."

"He knows it already. When I had cleared it all up I had an interview with him, and, finding that he would not tell me the story, I told it to him, on which he had to confess that I was right, and to add the very few details which were not yet quite clear to me. Your news of this morning, however, may open his lips."

"For Heaven's sake, tell me, then, what is this extraordinary mystery!"

"I will do so, and I will show you the steps by which I reached it. And let me say to you, first, that which it is hardest for me to say and for you to hear: there has been an understanding between Sir George Burnwell and your niece Mary. They have now fled together."

"My Mary? Impossible!"

"It is, unfortunately, more than possible; it is certain. Neither you nor your son knew the true character of this man when you admitted him into your family circle. He is one of the most dangerous men in England—a ruined gambler, an absolutely desperate villain, a man without heart or conscience. Your niece knew nothing of such men. When he breathed his vows to her, as he had done to a hundred before her, she flattered herself that she alone had touched his heart. The devil knows best what he said, but at least she became his tool, and was in the habit of seeing him nearly every evening."

"I cannot, and I will not, believe it!" cried the banker, with an ashen face.

"I will tell you, then, what occurred in your house last night. Your niece, when you had, as she thought, gone to your room, slipped down and talked to her lover through the window which leads into the stable lane. His footmarks had pressed right through the snow, so long had he stood there. She told him of the coronet. His wicked lust for gold kindled at the news, and he bent her to his will. I have no doubt that she loved you, but there are women in whom the love of a lover extinguishes all other loves, and I think that she must have been one. She had hardly listened to his instructions when she saw you coming down-stairs, on which she closed the window rapidly, and told you about one of the servants' escapade with her wooden-legged lover, which was all perfectly true.

"Your boy, Arthur, went to bed after his interview with you, but he slept badly on account of his uneasiness about his club debts. In the middle of the night he heard a soft tread pass his door, so he rose, and looking out, was surprised to see his cousin walking very stealthily along the passage, until she disappeared into your dressing-room. Petrified with astonishment, the lad slipped on some clothes, and waited there in the dark to see what would come of this strange affair. Presently she emerged from the room again, and in the light of the passage-lamp your son saw that she carried the precious coronet in her hands. She passed down the stairs, and he, thrilling with horror, ran along and slipped behind the curtain near your door, whence he could see what passed in the hall beneath. He saw her stealthily open the window, hand out the coronet to some one in the gloom, and then closing it once more hurry back to her room, passing quite close to where he stood hid behind the curtain.

"As long as she was on the scene he could not take any action without a horrible exposure of the woman whom he loved. But the instant that she was gone he realized how crushing a misfortune this would be for you, and how all-important it was to set it right. He rushed down, just as he was, in his bare feet, opened the window, sprang out into the snow, and ran down the lane, where he could see a dark figure in the moonlight. Sir George Burnwell tried to get away, but Arthur caught him, and there was a struggle between them, your lad tugging at one side of the coronet, and his opponent at the other. In the scuffle, your son struck Sir George, and cut him over the eye. Then something suddenly snapped, and your son, finding that he had the coronet in his hands, rushed back, closed the window, ascended to your room, and had just observed that the coronet had been twisted in the struggle, and was endeavoring to straighten it when you appeared upon the scene."

"Is it possible?" gasped the banker.

"You then roused his anger by calling him names

at a moment when he felt that he had deserved your warmest thanks. He could not explain the true state of affairs without betraying one who certainly deserved little enough consideration at his hands. He took the more chivalrous view, however, and preserved her secret."

"And that was why she shrieked and fainted when she saw the coronet," cried Mr. Holder. "Oh, my God! What a blind fool I have been! And his asking to be allowed to go out for five minutes! The dear fellow wanted to see if the missing piece were at the scene of the struggle. How cruelly I have misjudged him!"

"When I arrived at the house," continued Holmes, "I at once went very carefully round it to observe if there were any traces in the snow which might help me. I knew that none had fallen since the evening before, and also that there had been a strong frost to preserve impressions. I passed along the tradesmen's path, but found it all trampled down and indistinguishable. Just beyond it, however, at the far side of the kitchen door, a woman had stood and talked with a man, whose round impressions on one side showed that he had a wooden leg. I could even tell that they had been disturbed, for the woman had run back swiftly to the door, as was shown by the deep toe and light heel marks, while Wooden-leg had waited a little, and then had gone away. I thought at the time that this might be the maid and her sweetheart, of whom you had already spoken to me, and inquiry showed it was so. I passed round the garden without seeing anything more than random tracks, which I took to be the police; but when I got into the stable lane a very long and complex story was written in the snow in front of me.

"There was a double line of tracks of a booted man, and a second double line which I saw with delight belonged to a man with naked feet. I was at once convinced from what you had told me that the latter was your son. The first had walked both ways, but the other had run swiftly, and, as his tread was marked in places over the depression of the boot, it was obvious that he had passed after the other. I followed them up, and found that they led to the hall window, where Boots had worn all the snow away while waiting. Then I walked to the other end, which was a hundred yards or more down the lane. I saw where Boots had faced round, where the snow was cut up as though there had been a struggle, and, finally, where a few drops of blood had fallen, to show me that I was not mistaken. Boots had then run down the lane, and another little smudge of blood showed that it was he who had been hurt. When he came to the high-road at the other end, I found that the pavement had been cleared, so there was an end to that clue.

"On entering the house, however, I examined, as you remember, the sill and framework of the hall window with my lens, and I could at once see that some one had passed out. I could distinguish the outline of an instep where the wet foot had been placed in coming in. I was then beginning to be able to form an opinion as to what had occurred. A man had waited outside the window, some one had brought the gems; the deed had been overseen by your son, he had pursued the thief, had struggled with him, they had each tugged at the coronet, their united strength causing injuries which neither alone could have effected. He had returned with the prize, but had left a fragment in the grasp of his opponent. So far I was clear. The question now was, who was the man, and who was it brought him the coronet?

"It is an old maxim of mine that when you have excluded the impossible, whatever remains, however improbable, must be the truth. Now, I knew that it was not you who had brought it down, so there only remained your niece and the maids. But if it were the maids, why should your son allow himself to be accused in their place? There could be no possible reason. As he loved his cousin, however, there was an excellent explanation why he should retain her secret—the more so as the secret was a disgraceful one. When I remembered that you had seen her at that window, and how she had fainted on seeing the coronet again, my conjecture became a certainty.

"And who could it be who was her confederate? A lover evidently, for who else could outweigh the love and gratitude which she must feel to you? I knew that you went out little, and that your circle of friends was a very limited one. But among them was Sir George Burnwell. I had heard of him before as being a man of evil reputation among women. It must have been he who wore those boots and retained the missing gems. Even though he knew that Arthur had discovered him, he might still flatter himself that he was safe, for the lad could not say a word without compromising his own family.

"Well, your own good sense will suggest what measures I took next. I went in the shape of a loafer to Sir George's house, managed to pick up an acquaintance with his valet, learned that his master had cut his head the night before, and, finally, at the expense of six shillings, made all sure by buying a pair of his cast-off shoes. With these I journeyed down to Streatham, and saw that they exactly fitted the tracks."

"I saw an ill-dressed vagabond in the lane yesterday evening," said Mr. Holder.

"Precisely. It was I. I found that I had my man, so I came home and changed my clothes. It was a delicate part which I had to play then, for I saw that a prosecution must be avoided to avert scandal, and I knew that so astute a villain would see that our hands were tied in the matter. I went and saw him. At first, of course, he denied everything. But when I gave him every particular that had occurred, he tried to bluster, and took down a life-preserver from the wall. I knew my man, however, and I clapped a pistol to his head before he could strike. Then he became a little more reasonable. I told him that we would give him a price for the stones he held—£ 1000 apiece. That brought out the first signs of grief that he had shown. 'Why, dash it all!' said he, 'I've let them go at six hundred for the three!' I soon managed to get the address of the receiver who had them, on promising him that there would be no prosecution. Off I set to him, and after much chaffering I got our stones at £ 1000 apiece. Then I looked in upon your son, told him that all was right, and eventually got to my bed about two o'clock, after what I may call a really hard day's work."

"A day which has saved England from a great public scandal," said the banker, rising. "Sir, I cannot find words to thank you, but you shall not find me ungrateful for what you have done. Your skill has indeed exceeded all that I have heard of it. And now I must fly to my dear boy to apologize to him for the wrong which I have done him. As to what you tell me of poor Mary, it goes to my very heart. Not even your skill can inform me where she is now."

"I think that we may safely say," returned Holmes, "that she is wherever Sir George Burnwell is. It is equally certain, too, that whatever her sins are, they will soon receive a more than sufficient punishment."

L. T. MEADE AND ROBERT EUSTACE

The Mystery of the Felwyn Tunnel

I was making experiments of some interest at South
Kensington, and hoped that I had perfected a small
but not unimportant discovery, when, on returning
home one evening in late October in the year 1893,
I found a visiting card on my table. On it were
inscribed the words, "Mr. Geoffrey Bainbridge."
This name was quite unknown to me, so I rang
the bell and inquired of my servant who the visitor
had been. He described him as a gentleman who
wished to see me on most urgent business, and said
further that Mr. Bainbridge intended to call again
later in the evening. It was with both curiosity and
vexation that I awaited the return of the stranger.
Urgent business with me generally meant a hurried
rush to one part of the country or the other. I did
not want to leave London just then; and when at
half-past nine Mr. Geoffrey Bainbridge was ushered
into my room, I received him with a certain coldness
which he could not fail to perceive. He was a tall,
well-dressed, elderly man. He immediately plunged
into the object of his visit.

43

"I hope you do not consider my unexpected presence an intrusion, Mr. Bell," he said. "But I have heard of you from our mutual friends, the Greys of Uplands. You may remember once doing that family a great service."

"I remember perfectly well," I answered more cordially. "Pray tell me what you want; I shall listen with attention."

"I believe you are the one man in London who can help me," he continued. "I refer to a matter especially relating to your own particular study. I need hardly say that whatever you do will not be unrewarded."

"That is neither here nor there," I said; "but before you go any further, allow me to ask one question. Do you want me to leave London at present?"

He raised his eyebrows in dismay.

"I certainly do," he answered.

"Very well; pray proceed with your story."

He looked at me with anxiety.

"In the first place," he began, "I must tell you that I am chairman of the Lytton Vale Railway Company in Wales, and that it is on an important matter connected with our line that I have come to consult you. When I explain to you the nature of the mystery, you will not wonder, I think, at my soliciting your aid."

"I will give you my closest attention," I answered; and then I added, impelled to say the latter words by a certain expression on his face, "if I can see my way to assisting you I shall be ready to do so."

"Pray accept my cordial thanks," he replied. "I have come up from my place at Felwyn to-day on purpose to consult you. It is in that neighbourhood that the affair has occurred. As it is essential that you should be in possession of the facts of the whole matter, I will go over things just as they happened."

I bent forward and listened attentively.

"This day fortnight," continued Mr. Bainbridge, "our quiet little village was horrified by the news that the signalman on duty at the mouth of the Felwyn Tunnel had been found dead under the most mysterious circumstances. The tunnel is at the end of a long cutting between Llanlys and Felwyn stations. It is about a mile long, and the signal-box is on the Felwyn side. The place is extremely lonely, being six miles from the village across the mountains. The name of the poor fellow who met his death in this mysterious fashion was David Pritchard. I have known him from a boy, and he was quite one of the steadiest and most trustworthy men on the line. On Tuesday evening he went on duty at six o'clock; on Wednesday morning the day-man who had come to relieve him was surprised not to find him in the box. It was just getting daylight, and the 6.30 local was coming down, so he pulled the signals and let her through. Then he went out, and, looking up the line towards the tunnel, saw Pritchard lying beside the line close to the mouth of the tunnel. Roberts, the day-man, ran up to him and found, to his horror, that he was quite dead. At first Roberts naturally supposed that he had been cut down by a train, as there was a wound at the back of the head; but he was not lying on the metals. Roberts ran back to the box and telegraphed through to Felwyn Station. The message was sent on to the village, and at half-past seven o'clock the police inspector came up to my house with the news. He and I, with the local doctor, went off at once to the tunnel. We found the dead man lying beside the metals a few yards away from the mouth of the tunnel, and the doctor immediately gave him a careful examination. There was a depressed fracture at the back of the skull, which must have caused his death; but how he came by it was not so clear. On examining the whole place most carefully, we saw, further, that there were marks on the rocks at the steep side of the embankment as if some one had tried to scramble up them. Why the poor fellow had attempted such a climb, God only knows. In doing so he must have slipped and fallen back on to the line, thus causing the fracture of the skull. In no case could he have gone up more than eight or ten feet, as the banks of the cutting run sheer up, almost perpendicularly, beyond that point for more than a hundred and fifty feet. There are some sharp boulders beside the line, and it was possible that he might have fallen on one of these and so sustained the injury. The affair must have occurred some time between 11.45 p.m. and 6 a.m., as the engine-driver of the express at 11.45 p.m. states that the line was signaled clear, and he also caught sight of Pritchard in his box as he passed."

"This is deeply interesting," I said; "pray proceed."

Bainbridge looked at me earnestly; he then continued:—

"The whole thing is shrouded in mystery. Why should Pritchard have left his box and gone down to the tunnel? Why, having done so, should he have made a wild attempt to scale the side of the cutting, an impossible feat at any time? Had danger threatened, the ordinary course of things would have been to run up the line towards the signal-box. These points are quite unexplained. Another curious fact is that death appears to have taken place just before the day-man came on duty, as the light at the mouth of the tunnel had been put out, and it was one of the night signalman's duties to do this as soon as daylight appeared; it is possible, therefore, that Pritchard went down to the tunnel for that purpose. Against this theory, however, and an objection that seems to nullify it, is the evidence of Dr. Williams, who states that when he examined the body his opinion was that death had taken place some hours before. An inquest was held on the following day, but before it took place there was a new and most important development. I now come to what I consider the crucial point in the whole story.

"For a long time there had been a feud between Pritchard and another man of the name of Wynne, a platelayer on the line. The object of their quarrel was the blacksmith's daughter in the neighbouring village—a remarkably pretty girl and an arrant flirt. Both men were madly in love with her, and she played them off one against the other. The night but one before his death Pritchard and Wynne had met at the village inn, had quarrelled in the bar—Lucy, of course, being the subject of their difference. Wynne was heard to say (he was a man of powerful build and subject to fits of ungovernable rage) that he would have Pritchard's life. Pritchard swore a great oath that he would get Lucy on the following day to promise to marry him. This oath, it appears, he kept, and on his way to the signal-box on Tuesday

evening met Wynne, and triumphantly told him that
Lucy had promised to be his wife. The men had a
hand-to-hand fight on the spot, several people from
the village being witnesses of it. They were separated
with difficulty, each vowing vengeance on the other.
Pritchard went off to his duty at the signal-box and
Wynne returned to the village to drown his sorrows
at the public-house.

"Very late that same night Wynne was seen by
a villager going in the direction of the tunnel. The
man stopped him and questioned him. He explained
that he had left some of his tools on the line, and
was on his way to fetch them. The villager noticed
that he looked queer and excited, but not wishing
to pick a quarrel thought it best not to question
him further. It has been proved that Wynne never
returned home that night, but came back at an early
hour on the following morning, looking dazed and
stupid. He was arrested on suspicion, and at the
inquest the verdict was against him."

"Has he given any explanation of his own movements?" I asked.

"Yes; but nothing that can clear him. As a matter
of fact, his tools were nowhere to be seen on the
line, nor did he bring them home with him. His own
story is that being considerably the worse for drink,

he had fallen down in one of the fields and slept there till morning."

"Things look black against him," I said.

"They do; but listen, I have something more to add. Here comes a very queer feature in the affair. Lucy Ray, the girl who had caused the feud between Pritchard and Wynne, after hearing the news of Pritchard's death, completely lost her head, and ran frantically about the village declaring that Wynne was the man she really loved, and that she had only accepted Pritchard in a fit of rage with Wynne for not himself bringing matters to the point. The case looks very bad against Wynne, and yesterday the magistrate committed him for trial at the coming assizes. The unhappy Lucy Ray and the young man's parents are in a state bordering on distraction."

"What is your own opinion with regard to Wynne's guilt?" I asked.

"Before God, Mr. Bell, I believe the poor fellow is innocent, but the evidence against him is very strong. One of the favourite theories is that he went down to the tunnel and extinguished the light, knowing that this would bring Pritchard out of his box to see what was the matter, and that he then attacked him, striking the blow which fractured the skull."

"Has any weapon been found about, with which he could have given such a blow?"

"No; nor has anything of the kind been discovered on Wynne's person; that fact is decidedly in his favour."

"But what about the marks on the rocks?" I asked.

"It is possible that Wynne may have made them in order to divert suspicion by making people think that Pritchard must have fallen, and so killed himself. The holders of this theory base their belief on the absolute want of cause for Pritchard's trying to scale the rock. The whole thing is the most absolute enigma. Some of the country folk have declared that the tunnel is haunted (and there certainly has been such a rumour current among them for years). That Pritchard saw some apparition, and in wild terror sought to escape from it by climbing the rocks, is another theory, but only the most imaginative hold it."

"Well, it is a most extraordinary case," I replied.

"Yes, Mr. Bell, and I should like to get your opinion of it. Do you see your way to elucidate the mystery?"

"Not at present; but I shall be happy to investigate the matter to my utmost ability."

"But you do not wish to leave London at present?"

"That is so; but a matter of such importance

cannot be set aside. It appears, from what you say, that Wynne's life hangs more or less on my being able to clear away the mystery?"

"That is indeed the case. There ought not to be a single stone left unturned to get at the truth, for the sake of Wynne. Well, Mr. Bell, what do you propose to do?"

"To see the place without delay," I answered.

"That is right; when can you come?"

"Whenever you please."

"Will you come down to Felwyn with me to-morrow? I shall leave Paddington by the 7.10, and if you will be my guest I shall be only too pleased to put you up."

"That arrangement will suit me admirably," I replied. "I will meet you by the train you mention, and the affair shall have my best attention."

"Thank you," he said, rising. He shook hands with me and took his leave.

The next day I met Bainbridge at Paddington Station, and we were soon flying westward in the luxurious private compartment that had been reserved for him. I could see by his abstracted manner and his long lapses of silence that the mysterious affair at Felwyn Tunnel was occupying all his thoughts.

It was two o'clock in the afternoon when the

train slowed down at the little station of Felwyn. The station-master was at the door in an instant to receive us.

"I have some terribly bad news for you, sir," he said, turning to Bainbridge as we alighted; "and yet in one sense it is a relief, for it seems to clear Wynne."

"What do you mean?" cried Bainbridge. "Bad news? Speak out at once!"

"Well, sir, it is this: there has been another death at Felwyn signal-box. John Davidson, who was on duty last night, was found dead at an early hour this morning in the very same place where we found poor Pritchard."

"Good God!" cried Bainbridge, starting back, "what an awful thing! What, in the name of Heaven, does it mean, Mr. Bell? This is too fearful. Thank goodness you have come down with us."

"It is as black a business as I ever heard of, sir," echoed the station-master; "and what we are to do I don't know. Poor Davidson was found dead this morning, and there was neither mark nor sign of what killed him—that is the extraordinary part of it. There's a perfect panic abroad, and not a signal-man on the line will take duty to-night. I was quite in despair, and was afraid at one time that the line would have to be closed, but at last it occurred to

53

me to wire to Lytton Vale, and they are sending down an inspector. I expect him by a special every moment. I believe this is he coming now," added the station-master, looking up the line.

There was the sound of a whistle down the valley, and in a few moments a single engine shot into the station, and an official in uniform stepped on to the platform.

"Good-evening, sir," he said, touching his cap to Bainbridge; "I have just been sent down to inquire into this affair at the Felwyn Tunnel, and though it seems more of a matter for a Scotland Yard detective than one of ourselves, there was nothing for it but to come. All the same, Mr. Bainbridge, I cannot say that I look forward to spending to-night alone at the place."

"You wish for the services of a detective, but you shall have some one better," said Bainbridge, turning towards me. "This gentleman, Mr. John Bell, is the man of all others for our business. I have just brought him down from London for the purpose."

An expression of relief flitted across the inspector's face.

"I am very glad to see you, sir," he said to me, "and I hope you will be able to spend the night with me in the signal-box. I must say I don't much relish the idea of tackling the thing single-handed;

54

but with your help, sir, I think we ought to get to the bottom of it somehow. I am afraid there is not a man on the line who will take duty until we do. So it is most important that the thing should be cleared, and without delay."

I readily assented to the inspector's proposition, and Bainbridge and I arranged that we should call for him at four o'clock at the village inn and drive him to the tunnel.

We then stepped into the wagonette which was waiting for us, and drove to Bainbridge's house.

Mrs. Bainbridge came out to meet us, and was full of the tragedy. Two pretty girls also ran to greet their father, and to glance inquisitively at me. I could see that the entire family was in a state of much excitement.

"Lucy Ray has just left, father," said the elder of the girls. "We had much trouble to soothe her; she is in a frantic state."

"You have heard, Mr. Bell, all about this dreadful mystery?" said Mrs. Bainbridge as she led me towards the dining-room.

"Yes," I answered; "your husband has been good enough to give me every particular."

"And you have really come here to help us?"

"I hope I may be able to discover the cause," I answered.

55

"It certainly seems most extraordinary," continued Mrs. Bainbridge. "My dear," she continued, turning to her husband, "you can easily imagine the state we were all in this morning when the news of the second death was brought to us."

"For my part," said Ella Bainbridge, "I am sure that Felwyn Tunnel is haunted. The villagers have thought so for a long time, and this second death seems to prove it, does it not?" Here she looked anxiously at me.

"I can offer no opinion," I replied, "until I have sifted the matter thoroughly."

"Come, Ella, don't worry Mr. Bell," said her father; "if he is as hungry as I am, he must want his lunch."

We then seated ourselves at the table and commenced the meal. Bainbridge, although he professed to be hungry, was in such a state of excitement that he could scarcely eat. Immediately after lunch he left me to the care of his family and went into the village.

"It is just like him," said Mrs. Bainbridge; "he takes these sort of things to heart dreadfully. He is terribly upset about Lucy Ray, and also about the poor fellow Wynne. It is certainly a fearful tragedy from first to last."

"Well, at any rate," I said, "this fresh death will upset the evidence against Wynne."

56

"I hope so, and there is some satisfaction in the fact. Well, Mr. Bell, I see you have finished lunch; will you come into the drawing-room?"

I followed her into a pleasant room overlooking the valley of the Lytton.

By-and-by Bainbridge returned, and soon afterwards the dog-cart came to the door. My host and I mounted, Bainbridge took the reins, and we started off at a brisk pace.

"Matters get worse and worse," he said the moment we were alone. "If you don't clear things up to-night, Bell, I say frankly that I cannot imagine what will happen."

We entered the village, and as we rattled down the ill-paved streets I was greeted with curious glances on all sides. The people were standing about in groups, evidently talking about the tragedy and nothing else. Suddenly, as our trap bumped noisily over the paving-stones, a girl darted out of one of the houses and made frantic motions to Bainbridge to stop the horse. He pulled the mare nearly up on her haunches, and the girl came up to the side of the dog-cart.

"You have heard it?" she said, speaking eagerly and in a gasping voice. "The death which occurred this morning will clear Stephen Wynne, won't it, Mr. Bainbridge?—it will, you are sure, are you not?"

57

"It looks like it, Lucy, my poor girl," he answered. "But there, the whole thing is so terrible that I scarcely know what to think."

She was a pretty girl with dark eyes, and under ordinary circumstances must have had the vivacious expression of face and the brilliant complexion which so many of her country-women possess. But now her eyes were swollen with weeping and her complexion more or less disfigured by the agony she had gone through. She looked piteously at Bainbridge, her lips trembling. The next moment she burst into tears.

"Come away, Lucy," said a woman who had followed her out of the cottage; "Fie—for shame! don't trouble the gentlemen; come back and stay quiet."

"I can't, mother, I can't," said the unfortunate girl. "If they hang him, I'll go clean off my head. Oh, Mr. Bainbridge, do say that the second death has cleared him!"

"I have every hope that it will do so, Lucy," said Bainbridge, "but now don't keep us, there's a good girl; go back into the house. This gentleman has come down from London on purpose to look into the whole matter. I may have good news for you in the morning."

The girl raised her eyes to my face with a look of intense pleading. "Oh, I have been cruel and a fool, and I deserve everything," she gasped; "but, sir, for the love of Heaven, try to clear him."

I promised to do my best.

Bainbridge touched up the mare, she bounded forward, and Lucy disappeared into the cottage with her mother.

The next moment we drew up at the inn where the Inspector was waiting, and soon afterwards were bowling along between the high banks of the country lanes to the tunnel. It was a cold, still afternoon; the air was wonderfully keen, for a sharp frost had held the countryside in its grip for the last two days. The sun was just tipping the hills to westward when the trap pulled up at the top of the cutting. We hastily alighted, and the Inspector and I bade Bainbridge good-bye. He said that he only wished that he could stay with us for the night, assured us that little sleep would visit him, and that he would be back at the cutting at an early hour on the following morning; then the noise of his horse's feet was heard fainter and fainter as he drove back over the frost-bound roads. The Inspector and I ran along the little path to the wicket-gate in the fence, stamping our feet on the hard ground to restore circulation after our cold drive. The next moment we were looking down upon the scene of the mysterious deaths, and a weird and lonely place it looked. The tunnel was at one end of the rock cutting, the sides of which ran sheer down to the line for over a hundred and fifty feet. Above the tunnel's mouth the hills rose one upon the other. A more dreary place it would have been difficult to imagine. From a little clump of pines a delicate film of blue smoke rose straight up on the still air. This came from the chimney of the signal-box.

As we started to descend the precipitous path the Inspector sang out a cheery "Hullo!" The man on duty in the box immediately answered. His voice echoed and reverberated down the cutting, and the next moment he appeared at the door of the box. He told us that he would be with us immediately; but we called back to him to stay where he was, and the next instant the Inspector and I entered the box.

"The first thing to do," said Henderson the Inspector, "is to send a message down the line to announce our arrival."

This he did, and in a few moments a crawling goods train came panting up the cutting. After signalling her through we descended the wooden flight of steps which led from the box down to the line and walked along the metals towards the tunnel till we stood on the spot where poor Davidson had been found dead that morning. I examined the ground and all around it most carefully. Everything tallied exactly with the description I had received. There could be no possible way of approaching the spot except by going along the line, as the rocky sides of the cutting were inaccessible.

"It is a most extraordinary thing, sir," said the signalman whom we had come to relieve. "David-son had neither mark nor sign on him—there he lay stone dead and cold, and not a bruise nowhere; but Pritchard had an awful wound at the back of the head. They said he got it by climbing the rocks—here, you can see the marks for yourself, sir. But now, is it likely that Pritchard would try to climb rocks like these, so steep as they are?"

"Certainly not," I replied.

"Then how do you account for the wound, sir?" asked the man with an anxious face.

"I cannot tell you at present," I answered.

"And you and Inspector Henderson are going to spend the night in the signal-box?"

"Yes."

A horrified expression crept over the signalman's face.

"God preserve you both," he said; "I wouldn't do it—not for fifty pounds. It's not the first time I have heard tell that Felwyn Tunnel is haunted. But, there, I won't say any more about that. It's a black business, and has given trouble enough. There's poor

Wynne, the same thing as convicted of the murder
of Pritchard; but now they say that Davidson's death
will clear him. Davidson was as good a fellow as you
would come across this side of the country; but for
the matter of that, so was Pritchard. The whole thing
is terrible—it upsets one, that it do, sir."

"I don't wonder at your feelings," I answered;
"but now, see here, I want to make a most careful
examination of everything. One of the theories is
that Wynne crept down this rocky side and fractured Pritchard's skull. I believe such a feat to be
impossible. On examining these rocks I see that a
man might climb up the side of the tunnel as far as
from eight to ten feet, utilising the sharp projections
of rock for the purpose; but it would be out of the
question for any man to come down the cutting.
No; the only way Wynne could have approached
Pritchard was by the line itself. But, after all, the real
thing to discover is this," I continued: "what killed
Davidson? Whatever caused his death is, beyond
doubt, equally responsible for Pritchard's. I am now
going into the tunnel."

Inspector Henderson went in with me. The place
struck damp and chill. The walls were covered with
green, evil-smelling fungi, and through the brick-
work the moisture was oozing and had trickled

THE MYSTERY OF THE FELWYN TUNNEL

down in long lines to the ground. Before us was nothing but dense darkness.

When we re-appeared the signalman was lighting the red lamp on the post, which stood about five feet from the ground just above the entrance to the tunnel.

"Is there plenty of oil?" asked the Inspector.

"Yes, sir, plenty," replied the man. "Is there anything more I can do for either of you gentlemen?" he asked, pausing, and evidently dying to be off.

"Nothing," answered Henderson; "I will wish you good-evening."

"Good-evening to you both," said the man. He made his way quickly up the path and was soon lost to sight.

Henderson and I then returned to the signal-box. By this time it was nearly dark.

"How many trains pass in the night?" I asked of the Inspector.

"There's the 10.20 down express," he said, "it will pass here at about 10.40; then there's the 11.45 up, and then not another train till the 6.30 local to-morrow morning. We shan't have a very lively time," he added.

I approached the fire and bent over it, holding out my hands to try and get some warmth into them.

"It will take a good deal to persuade me to go

down to the tunnel, whatever I may see there," said the man. "I don't think, Mr. Bell, I am a coward in any sense of the word, but there's something very uncanny about this place, right away from the rest of the world. I don't wonder one often hears of signalmen going mad in some of these lonely boxes. Have you any theory to account for these deaths, sir?"

"None at present," I replied.

"This second death puts the idea of Pritchard being murdered quite out of court," he continued.

"I am sure of it," I answered.

"And so am I, and that's one comfort," continued Henderson. "That poor girl, Lucy Ray, although she was to be blamed for her conduct, is much to be pitied now; and as to poor Wynne himself, he protests his innocence through thick and thin. He was a wild fellow, but not the sort to take the life of a fellow-creature. I saw the doctor this afternoon while I was waiting for you at the inn, Mr. Bell, and also the police-sergeant. They both say they do not know what Davidson died of. There was not the least sign of violence on the body."

"Well, I am as puzzled as the rest of you," I said. "I have one or two theories in my mind, but none of them will quite fit the situation."

The night was piercingly cold, and, although there was not a breath of wind, the keen and frosty air penetrated into the lonely signal-box. We spoke little, and both of us were doubtless absorbed by our own thoughts and speculations. As to Henderson, he looked distinctly uncomfortable, and I cannot say that my own feelings were too pleasant. Never had I been given a tougher problem to solve, and never had I been so utterly at my wits' end for a solution.

Now and then the Inspector got up and went to the telegraph instrument, which intermittently clicked away in its box. As he did so he made some casual remark and then sat down again. After the 10.40 had gone through, there followed a period of silence which seemed almost oppressive. All at once the stillness was broken by the whirr of the electric bell, which sounded so sharply in our ears that we both started. Henderson rose.

"That's the 11.45 coming," he said, and, going over to the three long levers, he pulled two of them down with a loud clang. The next moment, with a rush and a scream, the express tore down the cutting, the carriage lights streamed past in a rapid flash, the ground trembled, a few sparks from the engine whirled up into the darkness, and the train plunged into the tunnel.

"And now," said Henderson, as he pushed back the levers, "not another train till daylight. My word, it is cold!"

It was intensely so. I piled some more wood on the fire and, turning up the collar of my heavy ulster, sat down at one end of the bench and leant my back against the wall. Henderson did likewise; we were neither of us inclined to speak. As a rule, whenever I have any night work to do, I am never troubled with sleepiness, but on this occasion I felt unaccountably drowsy. I soon perceived that Henderson was in the same condition.

"Are you sleepy?" I asked of him.

"Dead with it, sir," was his answer; "but there's no fear, I won't drop off."

I got up and went to the window of the box. I felt certain that if I sat still any longer I should be in a sound sleep. This would never do. Already it was becoming a matter of torture to keep my eyes open. I began to pace up and down; I opened the door of the box and went out on the little platform.

"What's the matter, sir?" inquired Henderson, jumping up with a start.

"I cannot keep awake," I said.

"Nor can I," he answered, "and yet I have spent nights and nights of my life in signal-boxes and never was the least bit drowsy; perhaps it's the cold."

"Perhaps it is," I said; "but I have been out on as freezing nights before, and—"

The man did not reply; he had sat down again; his head was nodding.

I was just about to go up to him and shake him, when it suddenly occurred to me that I might as well let him have his sleep out. I soon heard him snoring, and he presently fell forward in a heap on the floor. By dint of walking up and down, I managed to keep from dropping off myself, and in torture which I shall never be able to describe, the night wore itself away. At last, towards morning, I awoke Henderson.

"You have had a good nap," I said; "but never mind, I have been on guard and nothing has occurred."

"Good God! have I been asleep?" cried the man.

"Sound," I answered.

"Well, I never felt anything like it," he replied. "Don't you find the air very close, sir?"

"No," I said; "it is as fresh as possible; it must be the cold."

"I'll just go and have a look at the light at the tunnel," said the man; "it will rouse me."

He went on to the little platform, whilst I bent over the fire and began to build it up. Presently he returned with a scared look on his face. I could see by the light of the oil lamp which hung on the wall that he was trembling.

"Mr. Bell," he said, "I believe there is somebody

67

or something down at the mouth of the tunnel now."
As he spoke he clutched me by the arm. "Go and
look," he said; "whoever it is, it has put out the light."

"Put out the light?" I cried. "Why, what's the
time?"

Henderson pulled out his watch.

"Thank goodness, most of the night is gone," he
said; "I didn't know it was so late, it is half-past five."

"Then the local is not due for an hour yet?" I said.

"No; but who should put out the light?" cried
Henderson.

I went to the door, flung it open, and looked out.
The dim outline of the tunnel was just visible loom-
ing through the darkness, but the red light was out.

"What the dickens does it mean, sir?" gasped
the Inspector. "I know the lamp had plenty of oil in
it. Can there be any one standing in front of it, do
you think?"

We waited and watched for a few moments, but
nothing stirred.

"Come along," I said, "let us go down together
and see what it is."

"I don't believe I can do it, sir; I really don't!"

"Nonsense," I cried. "I shall go down alone if
you won't accompany me. Just hand me my stick,
will you?"

"For God's sake, be careful, Mr. Bell. Don't go

down, whatever you do. I expect this is what happened before, and the poor fellows went down to see
what it was and died there. There's some devilry at
work, that's my belief."

"That is as it may be," I answered shortly; "but
we certainly shall not find out by stopping here. My
business is to get to the bottom of this, and I am
going to do it. That there is danger of some sort, I
have very little doubt; but danger or not, I am going
down."

"If you'll be warned by me, sir, you'll just stay
quietly here."

"I must go down and see the matter out," was
my answer. "Now listen to me, Henderson. I see
that you are alarmed, and I don't wonder. Just stay
quietly where you are and watch, but if I call come
at once. Don't delay a single instant. Remember I
am putting my life into your hands. If I call 'Come,'
just come to me as quick as you can, for I may want
help. Give me that lantern."

He unhitched it from the wall, and taking it
from him, I walked cautiously down the steps on to
the line. I still felt curiously, unaccountably drowsy
and heavy. I wondered at this, for the moment was
such a critical one as to make almost any man wide
awake. Holding the lamp high above my head, I
walked rapidly along the line. I hardly knew what

69

I expected to find. Cautiously along the metals I made my way, peering right and left until I was close to the fatal spot where the bodies had been found. An uncontrollable shudder passed over me. The next moment, to my horror, without the slightest warning, the light I was carrying went out, leaving me in total darkness. I started back, and stumbling against one of the loose boulders reeled against the wall and nearly fell. What was the matter with me? I could hardly stand. I felt giddy and faint, and a horrible sensation of great tightness seized me across the chest. A loud ringing noise sounded in my ears. Struggling madly for breath, and with the fear of impending death upon me, I turned and tried to run from a danger I could neither understand nor grapple with. But before I had taken two steps my legs gave way from under me, and uttering a loud cry I fell insensible to the ground.

Out of an oblivion which, for all I knew, might have lasted for moments or centuries, a dawning consciousness came to me. I knew that I was lying on hard ground; that I was absolutely incapable of realizing, nor had I the slightest inclination to discover, where I was. All I wanted was to lie quite still and undisturbed. Presently I opened my eyes.

Some one was bending over me and looking into my face.

"Thank God, he is not dead," I heard in whispered tones. Then, with a flash, memory returned to me.

"What has happened?" I asked.

"You may well ask that, sir," said the Inspector gravely. "It has been touch and go with you for the last quarter of an hour; and a near thing for me too."

I sat up and looked around me. Daylight was just beginning to break, and I saw that we were at the bottom of the steps that led up to the signal-box. My teeth were chattering with the cold and I was shivering like a man with ague.

"I am better now," I said; "just give me your hand."

I took his arm, and holding the rail with the other hand staggered up into the box and sat down on the bench.

"Yes, it has been a near shave," I said; "and a big price to pay for solving a mystery."

"Do you mean to say you know what it is?" asked Henderson eagerly.

"Yes," I answered, "I think I know now; but first tell me how long was I unconscious?"

"A good bit over half an hour, sir, I should think. As soon as I heard you call out I ran down as you told me, but before I got to you I nearly fainted. I never had such a horrible sensation in my life. I felt as weak as a baby, but I just managed to seize you by the arms and drag you along the line to the steps, and that was about all I could do."

"Well, I owe you my life," I said; "just hand me that brandy flask, I shall be the better for some of its contents."

I took a long pull. Just as I was laying the flask down Henderson started from my side.

"There," he cried, "the 6.30 is coming." The electric bell at the instrument suddenly began to ring. "Ought I to let her go through, sir?" he inquired.

"Certainly," I answered. "That is exactly what we want. Oh, she will be all right."

"No danger to her, sir?"

"None, none; let her go through."

He pulled the lever and the next moment the train tore through the cutting.

"Now I think it will be safe to go down again," I said. "I believe I shall be able to get to the bottom of this business."

Henderson stared at me aghast.

"Do you mean that you are going down again to the tunnel?" he gasped.

"Yes," I said; "give me those matches. You had better come too. I don't think there will be much danger now; and there is daylight, so we can see what we are about."

The man was very loth to obey me, but at last I managed to persuade him. We went down the line, walking slowly, and at this moment we both felt our courage revived by a broad and cheerful ray of sunshine.

"We must advance cautiously," I said, "and be ready to run back at a moment's notice."

"God knows, sir, I think we are running a great risk," panted poor Henderson; "and if that devil or whatever else it is should happen to be about—why, daylight or no daylight—"

"Nonsense! man," I interrupted; "if we are careful, no harm will happen to us now. Ah! and here we are!" We had reached the spot where I had fallen. "Just give me a match, Henderson."

He did so, and I immediately lit the lamp. Opening the glass of the lamp, I held it close to the ground and passed it to and fro. Suddenly the flame went out.

"Don't you understand now?" I said, looking up at the Inspector.

"No, I don't, sir," he replied with a bewildered expression.

Suddenly, before I could make an explanation, we both heard shouts from the top of the cutting, and looking up I saw Bainbridge hurrying down the path. He had come in the dog-cart to fetch us.

"Here's the mystery," I cried as he rushed up to us, "and a deadlier scheme of Dame Nature's to frighten and murder poor humanity I have never seen."

As I spoke I lit the lamp again and held it just above a tiny fissure in the rock. It was at once extinguished.

"What is it?" said Bainbridge, panting with excitement.

"Something that nearly finished *me*," I replied. "Why, this is a natural escape of choke damp. Carbonic acid gas—the deadliest gas imaginable, because it gives no warning of its presence, and it has no smell. It must have collected here during the hours of the night when no train was passing, and gradually rising put out the signal light. The constant rushing of the trains through the cutting all day would temporarily disperse it."

As I made this explanation Bainbridge stood like one electrified, while a curious expression of mingled relief and horror swept over Henderson's face.

"An escape of carbonic acid gas is not an uncommon phenomenon in volcanic districts," I continued, "as I take this to be; but it is odd what should have started it. It has sometimes been known to follow earthquake shocks, when there is a profound disturbance of the deep strata."

"It is strange that you should have said that," said Bainbridge, when he could find his voice.

"What do you mean?"

"Why, that about the earthquake. Don't you remember, Henderson," he added, turning to the Inspector, "we had felt a slight shock all over South Wales about three weeks back?"

"Then that, I think, explains it," I said. "It is evident that Pritchard really did climb the rocks in a frantic attempt to escape from the gas and fell back on to these boulders. The other man was cut down at once, before he had time to fly."

"But what is to happen now?" asked Bainbridge. "Will it go on for ever? How are we to stop it?"

"The fissure ought to be drenched with lime water, and then filled up; but all really depends on what is the size of the supply and also the depth. It is an extremely heavy gas, and would lie at the bottom of a cutting like water. I think there is more here just now than is good for us," I added.

"But how," continued Bainbridge, as we moved a few steps from the fatal spot, "do you account for the interval between the first death and the second?"

"The escape must have been intermittent. If wind blew down the cutting, as probably was the case before this frost set in, it would keep the gas so diluted that its effects would not be noticed. There was enough down here this morning, before that train came through, to poison an army. Indeed, if it had not been for Henderson's promptitude, there would have been another inquest—on myself."

I then related my own experience.

"Well, this clears Wynne, without doubt," said Bainbridge; "but alas! for the two poor fellows who were victims. Bell, the Lytton Vale Railway Company owe you unlimited thanks; you have doubtless saved many lives, and also the Company, for the line must have been closed if you had not made your valuable discovery. But now come home with me to breakfast. We can discuss all those matters later on."

FERGUS HUME

The Ghost's Touch

I shall never forget the terrible Christmas I spent
at Ringshaw Grange in the year '93. As an army
doctor I have met with strange adventures in far
lands, and have seen some gruesome sights in the
little wars which are constantly being waged on the
frontiers of our empire; but it was reserved for an
old country house in Hants to be the scene of the
most noteworthy episode in my life. The experience was a painful one, and I hope it may never be
repeated; but indeed so ghastly an event is not likely
to occur again. If my story reads more like fiction
than truth, I can only quote the well-worn saying,
of the latter being stranger than the former. Many
a time in my wandering life have I proved the truth
of this proverb.

The whole affair rose out of the invitation which
Frank Ringan sent me to spend Christmas with
himself and his cousin Percy at the family seat near
Christchurch. At that time I was home on leave
from India; and shortly after my arrival I chanced
to meet with Percy Ringan in Piccadilly. He was an

Australian with whom I had been intimate some years before in Melbourne: a dapper little man with sleek fair hair and a transparent complexion, looking as fragile as a Dresden china image, yet with plenty of pluck and spirits. He suffered from heart disease, and was liable to faint on occasions; yet he fought against his mortal weakness with silent courage, and with certain precautions against overexcitement, he managed to enjoy life fairly well.

Notwithstanding his pronounced effeminacy, and somewhat truckling subserviency to rank and high birth, I liked the little man very well for his many good qualities. On the present occasion I was glad to see him, and expressed my pleasure.

'Although I did not expect to see you in England,' said I, after the first greetings had passed.

'I have been in London these nine months, my dear Lascelles,' he said, in his usual mincing way, 'partly by way of a change and partly to see my cousin Frank—who indeed invited me to come over from Australia.'

'Is that the rich cousin you were always speaking about in Melbourne?'

'Yes. But Frank is not rich. I am the wealthy Ringan, but he is the head of the family. You see, Doctor,' continued Percy, taking my arm and pursuing the subject in a conversational manner, 'my father, being a younger son, emigrated to Melbourne in the gold-digging days, and made his fortune out there. His brother remained at home on the estates, with very little money to keep up the dignity of the family; so my father helped the head of his house from time to time. Five years ago both my uncle and father died, leaving Frank and me as heirs, the one to the family estate, the other to the Australian wealth. So—'

'So you assist your cousin to keep up the dignity of the family as your father did before you.'

'Well, yes, I do,' admitted Percy, frankly. 'You see, we Ringans think a great deal of our birth and position. So much so, that we have made our wills in one another's favour.'

'How do you mean?'

'Well, if I die Frank inherits my money; and if he dies, I become heir to the Ringan estates. It seems strange that I should tell you all this, Lascelles; but you were so intimate with me in the old days that you can understand my apparent rashness.'

I could not forbear a chuckle at the reason assigned by Percy for his confidence, especially as it was such a weak one. The little man had a tongue like a town-crier, and could no more keep his private affairs to himself than a woman could guard a secret. Besides I saw very well that with his inherent snobbishness he desired to impress me with the position and antiquity of his family, and with the fact—undoubtedly true—that it ranked amongst the landed gentry of the kingdom.

However, the weakness, though in bad taste, was harmless enough, and I had no scorn for the confession of it. Still, I felt a trifle bored, as I took little interest in the chronicling of such small beer, and shortly parted from Percy after promising to dine with him the following week.

At this dinner, which took place at the Athenian Club, I met with the head of the Ringan family; or, to put it plainer, with Percy's cousin Frank. Like the Australian he was small and neat, but enjoyed much better health and lacked the effeminacy of the other. Yet on the whole I liked Percy the best, as there was a sly cast about Frank's countenance which I did not relish; and he patronized his colonial cousin in rather an offensive manner.

The latter looked up to his English kinsman with all deference, and would, I am sure, have willingly given his gold to regild the somewhat tarnished escutcheon of the Ringans. Outwardly, the two cousins were so alike as to remind one of Tweedledum and Tweedledee; but after due consideration I decided that Percy was the better-natured and more honourable of the two.

For some reason Frank Ringan seemed desirous of cultivating my acquaintance; and in one way and another I saw a good deal of him during my stay in London. Finally, when I was departing on a visit to some relatives in Norfolk he invited me to spend Christmas at Ringshaw Grange—not, as it afterwards appeared, without an ulterior motive.

'I can take no refusal,' said he, with a heartiness which sat ill on him. 'Percy, as an old friend of yours, has set his heart on my having you down; and—if I may say so—I have set my heart on the same thing.'

'Oh, you really must come, Lascelles,' cried Percy, eagerly. 'We are going to keep Christmas in the real old English fashion. Washington Irving's style, you know: holly, wassail-bowl, games, and mistletoe.'

'And perhaps a ghost or so,' finished Frank, laughing, yet with a side glance at his eager little cousin.

'Ah,' said I. 'So your Grange is haunted.'

'I should think so,' said Percy, before his cousin could speak, 'and with a good old Queen Anne ghost. Come down, Doctor, and Frank shall put you in the haunted chamber.'

'No!' cried Frank, with a sharpness which rather surprised me, 'I'll put no one in the Blue Room; the consequences might be fatal. You smile, Lascelles, but I assure you our ghost has been proved to exist!'

'That's a paradox; a ghost can't exist. But the story of your ghost—'

'Is too long to tell now,' said Frank, laughing. 'Come down to the Grange and you'll hear it.'

'Very good,' I replied, rather attracted by the idea of a haunted house, 'you can count upon me for Christmas. But I warn you, Ringan, that I don't believe in spirits. Ghosts went out with gas.'

'Then they must have come in again with electric light,' retorted Frank Ringan, 'for Lady Joan undoubtedly haunts the Grange. I don't mind; as it adds distinction to the house.'

'All old families have a ghost,' said Percy, importantly. 'It is very natural when one has ancestors.'

There was no more said on the subject for the time being, but the upshot of this conversation was that I presented myself at Ringshaw Grange two or three days before Christmas. To speak the truth, I came more on Percy's account than my own, as I knew the little man suffered from heart disease, and a sudden shock might prove fatal. If, in the unhealthy atmosphere of an old house, the inmates got talking of ghosts and goblins, it might be that the consequences would be dangerous to so highly strung and delicate a man as Percy Ringan.

For this reason, joined to a sneaking desire to
see the ghost, I found myself a guest at Ringshaw
Grange. In one way I regret the visit; yet in another
I regard it as providential that I was on the spot.
Had I been absent the catastrophe might have been
greater, although it could scarcely have been more
terrible.

Ringshaw Grange was a quaint Elizabethan
house, all gables and diamond casements, and oriel
windows, and quaint terraces, looking like an illus-
tration out of an old Christmas number. It was
embowered in a large park, the trees of which came
up almost to the doors, and when I saw it first in
the moonlight—for it was by a late train that I came
from London—it struck me as the very place for a
ghost.

Here was a haunted house of the right quality if
ever there was one, and I only hoped when I crossed
the threshold that the local spectre would be worthy
of its environment. In such an interesting house I
did not think to pass a dull Christmas; but—God
help me—I did not anticipate so tragic a Yuletide
as I spent.

As our host was a bachelor and had no female
relative to do the honours of his house the guests
were all of the masculine gender. It is true that
there was a housekeeper—a distant cousin I

understood—who was rather elderly but very juven-
ile as to dress and manner. She went by the name
of Miss Laura, but no one saw much of her as,
otherwise than attending to her duties, she remained
mostly in her own rooms.

So our party was composed of young men—none
save myself being over the age of thirty, and few
being gifted with much intelligence. The talk was
mostly of sport, of horse-racing, big game shooting
and yacht-sailing: so that I grew tired at times of
these subjects and retired to the library to read and
write. The day after I arrived Frank showed me over
the house.

It was a wonderful old barrack of a place, with
broad passages, twisting interminably like the laby-
rinth of Daedalus; small bedrooms furnished in an
old-fashioned manner, and vast reception apartments with polished floors and painted ceilings. Also
there were the customary number of family portraits
frowning from the walls; suits of tarnished armour;
and ancient tapestries embroidered with grim and
ghastly legends of the past.

The old house was crammed with treasures, rare
enough to drive an antiquarian crazy; and filled
with the flotsam and jetsam of many centuries, mel-
lowed by time into one soft hue, which put them
all in keeping with one another. I must say that I

was charmed with Ringshaw Grange, and no longer wondered at the pride taken by Percy Ringan in his family and their past glories.

'That's all very well,' said Frank, to whom I remarked as much; 'Percy is rich, and had he this place could keep it up in proper style; but I am as poor as a rat, and unless I can make a rich marriage, or inherit a comfortable legacy, house and furniture, park and timber may all come to the hammer.'

He looked gloomy as he spoke; and, feeling that I had touched on a somewhat delicate matter, I hastened to change the subject, by asking to be shown the famous Blue Chamber, which was said to be haunted. This was the true Mecca of my pilgrimage into Hants.

'It is along this passage,' said Frank, leading the way, 'and not very far from your own quarters. There is nothing in its looks likely to hint at the ghost—at all events by day—but it is haunted for all that.'

Thus speaking he led me into a large room with a low ceiling, and a broad casement looking out on to the untrimmed park, where the woodland was most sylvan. The walls were hung with blue cloth embroidered with grotesque figures in black braid or thread, I know not which. There was a large old-fashioned bed with tester and figured curtains and a quantity of cumbersome furniture of the early Georgian epoch. Not having been inhabited for many years the room had a desolate and silent look—if one may use such an expression—and to my mind looked gruesome enough to conjure up a battalion of ghosts, let alone one.

'I don't agree with you!' said I, in reply to my host's remark. 'To my mind this is the very model of a haunted chamber. What is the legend?'

'I'll tell it to you on Christmas Eve,' replied Ringan, as we left the room. 'It is rather a blood-curdling tale.'

'Do you believe it?' said I, struck by the solemn air of the speaker.

'I have had evidence to make me credulous,' he replied dryly, and closed the subject for the time being.

It was renewed on Christmas Eve when all our company were gathered round a huge wood fire in the library. Outside, the snow lay thick on the ground, and the gaunt trees stood up black and leafless out of the white expanse. The sky was of a frosty blue with sharply twinkling stars, and a hard-looking moon. On the snow the shadows of interlacing boughs were traced blackly as in Indian ink, and the cold was of Arctic severity.

But seated in the holly-decked apartment before

a noble fire which roared bravely up the wide chimney we cared nothing for the frozen world out of doors. We laughed and talked, sang songs and recalled adventures, until somewhere about ten o'clock we fell into a ghostly vein quite in keeping with the goblin-haunted season. It was then that Frank Ringan was called upon to chill our blood with his local legend. This he did without much pressing.

'In the reign of the good Queen Anne,' said he, with a gravity befitting the subject, 'my ancestor Hugh Ringan was the owner of this house. He was a silent misanthropic man, having been soured early in life by the treachery of a woman. Mistrusting the sex he refused to marry for many years; and it was not until he was fifty years of age that he was beguiled by the arts of a pretty girl into the toils of matrimony. The lady was Joan Challoner, the daughter of the Earl of Branscourt; and she was esteemed one of the beauties of Queen Anne's court.

'It was in London that Hugh met her, and thinking from her innocent and child-like appearance that she would make him a true-hearted wife, he married her after a six months' courtship and brought her with all honour to Ringshaw Grange. After his marriage he became more cheerful and less distrustful of his fellow-creatures. Lady Joan was all

to him that a wife could be, and seemed devoted
to her husband and child—for she early became a
mother—when one Christmas Eve all this happiness
came to an end.'

'Oh!' said I, rather cynically. 'So Lady Joan
proved to be no better than the rest of her sex.'

'So Hugh Ringan thought, Doctor; but he was as
mistaken as you are. Lady Joan occupied the Blue
Room, which I showed you the other day; and on
Christmas Eve, when riding home late, Hugh saw
a man descend from the window. Thunderstruck by
the sight, he galloped after the man and caught him
before he could mount a horse which was waiting
for him. The cavalier was a handsome young fellow
of twenty-five, who refused to answer Hugh's questions. Thinking, naturally enough, that he had to do
with a lover of his wife's, Hugh fought a duel with
the stranger and killed him after a hard fight.

'Leaving him dead on the snow he rode back
to the Grange, and burst in on his wife to accuse
her of perfidy. It was in vain that Lady Joan tried
to defend herself by stating that the visitor was her
brother, who was engaged in plots for the restoration of James II, and on that account wished to
keep secret the fact of his presence in England.
Hugh did not believe her, and told her plainly that
he had killed her lover; whereupon Lady Joan burst

out into a volley of reproaches and cursed her husband. Furious at what he deemed was her boldness
Hugh at first attempted to kill her, but not thinking
the punishment sufficient, he cut off her right hand.'

'Why?' asked everyone, quite unprepared for this
information.

'Because in the first place Lady Joan was very
proud of her beautiful white hands, and in the
second Hugh had seen the stranger kiss her hand—
her right hand—before he descended from the
window. For these reasons he mutilated her thus
terribly.'

'And she died.'

'Yes, a week after her hand was cut off. And she
swore that she would come back to touch all those
in the Blue Room—that is who slept in it—who
were foredoomed to death. She kept her promise,
for many people who have slept in that fatal room
have been touched by the dead hand of Lady Joan,
and have subsequently died.'

'Did Hugh find out that his wife was innocent?'

'He did,' replied Ringan, 'and within a month
after her death. The stranger was really her brother,
plotting for James II, as she had stated. Hugh was
not punished by man for his crime, but within a year
he slept in the Blue Chamber and was found dead
next morning with the mark of three fingers on his

right wrist. It was thought that in his remorse he had courted death by sleeping in the room cursed by his wife.'

'And there was a mark on him?'

'On his right wrist red marks like a burn; the impression of three fingers. Since that time the room has been haunted.'

'Does everyone who sleeps in it die?' I asked.

'No. Many people have risen well and hearty in the morning. Only those who are doomed to an early death are thus touched!'

'When did the last case occur?'

'Three years ago,' was Frank's unexpected reply. 'A friend of mine called Herbert Spencer would sleep in that room. He saw the ghost and was touched. He showed me the marks next morning— three red finger marks.'

'Did the omen hold good?'

'Yes. Spencer died three months afterwards. He was thrown from his horse.'

I was about to put further questions in a sceptical vein, when we heard shouts outside, and we all sprang to our feet as the door was thrown open to admit Miss Laura in a state of excitement.

'Fire! Fire!' she cried, almost distracted. 'Oh! Mr Ringan,' addressing herself to Percy, 'your room is on fire! I—'

We waited to hear no more, but in a body rushed up to Percy's room. Volumes of smoke were rolling out of the door, and flames were flashing within. Frank Ringan, however, was prompt and cool-headed. He had the alarm bell rung, summoned the servants, grooms, and stable hands, and in twenty minutes the fire was extinguished.

On asking how the fire had started, Miss Laura, with much hysterical sobbing, stated that she had gone into Percy's room to see that all was ready and comfortable for the night. Unfortunately the wind wafted one of the bed-curtains towards the candle she was carrying, and in a moment the room was in a blaze. After pacifying Miss Laura, who could not help the accident, Frank turned to his cousin. By this time we were back again in the library.

'My dear fellow,' he said, 'your room is swimming in water, and is charred with fire. I'm afraid you can't stay there tonight; but I don't know where to put you unless you take the Blue Room.'

'The Blue Room!' we all cried. 'What! The haunted chamber?'

'Yes; all the other rooms are full. Still, if Percy is afraid—'

'Afraid!' cried Percy indignantly. 'I'm not afraid at all. I'll sleep in the Blue Room with the greatest of pleasure.'

'But the ghost—'

'I don't care for the ghost,' interrupted the Australian, with a nervous laugh. 'We have no ghosts in our part of the world, and as I have not seen one, I do not believe there is such a thing.'

We all tried to dissuade him from sleeping in the haunted room, and several of us offered to give up our apartments for the night—Frank among the number. But Percy's dignity was touched, and he was resolute to keep his word. He had plenty of pluck, as I said before, and the fancy that we might think him a coward spurred him on to resist our entreaties.

The end of it was that shortly before midnight he went off to the Blue Room, and declared his intention of sleeping in it. There was nothing more to be said in the face of such obstinacy, so one by one we retired, quite unaware of the events to happen before the morning. So on that Christmas Eve the Blue Room had an unexpected tenant.

On going to my bedroom I could not sleep. The tale told by Frank Ringan haunted my fancy, and the idea of Percy sleeping in that ill-omened room made me nervous. I did not believe in ghosts myself, nor, so far as I knew, did Percy, but the little man suffered from heart disease—he was strung up to a high nervous pitch by our ghost stories—and if anything out of the common—even from natural causes—happened in that room, the shock might be fatal to its occupant.

I knew well enough that Percy, out of pride, would refuse to give up the room, yet I was determined that he should not sleep in it; so, failing persuasion, I employed stratagem. I had my medicine chest with me, and taking it from my portmanteau I prepared a powerful narcotic. I left this on the table and went along to the Blue Room, which, as I have said before, was not very far from mine.

A knock brought Percy to the door, clothed in pyjamas, and at a glance I could see that the ghostly atmosphere of the place was already telling on his nerves. He looked pale and disturbed, but his mouth was firmly set with an obstinate expression likely to resist my proposals. However, out of diplomacy, I made none, but blandly stated my errand, with more roughness, indeed, than was necessary.

'Come to my room, Percy,' I said, when he appeared, 'and let me give you something to calm your nerves.'

'I'm not afraid!' he said, defiantly.

'Who said you were?' I rejoined, tartly. 'You believe in ghosts no more than I do, so why should you be afraid? But after the alarm of fire your nerves are upset, and I want to give you something to put them right. Otherwise, you'll get no sleep.'

'I shouldn't mind a composing draught, certainly,' said the little man. 'Have you it here?'

'No, it's in my room, a few yards off. Come along.'

Quite deluded by my speech and manner, Percy followed me into my bedroom, and obediently enough swallowed the medicine. Then I made him sit down in a comfortable armchair, on the plea that he must not walk immediately after the draught. The result of my experiment was justified, for in less than ten minutes the poor little man was fast asleep under the influence of the narcotic. When thus helpless, I placed him on my bed, quite satisfied that he would not awaken until late the next day. My task accomplished, I extinguished the light, and went off myself to the Blue Room, intending to remain there for the night.

It may be asked why I did so, as I could easily have taken my rest on the sofa in my own room; but the fact is, I was anxious to sleep in a haunted chamber. I did not believe in ghosts, as I had never seen one, but as there was a chance of meeting here with an authentic phantom I did not wish to lose the opportunity.

Therefore when I saw that Percy was safe for the

night, I took up my quarters in the ghostly territory, with much curiosity, but—as I can safely aver—no fear. All the same, in case of practical jokes on the part of the feather-headed young men in the house, I took my revolver with me. Thus prepared, I locked the door of the Blue Room and slipped into bed, leaving the light burning. The revolver I kept under my pillow ready to my hand in case of necessity.

'Now,' said I grimly, as I made myself comfortable, 'I'm ready for ghosts, or goblins, or practical jokers.'

I lay awake for a long time, staring at the queer figures on the blue draperies of the apartment. In the pale flame of the candle they looked ghostly enough to disturb the nerves of anyone: and when the draught fluttered the tapestries the figures seemed to move as though alive. For this sight alone I was glad that Percy had not slept in that room. I could fancy the poor man lying in that vast bed with blanched face and beating heart, listening to every creak, and watching the fantastic embroideries waving on the walls. Brave as he was, I am sure the sounds and sights of that room would have shaken his nerves, I did not feel very comfortable myself, sceptic as I was.

When the candle had burned down pretty low I fell asleep. How long I slumbered I know not: but

I woke up with the impression that something or someone was in the room. The candle had wasted nearly to the socket and the flame was flickering and leaping fitfully, so as to display the room one moment and leave it almost in darkness the next. I heard a soft step crossing the room, and as it drew near a sudden spurt of flame from the candle showed me a little woman standing by the side of the bed. She was dressed in a gown of flowered brocade, and wore the towering head dress of the Queen Anne epoch. Her face I could scarcely see, as the flash of flame was only momentary: but I felt what the Scotch call a deadly grue as I realized that this was the veritable phantom of Lady Joan.

For the moment the natural dread of the super-natural quite overpowered me, and with my hands and arms lying outside the counterpane I rested inert and chilled with fear. This sensation of help-lessness in the presence of evil, was like what one experiences in a nightmare of the worst kind.

When again the flame of the expiring candle shot up, I beheld the ghost close at hand, and—as I felt rather than saw—knew that it was bending over me. A faint odour of musk was in the air, and I heard the soft rustle of the brocaded skirts echo through the semi-darkness. The next moment I felt my right wrist gripped in a burning grasp, and the sudden pain roused my nerves from their paralysis.

With a yell I rolled over, away from the ghost, wrenching my wrist from that horrible clasp, and, almost mad with pain I groped with my left hand for the revolver. As I seized it the candle flared up for the last time, and I saw the ghost gliding back towards the tapestries. In a second I raised the revolver and fired. The next moment there was a wild cry of terror and agony, the fall of a heavy body on the floor, and almost before I knew where I was I found myself outside the door of the haunted room. To attract attention I fired another shot from my revolver, while the Thing on the floor moaned in the darkness most horribly.

In a few moments guests and servants, all in various stages of undress, came rushing along the passage bearing lights. A babel of voices arose, and I managed to babble some incoherent explanation, and led the way into the room. There on the floor lay the ghost, and we lowered the candles to look at its face. I sprang up with a cry on recognizing who it was.

'Frank Ringan!'

It was indeed Frank Ringan disguised as a woman in wig and brocades. He looked at me with a ghostly face, his mouth working nervously. With an effort he raised himself on his hands and tried to speak—whether in confession or exculpation, I know not. But the attempt was too much for him, a choking cry escaped his lips, a jet of blood burst from his mouth, and he fell back dead.

Over the rest of the events of that terrible night I draw a veil. There are some things it is as well not to speak of. Only I may state that all through the horror and confusion Percy Ringan, thanks to my strong sleeping draught, slumbered as peacefully as a child, thereby saving his life.

With the morning's light came discoveries and explanations. We found one of the panels behind the tapestry of the Blue Room open, and it gave admittance into a passage which on examination proved to lead into Frank Ringan's bedroom. On the floor we discovered a delicate hand formed of steel, and which bore marks of having been in the fire. On my right wrist were three distinct burns, which I have no hesitation in declaring, were caused by the mechanical hand which we picked up near the dead man. And the explanation of these things came from Miss Laura, who was wild with terror at the death of her master, and said in her first outburst of grief and fear, what I am sure she regretted in her calmer moments.

'It's all Frank's fault,' she wept. 'He was poor and

wished to be rich. He got Percy to make his will in his favour, and wanted to kill him by a shock. He knew that Percy had heart disease and that a shock might prove fatal; so he contrived that his cousin should sleep in the Blue Room on Christmas Eve; and he himself played the ghost of Lady Joan with the burning hand. It was a steel hand, which he heated in his own room so as to mark with a scar those it touched.'

'Whose idea was this?' I asked, horrified by the devilish ingenuity of the scheme.

'Frank's!' said Miss Laura, candidly. 'He promised to marry me if I helped him to get the money by Percy's death. We found that there was a secret passage leading to the Blue Room; so some years ago we invented the story that it was haunted.'

'Why, in God's name?'

'Because Frank was always poor. He knew that his cousin in Australia had heart disease, and invited him home to kill him with fright. To make things safe he was always talking about the haunted room and telling the story so that everything should be ready for Percy on his arrival. Our plans were all carried out. Percy arrived and Frank got him to make the will in his favour. Then he was told the story of Lady Joan and her hand, and by setting fire to

Percy's room last night I got him to sleep in the Blue Chamber without any suspicion being aroused.'

'You wicked woman!' I cried. 'Did you fire Percy's room on purpose?'

'Yes. Frank promised to marry me if I helped him. We had to get Percy to sleep in the Blue Chamber, and I managed it by setting fire to his bedroom. He would have died with fright when Frank, as Lady Joan, touched him with the steel hand, and no one would have been the wiser. Your sleeping in that haunted room saved Percy's life, Dr Lascelles: yet Frank invited you down as part of his scheme, that you might examine the body: and declare the death to be a natural one.'

'Was it Frank who burnt the wrist of Herbert Spencer some years ago?' I asked.

'Yes!' replied Miss Laura, wiping her red eyes. 'We thought if the ghost appeared to a few other people, that Percy's death might seem more natural. It was a mere coincidence that Mr Spencer died three months after the ghost touched him.'

'Do you know you are a very wicked woman, Miss Laura?'

'I am a very unhappy one,' she retorted. 'I have lost the only man I ever loved; and his miserable cousin survives to step into his shoes as the master of Ringshaw Grange.'

That was the sole conversation I had with the wretched woman, for shortly afterwards she disappeared, and I fancy must have gone abroad, as she was never more heard of. At the inquest held on the body of Frank the whole strange story came out, and was reported at full length by the London press to the dismay of ghost-seers: for the fame of Ringshaw Grange as a haunted mansion had been great in the land.

I was afraid lest the jury should bring in a verdict of manslaughter against me, but the peculiar features of the case being taken into consideration I was acquitted of blame, and shortly afterwards returned to India with an unblemished character. Percy Ringan was terribly distressed on hearing of his cousin's death, and shocked by the discovery of his treachery. However, he was consoled by becoming the head of the family, and as he lives a quiet life at Ringshaw Grange there is not much chance of his early death from heart disease—at all events from a ghostly point of view.

The Blue Chamber is shut up, for it is haunted now by a worse spectre than that of Lady Joan, whose legend (purely fictitious) was so ingeniously set forth by Frank. It is haunted by the ghost of the cold-blooded scoundrel who fell into his own trap; and who met with his death in the very moment he was contriving that of another man. As to myself, I have given up ghost-hunting and sleeping in haunted rooms. Nothing will ever tempt me to experiment in that way again. One adventure of that sort is enough to last me a lifetime.

E. W. HORNUNG

The Christmas Story

I.

"Throne Hotel, Harrogate,
"*September 7th*, 1911.

"MY DEAR BRUCE,—The day before yesterday I finished that thing for the Christmas number of the *Vivid*, after nearly a fortnight's hard grind; late last night I destroyed it all but a redeeming bit that may come in for something else. You must make my peace with the *Vivid*, like the good agent and the still better pal that you always are to me. I don't know what they will say at being let in like this at the last moment; but I know what I should have said in their place if another author had traded on his contract to shoot in such stuff as I have been grinding out down here against the grain. It wouldn't have done, Bruce, not at any price *per* thousand words; and I don't mind telling you (or your telling them, if you like) that I wanted their money at least as much as they can possibly have wanted my name or yarn. But there are limits imposed upon the most mercenary of

103

us, not only by the saving vanity of the artisan,
but by the lowest and most calculating sort of
self-interest. If I had forced this thing upon the
Vivid, I should not have been able to hold up my
head while their Christmas Number was on the
stalls, and they would never have given me another
contract.

"I wish to goodness I had never accepted this
one, or at least that I had not been such a fool as
to take on the job in this penitential spot, in the
intervals of a cure which most people find quite
hard enough work in itself. It doesn't give the cure
a chance, while the cure is simply fatal to one's
work. I don't mean to inflict a long screed upon
you, but you are my only correspondent in these
days, and I should like just to give you a sample of
them in further extenuation of my breach of treaty.

"At 7.15 I am called from a couch against which
I have no complaint to make; but no cup of tea
assists me to my legs, and I only get my letters and
the papers on my way to the Old Pump Room at
eight o'clock. Oh, that Old Pump Room, and the
first whiff of it when the wind is the other way!
A foul libation of sulphur hot and strong, twenty
minutes of one's letters and the band, another
deadly draught and then back to breakfast with
what appetite one may. I glower from my solitary
table, and think I never saw a body of people who
appealed so little to my gregarious instincts; but

if they honour me with a thought, I am sure it is
quite as unflattering as my impression of them.
Indeed, I should expect to suffer heavily from an
impartial comparison, for they keep up their spirits
but I make no attempt in that direction. I doubt if I
have ever been detected smiling in this hotel. I see
my neighbours through sulphuric glasses, and they
see me under the influence of sulphur, probably
conning my programme for the day. This, of course,
includes another drink to cut up my morning, and
then some highly elaborate bath or skilled man-
handling to cut it short an hour before lunch. In
the afternoon my doctor would have me take an
enormous walk and climb some legendary rocks,
which I have not been man enough to find as yet.
After tea I am grist for some new mill in the Royal
Baths; after dinner I am a dead man, and the thing
I tore up last night was a dead man's effort.

"Yet I began with all the will in the world; my
very first act, or more correctly my last before
the cure began to kill me, was to hire a great
brute of a desk and a swivel-chair for my room;
on these I was to indite my little masterpiece for
the Christmas number of the *Vivid*. But you see
what my days have been; let me only add that, in
the odd moments I do spend at my hireling desk,
first all the coaches and *char-a-bancs* of Harrogate
start from under my window for the outlying
resorts, compelling me to shut it in spite of the

heat, and when they are gone a popular Punch
and Judy show gives a daily *matinée* on the green
across the road. Five minutes ago a band was
playing selections from the 'Pirates of Penzance,'
and as I write a sentimental cornet is blurting out
'Killarney' with explosive feeling. Can you wonder
that in these conditions I have done a long week's
work for the wastepaper basket? I hope the *Vivid*
people know that my loss is greater than theirs;
they can easily fill my place, but my vain effort
is both time and money lost. Also I almost wish
that these good folk downstairs knew what a load
I have been carrying all these dreary days; then
perhaps they might realise how a man may glower
and glower, and yet not be quite such a villain as
he looks.

"I never meant to let myself go like this, Bruce;
it only shows that I really do want to write, if a
congenial idea would but come in time. And that's
past praying for now, I fear; wasn't it the day after
to-morrow that we promised to deliver the MS?
I suppose I have a note of that somewhere; but
everything except the addled tale itself lies buried
beneath the dust of my defeat. I never was more
haunted and hunted by anything in all my literary
life; the last few days I have been going about
like a person in a bad dream, and doing the most
absentminded things. I always was given that way,
but I thought I had plumbed my nadir the other

morning when I threw my book into the clothes-
basket and marched downstairs with my dirty
pocket-handkerchief under my arm! Luckily for
me, the first person I saw was an old friend who
has just turned up at this hotel; she put me right,
and I had my first sound laugh since I got here.
It is a great thing to strike a friend in a place like
this. I believe you once met a soldier man named
Vereker, an old school-fellow of mine, at my
rooms in town? Well, this is his sister, and we were
tremendous pals when I used to stay with him
in the holidays a thousand years ago; now she's
here with their old father, a decrepit curmudgeon
who chains her to his side, but tells me between
ourselves that she's engaged to be married. She
doesn't mention it herself, or wear a ring, or look
the part in the least. I must take her on about it
when I get a chance.

"By Jove! I saw her in the road this instant as I
looked up from my hired desk. Good-bye, Bruce! I
must dash out and post this at once. Remember
that you're about my only friend; don't be hard on
me for letting you in with the *Vivid*, and do make
my peace with them if you can.

"YOURS EVER,
"P. A.

"N.B.—I'd have a fresh shot if they could give me
another week and I could only get an idea."

II.

"Throne Hotel, Harrogate,
"*September 7th,* 1911.

"DEAR BRUCE,—I do believe I've got it! If so it's a
great deal more (or less) than I deserve for one of
the rottenest things I ever did in all my days.

"I was just saying I was absent-minded—I
mean in the letter I only finished a few minutes
ago, though now you'll get this with it—but I've
lowered my own record since then. I should say I
had even beaten the man who went up to dress for
dinner at a country house, never came down, and
was found fast asleep in bed with the light out.
Did I tell you about him in my last? I know I was
beginning to, but I believe I went off about Ruth
Vereker instead; it was she who told me the story
for my consolation the other morning. But she
shall never hear the one I'm going to tell you now.

"I dashed down to post your letter—the other
one—and I rather thought I should run across
Miss Vereker on the way. She was coming along
the road when I left my room; but I was fool
enough to stop to light a cigarette in the hall,
thinking of course that she was on the way in. She
cannot have been on her way in, because she never
came in, and when I went out I could see nothing

of her—anywhere. It was very annoying, because it was a chance of getting her apart from the old man and having a gossip about prehistoric times. However, I had come down to post your letter, and I could have sworn I did post it, in the pillar-box on the edge of the green, just opposite. It was not until I got up here again that I found your letter still in my hand, but no cigarette between my lips! I could not have been more shocked and ashamed if I had caught myself with the letter actually between my teeth!

"Of course, I had posted the infernal lighted cigarette, and no doubt it will burn a hole in an envelope or so. I must be thankful that nobody seems to have seen me do it, for who would believe that one could play such a trick unintentionally? No great harm is likely to be done; it isn't as though I had put in lighted matches; but don't you see the possibilities of the thing? These pillar-boxes must get pretty hot in the sun; that one was, now I think of it; and suppose the things inside got like tinder, suppose some thin envelope—I know it sounds ridiculous, but I think I'll just have a look out and see . . .

"Bruce! Bruce! How I wish to goodness I could get you here by writing down your name! I shall never be able to tell you in a letter what I've been through since I last laid down my pen. Yet for the sake of practice, and in case you care to submit the idea to the *Vivid* (without giving me away), I mean to try.

"I got up and looked out; the pillar-box is only just over the way, almost absolutely underneath my window; and—smoke was coming out of the slot! It was only just beginning, but in a minute it was quite thick, and in less than half a minute it had been seen by the people down below. An old gentleman saw it first—I was just in time to see the old gentleman. He had come out to post a letter, and he was greeted by a puff of smoke from the pillar-box! He started back as though the thing had sworn at him; and, indeed, it had a grotesquely human look about it that even I could appreciate in my horror. We all know mouths like letter-boxes, but here was a letter-box exactly like a mouth opened wide to blow a satisfactory cloud. Later in the proceedings, when the smoke came fast and furious, lit by leaping flames, it reminded me of a negro I once saw swallowing lighted fusees at the Law Courts end of old Holywell Street.

"Meanwhile the old gentleman had shouted for help, police, the fire-brigade, and everything else that he could lay his tongue to except a can of water. In a few seconds he had succeeded in collecting a crowd as excited and as helpless as himself. The Punch and Judy show, in the act of starting a fresh performance, lost its entire audience, who, however, were accompanied to

the scene by Toby and the actor-manager with
the squeaker in his mouth. A motor stopped
in passing, and the occupants roared with
laughter, without getting out or doing a thing. No
policeman appeared; no policeman have I ever
seen (or recognised as such) in happy Harrogate.
And there was I looking down upon the grotesque
jumble from my upper window—I, the incredibly
unwitting author of it all!

"What was I to do? What would *you* have done?
I started to go down, not to confess my fault, only
to hear what they were saying; but on the stairs
it struck me that somebody might have seen me
after all, that I might conceivably be recognised
as the culprit and denounced *coram populo*. I was
not going to run the risk of that. I turned tail and
came slinking up again, and here I still am with
all the sensations of a hunted criminal. It may be
that I shall treat that perennial type with some
freshness, the next time I come to handle him.

"In the single minute of my absence the affair
had entered on a new phase; our sturdy little
Yorkshire porter had made his appearance with
the can of water which had seemed the one thing
needful. Yet it is not so easy to pour water into
a pillar-box; the slot slopes the wrong way, and
the porter could only dash cans of water at the
gaping mouth, and more ran down outside than
in. Relays of cans were requisitioned before that

pillar-box ceased to belch forth smoke and steam; and by that time it seemed to me that the fire had practically burnt itself out. At all events, when a postman arrived (I hear they telephoned at last to the post-office from this hotel) the correspondence extracted was a charred litter, so far as I could see from my rather excellent coign of vantage; some of it fluttered away in black flakes, and I hear that practically everything in the box was destroyed. I have just been down to lunch, and discussed the matter with many to whom I fear I had never even nodded before. But there is nothing like a little excitement for bringing people together; only I shuddered to think what they would have said or done had they dreamt that the entire conflagration was my handiwork. There was the keenest possible indignation against the author of the outrage, whoever he might be; I was obliged to join in it to some extent myself, or run the risk of incurring suspicion by my apathy. My old friend Squire Vereker was particularly scandalised and incensed; he thumped the floor with the stick on which he leans, and said he would give something to see the ruffian flogged within an inch of his life.

"'That's what we want in these days,' said he: 'the cat, and plenty of it, instead of which there's hardly any. This modern craze of coddling criminals is all confounded nonsense. It breeds 'em, sir; they thrive and multiply on it. If I wasn't on my last legs I'd like to have the flogging of this hound myself.'

"'They've got to catch him first,' I suggested, with an unpleasant attack of goose-skin under my clothes.

"'So they have, sir, and I don't suppose they'll do it. They never seem to me to catch anybody nowadays. I only hope the rascal won't fall in with Ruth; she's gone off on a long walk by herself— went without her lunch, if you please, and left me to get mine by myself. She might as well be married and done with me.'

"The rascal asked in which direction she had gone, but that the old curmudgeon could not say; nor has it anything to do with the case, my dear Bruce, though I feel more than ever that she must be having a precious thin time of it with the exacting old gentleman. The point is, however, that here I have a jolly good idea of the very kind I was wanting all along. It would make at least a very much better story than the one I destroyed. That's one reason why I've written it at such length for your benefit; you might get whole chunks typewritten (again, of course, without giving me away) and try them on the *Vivid*. It's not what they asked for, and they needn't have it if they don't like; but, if they do, let me have all this back and I can work it up in no time. It's simply a question of treatment now.

"What would you say? The more or less innocent criminal is always a fascinating fellow, though I can't profess to handle him like Anstey in 'The Black Poodle,' or Wells in some of his short stories. Still, that sort of thing at due distance. Suppose I *had* gone down into the street, and suppose somebody *had* spotted me as the dastardly offender playing a gratuitously double part? Should I have taken to my heels, and if so in what direction? Far afield in the heroine's passing motor-car, or back into the hotel, up in the lift, and so out upon the roof? The essentially innocent soul, in the grotesquely desperate situation; that's what we want, of course with the right sort of heroine to help him out in the end. Ruth Vereker would be the very one for the job. I would consult her about it, only I don't want her to know I was such an abject idiot, or to think that I wouldn't have owned up if there had seemed any point in it. On the whole I think I'll go and try to find those wonderful rocks my doctor keeps preaching about. I feel like a walk for once, and they might be a very good place for my man to fly to. She would follow him there. But now I think I've given you as much as you can master to-morrow morning if you're going to look after any other fellow's work as well as mine. I shall still let my first letter go on its own, but I'll mark it I., and this one II., so that you may get hold of the right end of the stick

first. And then I hope the wrong end won't seem
as wrong as it might have been.

"But this time I go to the General Post Office.
And I shall only light up on my way to those
rocks.

"YOURS,

"PHILIP."

III.

"Throne Hotel, Harrogate,
"*September 8th*, 1911.

"DEAR OLD BRUCE,—What wondrous weather
we are still having! I have shoved this delightful
desk close up to the open window, to see a bit
more of what's going on, and really the life and
spirit of this place are most exhilarating. The last
char-a-banc has just departed for the day; if I had
not better fish to fry I might have made one of its
merry load. The Punch and Judy man is mustering
his first audience; it would be too much to say
that his squeak attracts me, but I do not resent it
as I did. And I have just thrown half-a-crown to
a harpist in a flat-brimmed bowler, a fiddler of
more than faulty intonation, and a lady vocalist in
a feather boa who has been singing me songs of
Araby in a way that would indeed have charmed

me to a tear this time yesterday. But all's well with
Harrogate and me this morning, and really the
people in this hotel are as nice a crowd as one
could wish to meet in a casual sort of way. You
perceive, of course, that I have worked out my new
idea to my own satisfaction? Well, I should say I
have! I am wrong, however, for it has worked itself
out in a fashion that would never have occurred
to me in my most deliberately ingenious moments.
Fact, my dear fellow, has once more demonstrated
its superiority to fiction even of the ultra-Wells or
imitation-Anstey type.

"In spite of all the thousands of words I fired
at you yesterday, you must bear with another
thousand if you want to know the astounding
conclusion of the whole matter. But don't you
show this lot to the *Vivid*. It is for the private eye
of the pal whom I value more than any agent.

"I posted both my other letters, as I told you I
should, at the Post Office here while the afternoon
of yesterday was still young; then I set off for those
wretched rocks of which you have heard so much.
You will hear no more of them; they have not seen
me yet I had won through the Valley Gardens, and
the encampment of curists listening to the band
in their tent-chairs, when on the asphalt slope
between the Gardens and the Moor I met Miss
Vereker face to face. I was naturally pleased, after
the way I had just missed her in the morning;

my only trouble was that she was so near home, and rather fidgety about her father, though I was able to assure her that he was all right. She said she must get back to give him his tea after his rest; but I told her I thought he had not retired so soon as usual after lunch, as there had been some little excitement in the hotel owing to a very small fire in the vicinity. I was afraid I was going to be pressed for particulars, but Ruth seemed somewhat full of her own affairs, though I could not help thinking that in a way she was glad to see me. I was naturally delighted to have fallen in with her; and yet she seemed surprised when I importuned her to turn back for the least little stroll on the Moor.

"'But don't you want to think about your story, Phil?'

"'No, thank you! I've torn that story up. I want to forget about it. I'm going to do another one instead, if they'll give me time.'

"'But aren't you almost too conscientious?'

"'Not a bit. It's mere policy not to supply an order with stuff that one knows is bad. Besides, it was making an old man of me, that story. You don't know what it is to tinker and tinker away, and yet to feel at the back of your head that you're doing no good all the time.'

"Ruth had given in, and we were walking now in the direction of the Moor; but we went so far without further speech, and something in her figure and carriage, her colouring and her hair, had spirited me back so many years that I had lost my own thread before she took it up.

"'I'm glad it was only that,' she said.

"'What do you mean?'

"'You didn't seem the least bit glad to see us again. I thought you'd forgotten us at first.'

"'Forgotten you!' I cried. 'That only shows what a beast that infernal story was making of me. My wretched work always does drive me to one extreme or the other; if it had been going well you'd have heard about nothing else, and found me the most awful bore.'

"'I don't think I should. I haven't had so many opportunities of hearing you talk about your work. It's about a hundred years since we met.'

"'I shouldn't have forgotten you if it were a thousand. Besides, I heard all about you from Dick last time he was home from India. Do you remember the first time I came to stay with him in the holidays?'

"'I've got the verses you sent me afterwards about everything we'd done.'

"'You haven't! I remember having an awful row with Dick because I would always go about with you.'

"'Do you remember the day we hid from him in the loft?'

118

"'Rather! Poor old Dick! I didn't quite play the game by him. But it all seems like yesterday.'

"And it really did, Bruce, for we had been the most tremendous pals in our early days, and for years afterwards, until her brother went to India; but since then we have hardly ever met until this time. Yet it all came back, here on the Moor; we called up memory against memory, and laugh for laugh, exactly as though it were a game; and all the years since the end of those days seemed to drop out of our lives, or mine at least, and give me back my youth. You may say I flatter and deceive myself; you may say what you like! I never felt a younger man than yesterday afternoon, and I never sat beside a younger woman than Ruth Vereker, with her wonderful colouring and her gold-brown hair, as crisp and bonny as the day she put it up.

"I must tell you that this so-called Moor is a sort of miniature heath, only planted with tiny clumps of trees as well; and we sat under one, on a seat thoughtfully provided by the local corporation, and as carefully covered with the names and initials of local louts. It wasn't in the least secluded or romantic; a train runs close at hand, cars hoot nearer still, nurses and children with harsh Yorkshire accents lurk behind every bush if they are not actually sitting beside you. We had our seat to ourselves; so far we were fortunate; and a hideous reservoir, with a row of raw villas inverted in its glassy depths, might have been a magic blend of Venice and Vallombrosa as seen between a neighbouring clump of birches and a more distant ridge of pines.

"It was with a kind of thud that we came back to Harrogate and 1911.

"'Why on earth did you get engaged, Ruth?'

"Was it that her colouring gained in brilliance, or merely that the afternoon sun swept the cheek nearer mine?

"'Who told you I was engaged?' she asked.

"'Your father. Isn't it true?'

"'Only just.'

"'Only just!' I echoed. 'It must be one thing or the other, Ruth?'

"'Then it's true enough, I suppose,' she said. 'I—I couldn't keep him waiting any longer—and now I've done it!'

"She looked adorably unhappy about it all.

"'When did you do it?' I demanded.

"'Only this morning,' she sighed.

"'What?' I cried. 'Is the fellow here in Harrogate?'

"She shook her head.

"'Then where is he, and who is he, Ruth? Is he an old friend,' I asked, jealously, 'who can talk over old days as well as I can? If so, I may remember him,' I had the wit to say hastily.

"'He is an old friend,' she answered, 'but of course not in the sense that you are, Phil. We weren't children together. He lives abroad, and I sent him his answer this morning.'

"I leapt to my legs.

"'You posted it?'

"'Yes.'

"'About twelve o'clock—opposite the hotel?'

"'Yes,' she whispered. 'It's done!'

"'It isn't!' I cried. 'Your letter never went; it was destroyed, with everything else that was in that pillar-box at that time; didn't I tell you there had been a fire? That was the one I meant, and—and it *isn't* done Ruth—and it never shall be!'

"That, my dear Bruce, is the end of the story I began to tell you yesterday, little dreaming what the end was to be. This much I owe you, and have leave to tell *you* word for word. The rest is silence, until you come down and see her for yourself. But you will plainly see that I cannot give it to the *Vivid* after all—unless—but to-morrow is Saturday, and a fine train leaves St. Pancras at 11.30. Come!

"PHIL."

Blind Man's Hood

Although one snowflake had already sifted past the lights, the great doors of the house stood open. It seemed less a snowflake than a shadow; for a bitter wind whipped after it, and the doors creaked. Inside, Rodney and Muriel Hunter could see a dingy narrow hall paved in dull red tiles, with a Jacobean staircase at the rear. (At that time, of course, there was no dead woman lying inside.)

To find such a place in the loneliest part of the Weald of Kent—a seventeenth-century country house whose floors had grown humped and its beams scrubbed by the years—was what they had expected. Even to find electricity was not surprising. But Rodney Hunter thought he had seldom seen so many lights in one house, and Muriel had been wondering about it ever since their car turned the bend in the road. "Clearlawns" lived up to its name. It stood in the midst of a slope of flat grass, now wiry white with frost, and there was no tree or shrub within twenty yards of it. Those lights contrasted with a certain inhospitable and damp air about the house, as though the owner were compelled to keep them burning.

"But why is the front door *open*?" insisted Muriel.

In the drive-way, the engine of their car coughed and died. The house was now a secret blackness of gables, emitting light at every chink, and silhouetting the stalks of the wisteria vines which climbed it. On either side of the front door were little-paned windows whose curtains had not been drawn. Towards their left they could see into a low dining-room, with table and sideboard set for a cold supper; towards their right was a darkish library moving with the reflections of a bright fire.

The sight of the fire warmed Rodney Hunter, but it made him feel guilty. They were very late. At five o'clock, without fail, he had promised Jack Bannister, they would be at "Clearlawns" to inaugurate the Christmas party.

Engine-trouble in leaving London was one thing; idling at a country pub along the way, drinking hot ale and listening to the wireless sing carols until a sort of Dickensian jollity stole into you, was something else. But both he and Muriel were young; they were very fond of each other, and of things in general; and they had worked themselves into a glow of Christmas, which—as they stood before the creaking doors of "Clearlawns"—grew oddly cool.

There was no real reason, Rodney thought, to feel disquiet. He hoisted their luggage, including a big box of presents for Jack and Molly's children, out of the rear of the car. That his footsteps should sound loud on the gravel was only natural. He put his head into the doorway and whistled. Then he began to bang the knocker. Its sound seemed to seek out every corner of the house and then come back like a questing dog; but there was no response.

"I'll tell you something else," he said. "There's nobody in the house."

Muriel ran up the three steps to stand beside him. She had drawn her fur coat close around her, and her face was bright with cold.

"But that's impossible!" she said. "I mean, even if they're out, the servants—! Molly told me she keeps a cook and two maids. Are you sure we've got the right place?"

"Yes. The name's on the gate, and there's no other house within a mile."

With the same impulse they craned their necks to look through the windows of the dining-room on the left. Cold fowl on the sideboard, a great bowl of chestnuts; and, now they could see it, another good fire, before which stood a chair with a piece of knitting put aside on it. Rodney tried the knocker again, vigorously, but the sound was all wrong. It was as though they were even more lonely in that core of light, with the east wind rushing across the Weald, and the door creaking again.

"I suppose we'd better go in," said Rodney. He added, with a lack of Christmas spirit: "Here, this is a devil of a trick! What do you think has happened? I'll swear that fire has been made up in the last fifteen minutes."

He stepped into the hall and set down the bags. As he was turning to close the door, Muriel put her hand on his arm.

"I say, Rod. Do you think you'd better close it?"

"Why not?"

"I—I don't know."

"The place is getting chilly enough as it is," he pointed out, unwilling to admit that the same thought had occurred to him. He closed both doors and shot their bar into place; and, at the same moment, a girl came out of the door to the library on the right.

She was such a pleasant-faced girl that they both felt a sense of relief. Why she had not answered the knocking had ceased to be a question; she filled a void. She was pretty, not more than twenty-one or two, and had an air of primness which made Rodney Hunter vaguely associate her with a governess or a secretary, though Jack Bannister had never mentioned any such person. She was plump, but with a curiously narrow waist; and she wore brown. Her brown hair was neatly parted, and her brown eyes—long eyes, which might have given a hint of secrecy or curious smiles if they had not been so placid—looked concerned. In one hand she carried what looked like a small white bag of linen or cotton. And she spoke with a dignity which did not match her years.

"I am most terribly sorry," she told them. "I *thought* I heard someone, but I was so busy that I could not be sure. Will you forgive me?"

She smiled. Hunter's private view was that his knocking had been loud enough to wake the dead; but he murmured conventional things. As though conscious of some faint incongruity about the white bag in her hand, she held it up.

"For Blind Man's Buff," she explained. "They do cheat so, I'm afraid, and not only the children. If one uses an ordinary handkerchief tied round the eyes, they always manage to get a corner loose. But if you take this, and you put it fully over a person's head, and you tie it round the neck"—a sudden gruesome image ocurred to Rodney Hunter—"then it works so much better, don't you think?" Her eyes seemed to turn inward, and to grow absent. "But I must not keep you talking here. You are—"

"My name is Hunter. This is my wife. I'm afraid we've arrived late, but I understood Mr. Bannister was expecting—"

"He did not tell you?" asked the girl in brown.

"Tell me what?"

"Everyone here, including the servants, is always out of the house at this hour on this particular date. It is the custom; I believe it has been the custom for more than sixty years. There is some sort of special church service."

Rodney Hunter's imagination had been devising all sorts of fantastic explanations: the first of them being that this demure lady had murdered the members of the household, and was engaged in disposing of the bodies. What put this nonsensical notion into his head he could not tell, unless it was his own profession of detective-story writing. But he felt relieved to hear a commonplace explanation. Then the woman spoke again.

"Of course, it is a pretext, really. The rector, that dear man, invented it all those years to save embarrassment. What happened here had nothing to do with the murder, since the dates were so different; and I suppose most people have forgotten now why the tenants *do* prefer to stay away during seven and eight o'clock on Christmas Eve. I doubt if Mrs. Bannister even knows the real reason, though

I should imagine Mr. Bannister must know it. But what happens here cannot be very pleasant, and it wouldn't do to have the children see it—would it?"

Muriel spoke with such directness that her husband knew she was afraid. "Who are you?" Muriel said. "And what on earth are you talking about?"

"I am quite sane, really," their hostess assured them, with a smile that was half-cheery and half-coy. "I daresay it must be all very confusing to you, poor dear. But I am forgetting my duties. Please come in and sit down before the fire, and let me offer you something to drink."

She took them into the library on the right, going ahead with a walk that was like a bounce, and looking over her shoulder out of those long eyes. The library was a long, low room with beams. The windows towards the road were uncurtained; but those in the side-wall, where a faded red-brick fireplace stood, were bay windows with draperies closed across them. As their hostess put them before the fire. Hunter could have sworn he saw one of the draperies move.

"You need not worry about it," she assured him, following his glance towards the bay. "Even if you looked in there, you might not see anything now. I believe some gentleman did try it once, a long time ago. He stayed in the house for a wager. But when he pulled the curtain back, he did not see anything in the bay—at least, anything quite. He felt some hair, and it moved. That is why they have so many lights nowadays."

Muriel had sat down on a sofa, and was lighting a cigarette: to the rather prim disapproval of their hostess, Hunter thought.

"May we have a hot drink?" Muriel asked crisply. "And then, if you don't mind, we might walk over and meet the Bannisters coming from church."

"Oh, please don't do that!" cried the other. She had been standing by the fireplace, her hands folded and turned outwards. Now she ran across to sit down beside Muriel; and the swiftness of her movement, no less than the touch of her hand on Muriel's arm, made the latter draw back.

Hunter was now completely convinced that their hostess was out of her head. Why she held such fascination for him, though, he could not understand. In her eagerness to keep them there, the girl had come upon a new idea. On a table behind the sofa, book-ends held a row of modern novels. Conspicuously displayed—probably due to Molly Bannister's tact—were two of Rodney Hunter's detective stories. The girl put a finger on them.

"May I ask if you wrote these?"

He admitted it.

"Then," she said with sudden composure, "it would probably interest you to hear about the murder. It was a most perplexing business, you know; the police could make nothing of it, and no-one ever has been able to solve it." An arresting eye fixed on his. "It happened out in the hall there. A poor woman was killed where there was no-one to kill her, and no-one could have done it. But she was murdered."

Hunter started to get up from his chair; then he changed his mind, and sat down again. "Go on," he said.

"You must forgive me if I am a little uncertain about dates," she urged. "I think it was in the early eighteen-seventies, and I am sure it was in early February—because of the snow. It was a bad winter then; the farmers' live-stock all died. My people have been bred up in this district for years, and I know that. The house here was much as it is now, except that there was none of this lighting (only paraffin lamps, poor girl!); and you were obliged to pump up what water you wanted; and people read the newspaper quite through, and discussed it for days.

"The people were a little different to look at, too. I am sure I do not understand why we think beards

are so strange nowadays; they seem to think that
men who had beards never had any emotions. But
even young men wore them then, and looked handsome enough. There was a newly-married couple
living in this house at the time: at least, they had
been married only the summer before. They were
named Edward and Jane Waycross, and it was considered a good match everywhere.

"Edward Waycross did not have a beard, but
he had bushy side-whiskers which he kept curled.
He was not a handsome man, either, being somewhat dry and hard-favoured; but he was a religious
man, and a good man, and an excellent man of
business, they say; a manufacturer of agricultural
implements at Hawkhurst. He had determined that
Jane Anders (as she was) would make him a good
wife, and I dare say she did. The girl had several
suitors. Although Mr. Waycross was the best match,
I know it surprised people a little when she accepted
him, because she was thought to have been fond of
another man—a more striking man, whom many of
the young girls were after. This was Jeremy Wilkes:
who came of a very good family, but was considered
wicked. He was no younger than Mr. Waycross, but
he had a great black beard, and wore white waist-
coats with gold chains, and drove a gig. Of course,

there had been gossip, but that was because Jane Anders was considered pretty."

Their hostess had been sitting back against the sofa, quietly folding the little white bag with one hand, and speaking in a prim voice. Now she did something which turned her hearers cold.

You have probably seen the same thing done many times. She had been touching her cheek lightly with the fingers of the other hand. In doing so, she touched the flesh at the corner under her lower eyelid, and accidentally drew down the corner of that eyelid—which should have exposed the red part of the inner lid at the corner of the eye. It was not red. It was of a sickly pale colour.

"In the course of his business dealings," she went on, "Mr. Waycross had often to go to London, and usually he was obliged to remain overnight. But Jane Waycross was not afraid to remain alone in the house. She had a good servant, a staunch old woman, and a good dog. Even so, Mr. Waycross commended her for her courage."

The girl smiled. "On the night I wish to tell you of, in February, Mr. Waycross was absent. Unfortunately, too, the old servant was absent; she had been called away as a midwife to attend her cousin, and Jane Waycross had allowed her to go. This was known in the village, since all such affairs are well known, and some uneasiness was felt—this house being isolated, as you know. But she was not afraid.

"It was a very cold night, with a heavy fall of snow which had stopped about nine o'clock. You must know, beyond doubt, that poor Jane Waycross was alive after it had stopped snowing. It must have been nearly half-past nine when a Mr. Moody—a very good and sober man who lived in Hawkhurst—was driving home along the road past this house. As you know, it stands in the middle of a great bare stretch of lawn; and you can see the house clearly from the road. Mr. Moody saw poor Jane at the window of one of the upstairs bedrooms, with a candle in her hand, closing the shutters. But he was not the only witness who saw her alive.

"On that same evening, Mr. Wilkes (the handsome gentleman I spoke to you of a moment ago) had been at a tavern in the village of Five Ashes with Dr. Sutton, the local doctor, and a racing gentleman named Pawley. At about half-past eleven they started to drive home in Mr. Wilkes's gig to Cross-in-Hand. I am afraid they had all been drinking, but they were all in their sober senses. The landlord of the tavern remembered the time because he had stood in the doorway to watch the gig, which had fine yellow wheels, go spanking away as though there were no snow; and Mr. Wilkes in one of the new round hats with a curly brim.

"There was a bright moon. 'And no danger', Dr. Sutton always said afterwards; 'shadows of trees and fences as clear as though a silhouette-cutter had made 'em for sixpence.' But when they were passing this house Mr. Wilkes pulled up sharp. There was a bright light in the window of one of the downstairs rooms—this room, in fact. They sat out there looking round the hood of the gig, and wondering.

"Mr. Wilkes spoke: 'I don't like this,' he said. 'You know, gentlemen, that Waycross is still in London; and the lady in question is in the habit of retiring early. I am going up there to find out if anything is wrong.'

"With that he jumped out of the gig, his black beard jutting out and his breath smoking. He said: 'And if it is a burglar, then by Something, gentlemen'—I will not repeat the word he used—'by Something, gentlemen, I'll settle him.' He walked through the gate and up to the house—they could follow every step he made—and looked into the windows of this room here. Presently he returned looking relieved (they could see him by the light of the gig lamps), but wiping the moisture off his forehead.

"'It is all right,' he said to them; 'Waycross has

come home. But, by Something, gentlemen, he is growing thinner these days, or it is shadows.'

"Then he told them what he had seen. If you look through the front windows—there—you can look sideways and see out through the doorway into the main hall. He said he had seen Mrs. Waycross standing in the hall with her back to the staircase, wearing a blue dressing-wrap over her nightgown, and her hair down round her shoulders. Standing in front of her, with his back to Mr. Wilkes, was a tallish, thin man like Mr. Waycross, with a long greatcoat and a tall hat like Mr. Waycross's. *She* was carrying either a candle or a lamp; and he remembered how the tall hat seemed to wag back and forth, as though the man were talking to her or putting out his hands towards her. For he said he could not see the woman's face.

"Of course, it was not Mr. Waycross; but how were they to know that?

"At about seven o'clock next morning, Mrs. Randall, the old servant, returned. (A fine boy had been born to her cousin the night before.) Mrs. Randall came home through the white dawn and the white snow, and found the house all locked up. She could get no answer to her knocking. Being a woman of great resolution, she eventually broke a window and got in. But, when she saw what was in the front hall, she went out screaming for help.

"Poor Jane was past help. I know I should not speak of these things; but I must. She was lying on her face in the hall. From the waist down her body was much charred and—unclothed, you know, because fire had burnt away most of the nightgown and the dressing-wrap. The tiles of the hall were soaked with blood and paraffin oil, the oil having come from a broken lamp with a thick blue-silk shade which was lying a little distance away. Near it was a china candlestick with a candle. This fire had also charred a part of the paneling of the wall, and a part of the staircase. Fortunately, the floor is of brick tiles, and there had not been much paraffin left in the lamp, or the house would have been set afire.

"But she had not died from burns alone. Her throat had been cut with a deep slash from some very sharp blade. But she had been alive for a while to feel both things, for she had crawled forward on her hands while she was burning. It was a cruel death, a horrible death for a soft person like that."

There was a pause. The expression on the face of the narrator, the plump girl in the brown dress, altered slightly. So did the expression of her eyes. She was sitting beside Muriel; and moved a little closer.

"Of course, the police came. I do not understand such things, I am afraid, but they found that the house had not been robbed. They also noticed the odd thing I have mentioned, that there was both a lamp *and* a candle in a candlestick near her. The lamp came from Mr. and Mrs. Waycross's bedroom upstairs, and so did the candlestick; there were no other lamps or candles downstairs except the lamps waiting to be filled next morning in the back kitchen. But the police thought she would not have come downstairs carrying both the lamp *and* the candle as well.

"She must have brought the lamp, because that was broken. When the murderer took hold of her, they thought, she had dropped the lamp, and it went out; the paraffin spilled, but did not catch fire. Then this man in the tall hat, to finish his work after he had cut her throat, went upstairs, and got a candle, and set fire to the spilled oil. I am stupid at these things; but even I should have guessed that this must mean someone familiar with the house. Also, if she came downstairs, it must have been to let someone in at the front door; and that could not have been a burglar.

"You may be sure all the gossips were like police from the start, even when the police hem'd and haw'd, because they knew Mrs. Waycross must have opened the door to a man who was not her husband. And immediately they found an indication of this, in the mess that the fire and blood had made in the hall. Some distance away from poor Jane's body there was a medicine-bottle, such as chemists use. I think it had been broken in two pieces; and on one intact piece they found sticking some fragments of a letter that had not been quite burned. It was in a man's handwriting, not her husband's, and they made out enough of it to understand. It was full of—expressions of love, you know, and it made an appointment to meet her there on that night."

Rodney Hunter, as the girl paused, felt impelled to ask a question.

"Did they know whose handwriting it was?"

"It was Jeremy Wilkes's," replied the other simply. "Though they never proved that, never more than slightly suspected it, and the circumstances did not bear it out. In fact, a knife stained with blood was actually found in Mr. Wilkes's possession. But the police never brought it to anything, poor souls. For, you see, not Mr. Wilkes—or anyone else in the world—could possibly have done the murder."

"I don't understand that," said Hunter, rather sharply.

"Forgive me if I am stupid about telling things,"

urged their hostess in a tone of apology. She seemed to be listening to the chimney growl under a cold sky, and listening with hard, placid eyes. "But even the village gossips could tell that. When Mrs. Randall came here to the house on that morning, both the front and the back doors were locked and securely bolted on the inside. All the windows were locked on the inside. If you will look at the fastenings in this dear place, you will know what that means.

"But, bless you, that was the least of it! I told you about the snow. The snowfall had stopped at nine o'clock in the evening, hours and hours before Mrs. Waycross was murdered. When the police came, there were only two separate sets of footprints in the great unmarked half-acre of snow round the house. One set belonged to Mr. Wilkes, who had come up and looked in through the window the night before. The other belonged to Mrs. Randall. The police could follow and explain both sets of tracks; but there were no other tracks at all, and no-one was hiding in the house.

"Of course, it was absurd to suspect Mr. Wilkes. It was not only that he told a perfectly straight story about the man in the tall hat; but both Dr. Sutton and Mr. Pawley, who drove back with him from Five Ashes, were there to swear he could not have done it. You understand, he came no closer to the house than the windows of this room. They could watch every step he made in the moonlight, and they did. Afterwards he drove home with Dr. Sutton and slept there; or, I should say, they continued their terrible drinking until daylight. It is true that they found in his possession a knife with blood on it, but he explained that he had used the knife to gut a rabbit.

"It was the same with poor Mrs. Randall, who had been up all night about her midwife's duties, though naturally it was even more absurd to think of *her*. But there were no other footprints at all, either coming to or going from the house, in all that stretch of snow; and all the ways in or out were locked on the inside."

It was Muriel who spoke then, in a voice that tried to be crisp, but wavered in spite of her. "Are you telling us that all this is true?" she demanded.

"I am teasing you a little, my dear," said the other. "But really and truly, it all did happen. Perhaps I will show you in a moment."

"I suppose it was really the husband who did it?" asked Muriel in a bored tone.

"Poor Mr. Waycross!" said their hostess tenderly. "He spent that night in a temperance hotel near Charing Cross Station, as he always did, and, of course, he never left it. When he learned about his wife's duplicity"—again Hunter thought she was going to pull down a corner of her eyelid—"it nearly drove him out of his mind, poor fellow. I think he gave up agricultural machinery and took to preaching, but I am not sure. I know he left the district soon afterwards, and before he left he insisted on burning the mattress of their bed. It was a dreadful scandal."

"But in that case," insisted Hunter, "who did kill her? And, if there were no footprints and all the doors were locked, how did the murderer come or go? Finally, if all this happened in February, what does it have to do with people being out of the house on Christmas Eve?"

"Ah, that is the real story. That is what I meant to tell you."

She grew very subdued.

"It must have been very interesting to watch the people alter and grow older, or find queer paths, in the years afterwards. For, of course, nothing did happen as yet. The police presently gave it all up; for decency's sake it was allowed to rest. There was a new pump built in the market square; and the news of the Prince of Wales's going to India in '75 to talk about; and presently a new family came to live at 'Clearlawns', and began to raise their children. The trees and the rains in summer were just the same, you know. It must have been seven or eight years before anything happened, for Jane Waycross was very patient.

"Several of the people had died in the meantime. Mrs. Randall had, in a fit of quinsy; and so had Dr. Sutton, but that was a great mercy, because he fell by the way when he was going to perform an amputation with too much of the drink in him. But Mr. Pawley had prospered—and, above all, so had Mr. Wilkes. He had become an even finer figure of a man, they tell me, as he drew near middle age. When he married he gave up all his loose habits. Yes, he married; it was the Tinsley heiress, Miss Linshaw, whom he had been courting at the time of the murder; and I have heard that poor Jane Waycross, even after *she* was married to Mr. Waycross, used to bite her pillow at night, because she was so horribly jealous of Miss Linshaw.

"Mr. Wilkes had always been tall, and now he was finely stout. He always wore frock-coats. Though he had lost most of his hair, his beard was full and curly; he had twinkling black eyes, and twinkling ruddy cheeks, and a bluff voice. All the children ran to him. They say he broke as many feminine hearts as before. At any wholesome entertainment he was always the first to lead the cotillion or applaud the fiddler, and I do not know what hostesses would have done without him.

143

"On Christmas Eve, then—remember, I am not sure of the date—the Fentons gave a Christmas party. The Fentons were the very nice family who had taken this house afterwards, you know. There was to be no dancing, but all the old games. Naturally, Mr. Wilkes was the first of all to be invited, and the first to accept; for everything was all smoothed away by time, like the wrinkles in last year's counterpane; and what's past *is* past, or so they say. They had decorated the house with holly and mistletoe, and guests began to arrive as early as two in the afternoon.

"I had all this from Mrs. Fenton's aunt (one of the Warwickshire Abbotts), who was actually staying here at the time. In spite of such a festal season, the preparations had not been going at all well that day, though such preparations usually did. Miss Abbott complained that there was a nasty earthy smell in the house. It was a dark and raw day, and the chimneys did not seem to draw as well as they should. What is more, Mrs. Fenton cut her finger when she was carving the cold fowl, because she said one of the children had been hiding behind the window-curtains in here, and peeping out at her; she was very angry. But Mr. Fenton, who was going about the house in his carpet slippers before the arrival of the guests, called her 'Mother' and said that it was Christmas.

"It is certainly true that they forgot all about this when the fun of the games began. Such squeal-ings you never heard!—or so I am told. Foremost of all at Bobbing for Apples or Nuts in May was Mr. Jeremy Wilkes. He stood, gravely paternal, in the midst of everything, with his ugly wife beside him, and stroked his beard. He saluted each of the ladies on the cheek under the mistletoe; there was also some scampering to salute him; and, though he *did* remain for longer than was necessary behind the window-curtains with the younger Miss Twigelow, his wife only smiled. There was only one unpleasant incident, soon forgotten. Towards dusk a great gusty wind began to come up, with the chimneys smoking worse than usual. It being nearly dark, Mr. Fenton said it was time to fetch in the Snapdragon Bowl, and watch it flame. You know the game? It is a great bowl of lighted spirit, and you must thrust in your hand and pluck out a raisin from the bottom with-out scorching your fingers. Mr. Fenton carried it in on a tray in the half-darkness; it was flickering with that bluish flame you have seen on Christmas pud-dings. Miss Abbott said that once, in carrying it, he started and turned round. She said that for a second she thought there was a face looking over his shoulder, and it wasn't a nice face.

"Later in the evening, when the children were sleepy and there was tissue-paper scattered all over the house, the grown-ups began their games in earnest. Someone suggested Blind Man's Buff. They were mostly using the hall and this room here, as having more space than the dining-room. Various members of the party were blindfolded with men's handkerchiefs; but there was a dreadful amount of cheating. Mr. Fenton grew quite annoyed about it, because the ladies almost always caught Mr. Wilkes when they could; Mr. Wilkes was laughing and perspiring heartily, and his great cravat with the silver pin had almost come loose.

"To make it certain nobody could cheat, Mr. Fenton got a little white linen bag—like this one. It was the pillow-cover off the baby's cot, really; and he said nobody could look through that if it were tied over the head.

"I should explain that they have been having some trouble with the lamp in this room. Mr. Fenton said: 'Confound it, Mother, what is wrong with that lamp? Turn up the wick, will you?' It was really quite a good lamp from Spence and Minstead's, and should not have burned dull as it did. In the confusion, while Mrs. Fenton was trying to make the light better, and he was looking over her shoulder at her, Mr. Fenton had been rather absently fastening the bag on the head of the last person caught. He has said since that he did not notice who it was. No-one else noticed, either, the light being so dim and there being such a large number of people. It seemed to be a girl in a broad bluish kind of dress, standing over near the door.

"Perhaps you know how people act when they have just been blindfolded in this game. First they usually stand very still, as though they were smelling or sensing in which direction to go. Sometimes they make a sudden jump, or sometimes they begin to shuffle gently forward. Everyone noticed what an air of *purpose* there seemed to be about this person whose face was covered; she went forward very slowly, and seemed to crouch down a bit.

"It began to move towards Mr. Wilkes in very short but quick little jerks, the white bag bobbing on its face. At this time Mr. Wilkes was sitting at the end of the table, laughing, with his face pink above the beard, and a glass of our Kentish cider in his hand. I want you to imagine this room as being very dim, and much more cluttered, what with all the tassels they had on the furniture then; and the high-piled hair of the ladies, too. The hooded person got to the edge of the table. It began to edge along towards Mr. Wilkes's chair; and then it jumped.

"Mr. Wilkes got up and skipped (yes, skipped) out of its way, laughing. It waited quietly, after which it went, in the same slow way, towards him again. It nearly got him again, by the edge of the potted plant. All this time it did not say anything, you understand, although everyone was applauding it and crying encouraging advice. It kept its head down. Miss Abbott says she began to notice an unpleasant faint smell of burnt cloth or something worse, which turned her half-ill. By the time the hooded person came stooping clear across the room, as certainly as though it could see him, Mr. Wilkes was not laughing any longer.

"In the corner by one bookcase, he said out loud: 'I'm tired of this silly, rotten game; go away, do you hear?' Nobody there had ever heard him speak like that, in such a loud, wild way, but they laughed and thought it must be the Kentish cider. 'Go away!' cried Mr. Wilkes again, and began to strike at it with his fist. All this time, Miss Abbott says, she had observed his face gradually changing. He dodged again, very pleasant and nimble for such a big man, but with the perspiration running down his face. Back across the room he went again, with it following him; and he cried out something that most naturally shocked them all inexpressibly.

"He screamed out: 'For God's sake, Fenton, take it off me!'

"And for the last time the thing jumped.

"They were over near the curtains of that bay window, which were drawn as they are now. Miss Twigelow, who was nearest, says that Mr. Wilkes could not have seen anything, because the white bag was still drawn over the woman's head. The only thing she noticed was that at the lower part of the bag, where the face must have been, there was a curious kind of discoloration, a stain of some sort which had not been there before: something seemed to be seeping through. Mr. Wilkes fell back between the curtains, with the hooded person after him, and screamed again. There was a kind of thrashing noise in or behind the curtains; then they fell straight again, and everything grew quiet.

"Now, our Kentish cider is very strong, and for a moment Mr. Fenton did not know what to think. He tried to laugh at it, but the laugh did not sound well. Then he went over to the curtains, calling out gruffly to them to come out of there and not play the fool. But, after he had looked inside the curtains, he turned round very sharply and asked the rector to get the ladies out of the room. This was done, but Miss Abbott often said that she had one quick peep inside. Though the bay windows were locked on the inside, Mr. Wilkes was now alone on the window seat. She could see his beard sticking up, and the blood. He was dead, of course. But, since he had murdered Jane Waycross, I sincerely think he deserved to die."

For several seconds, the two listeners did not move. She had all too successfully conjured up this room in the late 'seventies, whose stuffiness still seemed to pervade it now.

"But look here!" protested Hunter, when he could fight down an inclination to get out of the room quickly. "You say he killed her after all? And yet you told us he had an absolute alibi. You said he never went closer to the house than the windows . . ."

"No more he did, my dear," said the other.

"He was courting the Linshaw heiress at the time," she resumed; "and Miss Linshaw was a very proper young lady who would have been horrified if she had heard about him and Jane Waycross. She would have broken off the match, naturally. But poor Jane Waycross meant her to hear. She was much in love with Mr. Wilkes, and she was going to tell the whole matter publicly: Mr. Wilkes had been trying to persuade her not to do so."

"But—"

"Oh, don't you see what happened?" cried the other in a pettish tone. "It is so dreadfully simple. I am not clever at these things, but I should have seen it in a moment: even if I did not already know. I told you everything so that you should be able to guess.

"When Mr. Wilkes and Dr. Sutton and Mr. Pawley drove past here in the gig that night, they saw a bright light burning in the windows of this room. I told you that. But the police never wondered, as anyone should, what caused that light. Jane Waycross never came into this room, as you know; she was out in the hall, carrying either a lamp or a candle. But that lamp in the thick blue-silk shade, held out there in the hall, would not have caused a bright light to shine through this room and illuminate it. Neither would a tiny candle; it is absurd. And I told you there were no other lamps in the house except some empty ones waiting to be filled in the back kitchen. There is only one thing they could have seen. They saw the great blaze of the paraffin oil round Jane Waycross's body.

"Didn't I tell you it was dreadfully simple? Poor Jane was upstairs waiting for her lover. From the upstairs window she saw Mr. Wilkes's gig drive along the road in the moonlight, and she did not know there were other men in it; she thought he was alone. She came downstairs—

"It is an awful thing that the police did not think more about that broken medicine-bottle lying in the hall, the large bottle that was broken in just two long pieces. She must have had a use for it; and, of course, she had. You knew that the oil in the lamp was almost exhausted, although there was a great blaze round the body. When poor Jane came downstairs, she was carrying the unlighted lamp in one hand; in the other hand she was carrying a lighted candle, and an old medicine-bottle containing paraffin oil. When she got downstairs, she meant to fill the lamp from the medicine-bottle, and then light it with the candle.

"But she was too eager to get downstairs, I am afraid. When she was more than half-way down, hurrying, that long nightgown tripped her. She pitched forward down the stairs on her face. The medicine-bottle broke on the tiles under her, and poured a lake of paraffin round her body. Of course, the lighted candle set the paraffin blazing when it fell; but that was not all. One intact side of that broken bottle, long and sharp and cleaner than any blade, cut into her throat when she fell on the smashed bottle. She was not quite stunned by the fall. When she felt herself burning, and the blood almost as hot, she tried to save herself. She tried to crawl forward on her hands, forward into the hall, away from the blood and oil and fire.

"That was what Mr. Wilkes really saw when he looked in through the window.

"You see, he had been unable to get rid of the two fuddled friends, who insisted on clinging to him and drinking with him. He had been obliged to drive them home. If he could not go to 'Clearlawns' now, he wondered how at least he could leave a message; and the light in the window gave him an excuse.

"He saw pretty Jane propped up on her hands in the hall, looking out at him beseechingly while the blue flame ran up and turned yellow. You might have thought he would have pitied, for she loved him very much. Her wound was not really a deep wound. If he had broken into the house at that moment, he might have saved her life. But he preferred to let her die; because now she would make no public scandal and spoil his chances with the rich Miss Linshaw. That was why he returned to his friends and told a lie about a murderer in a tall hat. It is why, in heaven's truth, he murdered her himself. But when he returned to his friends, I do not wonder that they saw him mopping his forehead. You know now how Jane Waycross came back for him, presently."

There was another heavy silence.

The girl got to her feet, with a sort of bouncing motion which was as suggestive as it was vaguely familiar. It was thought she were about to run. She stood there, a trifle crouched in her prim brown dress, so oddly narrow at the waist after an old-fashioned pattern; and in the play of light on her face Rodney Hunter fancied that its prettiness was only a shell.

"The same thing happened afterwards, on some Christmas Eves," she explained. "They played Blind Man's Buff over again. That is why people who live here do not care to risk it nowadays. It happens at a quarter-past-seven—"

Hunter stared at the curtains. "But it was a quarter-past seven when we got here!" he said. "It must now be—"

"Oh, yes," said the girl, and her eyes brimmed over. "You see, I told you you had nothing to fear; it was all over then. But that is not why I thank you. I begged you to stay, and you did. You have listened to me, as no-one else would. And now I have told it at last, and now I think both of us can sleep."

Not a fold stirred or altered in the dark curtains that closed the window bay; yet, as though a blurred lens had come into focus, they now seemed innocent and devoid of harm. You could have put a

154

Christmas-tree there. Rodney Hunter, with Muriel following his gaze, walked across and threw back the curtains. He saw a quiet window-seat covered with chintz, and the rising moon beyond the window. When he turned round, the girl in the old-fashioned dress was not there. But the front doors were open again, for he could feel a current of air blowing through the house.

With his arm round Muriel, who was white-faced, he went out into the hall. They did not look long at the scorched and beaded stains at the foot of the paneling, for even the scars of fire seemed gentle now. Instead, they stood in the doorway looking out, while the house threw its great blaze of light across the frosty Weald. It was a welcoming light. Over the rise of a hill, black dots trudging in the frost showed that Jack Bannister's party was returning; and they could hear the sound of voices carrying far. They heard one of the party carelessly singing a Christmas carol for glory and joy, and the laughter of children coming home.

Dorothy L. Sayers

The Necklace of Pearls

Sir Septimus Shale was accustomed to assert his
authority once in the year and once only. He allowed
his young and fashionable wife to fill his house with
diagrammatic furniture made of steel; to collect
advanced artists and anti-grammatical poets; to
believe in cocktails and relativity and to dress as
extravagantly as she pleased; but he did insist on an
old-fashioned Christmas. He was a simple-hearted
man, who really liked plum-pudding and cracker
mottoes, and he could not get it out of his head
that other people, 'at bottom', enjoyed these things
also. At Christmas, therefore, he firmly retired to
his country house in Essex, called in the servants to
hang holly and mistletoe upon the cubist electric fit-
tings; loaded the steel sideboard with delicacies from
Fortnum & Mason; hung up stockings at the heads
of the polished walnut bedsteads; and even, on this
occasion only, had the electric radiators removed
from the modernist grates and installed wood
fires and a Yule log. He then gathered his family
and friends about him, filled them with as much

Dickensian good fare as he could persuade them to swallow, and, after their Christmas dinner, set them down to play 'Charades' and 'Clumps' and 'Animal, Vegetable, and Mineral' in the drawing-room, concluding these diversions by 'Hide-and-Seek' in the dark all over the house. Because Sir Septimus was a very rich man, his guests fell in with this invariable programme, and if they were bored, they did not tell him so.

Another charming and traditional custom which he followed was that of presenting to his daughter Margharita a pearl on each successive birthday – this anniversary happening to coincide with Christmas Eve. The pearls now numbered twenty, and the collection was beginning to enjoy a certain celebrity, and had been photographed in the Society papers. Though not sensationally large – each one being about the size of a marrowfat pea – the pearls were of very great value. They were of exquisite colour and perfect shape and matched to a hair's-weight. On this particular Christmas Eve, the presentation of the twenty-first pearl had been the occasion of a very special ceremony. There was a dance and there were speeches. On the Christmas night following, the more restricted family party took place, with the turkey and the Victorian games. There were eleven guests, in addition to Sir Septimus and Lady Shale and their daughter, nearly all related or connected to them in some way: John Shale, a brother, with his wife and their son and daughter Henry and Betty; Betty's fiancé, Oswald Truegood, a young man with parliamentary ambitions; George Comphrey, a cousin of Lady Shale's, aged about thirty and known as a man about town; Lavinia Prescott, asked on George's account; Joyce Trivett, asked on Henry Shale's account; Richard and Beryl Dennison, distant relations of Lady Shale, who lived a gay and expensive life in town on nobody precisely knew what resources; and Lord Peter Wimsey, asked, in a touching spirit of unreasonable hope, on Margharita's account. There were also, of course, William Norgate, secretary to Sir Septimus, and Miss Tomkins, secretary to Lady Shale, who had to be there because, without their calm efficiency, the Christmas arrangements could not have been carried through.

Dinner was over – a seemingly endless succession of soup, fish, turkey, roast beef, plum-pudding, mince-pies, crystallized fruit, nuts, and five kinds of wine, presided over by Sir Septimus, all smiles, by Lady Shale, all mocking deprecation, and by Margharita, pretty and bored, with the necklace of twenty-one pearls gleaming softly on her slender throat. Gorged and dyspeptic and longing only for the horizontal position, the company had been shepherded into the drawing-room and set to play 'Musical Chairs' (Miss Tomkins at the piano), 'Hunt the Slipper' (slipper provided by Miss Tomkins), and 'Dumb Crambo' (costumes by Miss Tomkins and Mr William Norgate). The back drawing-room (for Sir Septimus clung to these old-fashioned names) provided an admirable dressing-room, being screened by folding doors from the large drawing-room in which the audience sat on aluminium chairs, scrabbling uneasy toes on a floor of black glass under the tremendous illumination of electricity reflected from a brass ceiling.

It was William Norgate who, after taking the temperature of the meeting, suggested to Lady Shale that they should play at something less athletic. Lady Shale agreed and, as usual, suggested bridge. Sir Septimus, as usual, blew the suggestion aside.

'Bridge? Nonsense! Nonsense! Play bridge every day of your lives. This is Christmas time. Something we can all play together. How about "Animal, Vegetable, and Mineral"?'

This intellectual pastime was a favourite with Sir Septimus; he was rather good at putting pregnant questions. After a brief discussion, it became evident that this game was an inevitable part of the programme. The party settled down to it, Sir Septimus undertaking to 'go out' first and set the thing going.

Presently they had guessed among other things Miss Tomkins's mother's photograph, a gramophone record of 'I want to be happy' (much scientific research into the exact composition of records, settled by William Norgate out of the *Encyclopaedia Britannica*), the smallest stickleback in the stream at the bottom of the garden, the new planet Pluto, the scarf worn by Mrs Dennison (very confusing, because it was not silk, which would be animal, or artificial silk, which would be vegetable, but made of spun glass – mineral, a very clever choice of subject), and had failed to guess the Prime Minister's wireless speech – which was voted not fair, since nobody could decide whether it was animal by nature or a kind of gas. It was decided that they should do one more word and then go on to 'Hide-and-Seek'. Oswald Truegood had retired into the back room and shut the door behind him while the party discussed the next subject of examination, when suddenly Sir Septimus broke in on the argument by calling to his daughter:

'Hullo, Margy! What have you done with your necklace?'

'I took it off, Dad, because I thought it might get

broken in "Dumb Crambo". It's over here on this table. No, it isn't. Did you take it, mother?'

'No, I didn't. If I'd seen it, I should have. You are a careless child.'

'I believe you've got it yourself, Dad. You're teasing.'

Sir Septimus denied the accusation with some energy. Everybody got up and began to hunt about. There were not many places in that bare and polished room where a necklace could be hidden. After ten minutes' fruitless investigation, Richard Dennison, who had been seated next to the table where the pearls had been placed, began to look rather uncomfortable.

'Awkward, you know,' he remarked to Wimsey.

At this moment, Oswald Truegood put his head through the folding-doors and asked whether they hadn't settled on something by now, because he was getting the fidgets.

This directed the attention of the searchers to the inner room. Margharita must have been mistaken. She had taken it in there, and it had got mixed up with the dressing-up clothes somehow. The room was ransacked. Everything was lifted up and shaken. The thing began to look serious. After half an hour of desperate energy it became apparent that the pearls were nowhere to be found.

'They must be somewhere in these two rooms, you know,' said Wimsey. 'The back drawing-room has no door and nobody could have gone out of the front drawing-room without being seen. Unless the windows –'

No. The windows were all guarded on the outside by heavy shutters which it needed two footmen to take down and replace. The pearls had not gone out that way. In fact, the mere suggestion that they had left the drawing-room at all was disagreeable. Because – because –

It was William Norgate, efficient as ever, who coldly and boldly, faced the issue.

'I think, Sir Septimus, it would be a relief to the minds of everybody present if we could all be searched.

Sir Septimus was horrified, but the guests, having found a leader, backed up Norgate. The door was locked, and the search was conducted – the ladies in the inner room and the men in the outer.

Nothing resulted from it except some very interesting information about the belongings habitually carried about by the average man and woman. It was natural that Lord Peter Wimsey should possess a pair of forceps, a pocket lens, and a small folding foot-rule – was he not a Sherlock Holmes in high life? But that Oswald Truegood should have

163

two liver-pills in a screw of paper and Henry Shale a pocket edition of *The Odes of Horace* was unexpected. Why did John Shale distend the pockets of his dress-suit with a stump of red sealing-wax, an ugly little mascot, and a five-shilling piece? George Comphrey had a pair of folding scissors, and three wrapped lumps of sugar, of the sort served in restaurants and dining-cars – evidence of a not uncommon form of kleptomania; but that the tidy and exact Norgate should burden himself with a reel of white cotton, three separate lengths of string, and twelve safety-pins on a card seemed really remarkable till one remembered that he had superintended all the Christmas decorations. Richard Dennison, amid some confusion and laughter, was found to cherish a lady's garter, a powder-compact, and half a potato; the last-named, he said, was a prophylactic against rheumatism (to which he was subject), while the other objects belonged to his wife. On the ladies' side, the more striking exhibits were a little book on palmistry, three invisible hair-pins, and a baby's photograph (Miss Tomkins); a Chinese trick cigarette-case with a secret compartment (Beryl Dennison); a *very* private letter and an outfit for mending stocking-ladders (Lavinia Prescott); and a pair of eyebrow tweezers and a small packet of white powder, said to be for headaches (Betty Shale). An agitating moment followed the production from Joyce Trivett's handbag of a small string of pearls – but it was promptly remembered that these had come out of one of the crackers at dinner-time, and they were, in fact, synthetic. In short, the search was unproductive of anything beyond a general shame-facedness and the discomfort always produced by undressing and re-dressing in a hurry at the wrong time of the day.

It was then that somebody, very grudgingly and haltingly, mentioned the horrid word 'Police'. Sir Septimus, naturally, was appalled by the idea. It was disgusting. He would not allow it. The pearls must be somewhere. They must search the rooms again. Could not Lord Peter Wimsey, with his experience of – er – mysterious happenings, do something to assist them?

'Eh?' said his lordship. 'Oh, by Jove, yes – by all means, certainly. That is to say, provided nobody supposes – eh, what? I mean to say, you don't know that I'm not a suspicious character, do you, what?'

Lady Shale interposed with authority.

'We don't think *anybody* ought to be suspected,' she said, 'but, if we did, we'd know it couldn't be you. You know *far* too much about crimes to want to commit one.'

'All right,' said Wimsey. 'But after the way

the place has been gone over –' He shrugged his shoulders.

'Yes, I'm afraid you won't be able to find any footprints,' said Margharita. 'But we may have overlooked something.'

Wimsey nodded.

'I'll try. Do you all mind sitting down on your chairs in the outer room and staying there. All except one of you – I'd better have a witness to anything I do or find. Sir Septimus – you'd be the best person, I think.'

He shepherded them to their places and began a slow circuit of the two rooms, exploring every surface, gazing up to the polished brazen ceiling, and crawling on hands and knees in the approved fashion across the black and shining desert of the floors. Sir Septimus followed, staring when Wimsey stared, bending with his hands upon his knees when Wimsey crawled, and puffing at intervals with astonishment and chagrin. Their progress rather resembled that of a man taking out a very inquisitive puppy for a very leisurely constitutional. Fortunately, Lady Shale's taste in furnishing made investigation easier; there were scarcely any nooks or corners where anything could be concealed.

They reached the inner drawing-room, and here the dressing-up clothes were again minutely examined, but without result. Finally, Wimsey lay down flat on his stomach to squint under a steel cabinet which was one of the very few pieces of furniture which possessed short legs. Something about it seemed to catch his attention. He rolled up his sleeve and plunged his arm into the cavity, kicked convulsively in the effort to reach farther than was humanly possible, pulled out from his pocket and extended his folding foot-rule, fished with it under the cabinet, and eventually succeeded in extracting what he sought.

It was a very minute object – in fact, a pin. Not an ordinary pin, but one resembling those used by entomologists to impale extremely small moths on the setting-board. It was about three-quarters of an inch in length, as fine as a very fine needle, with a sharp point and a particularly small head.

'Bless my soul!' said Sir Septimus. 'What's that?'

'Does anybody here happen to collect moths or beetles or anything?' asked Wimsey, squatting on his haunches and examining the pin.

'I'm pretty sure they don't,' replied Sir Septimus. 'I'll ask them.'

'Don't do that.' Wimsey bent his head and started at the floor, from which his own face started meditatively back at him.

'I see,' said Wimsey presently. 'That's how it was done. All right, Sir Septimus. I know where the pearls are, but I don't know who took them. Perhaps it would be as well – for everybody's satisfaction – just to find out. In the meantime they are perfectly safe. Don't tell anyone that we've found this pin or that we've discovered anything. Send all these people to bed. Lock the drawing-room door and keep the key, and we'll get our man – or woman – by breakfast-time.'

'God bless my soul,' said Sir Septimus, very much puzzled.

Lord Peter Wimsey kept careful watch that night upon the drawing-room door. Nobody, however, came near it. Either the thief suspected a trap or he felt confident that any time would do to recover the pearls. Wimsey, however, did not feel that he was wasting his time. He was making a list of people who had been left alone in the back drawing-room during the playing of 'Animal, Vegetable, and Mineral'. The list ran as follows:

Sir Septimus Shale

Lavinia Prescott

William Norgate

Joyce Trivett and Henry Shale (together, because they
   had claimed to be incapable of guessing anything
   unaided)

Mrs Dennison

Betty Shale

George Comphrey

Richard Dennison

Miss Tomkins

Oswald Truegood

He also made out a list of the persons to whom
pearls might be useful or desirable. Unfortunately,
this list agreed in almost all respects with the first
(always excepting Sir Septimus) and so was not very
helpful. The two secretaries had both come well
recommended, but that was exactly what they would
have done had they come with ulterior designs;
the Dennisons were notorious livers from hand to
mouth; Betty Shale carried mysterious white pow-
ders in her handbag, and was known to be in with a
rather rapid set in town; Henry was a harmless dil-
ettante, but Joyce Trivett could twist him round her
little finger and was what Jane Austen liked to call
'expensive and dissipated'; Comphrey speculated;
Oswald Truegood was rather frequently present at
Epsom and Newmarket – the search for motives was
only too fatally easy.

When the second housemaid and the under-footman appeared in the passage with household implements, Wimsey abandoned his vigil, but he was down early to breakfast. Sir Septimus with his wife and daughter were down before him, and a certain air of tension made itself felt. Wimsey, standing on the hearth before the fire, made conversation about the weather and politics.

The party assembled gradually, but, as though by common consent, nothing was said about pearls until after breakfast, when Oswald Truegood took the bull by the horns.

'Well now!' said he. 'How's the detective getting along? Got your man, Wimsey?'

'Not yet,' said Wimsey easily.

Sir Septimus, looking at Wimsey as though for his cue, cleared his throat and dashed into speech.

'All very tiresome,' he said, 'all very unpleasant. Hr'rm. Nothing for it but the police, I'm afraid. Just at Christmas, too. Hr'rm. Spoilt the party. Can't stand seeing all this stuff about the place.' He waved his hand towards the festoons of evergreens and coloured paper that adorned the walls. 'Take it all down, eh, what? No heart in it. Hr'rm. Burn the lot.'

'What a pity, when we worked so hard over it,' said Joyce.

'Oh, leave it, Uncle,' said Henry Shale. 'You're bothering too much about the pearls. They're sure to turn up.'

'Shall I ring for James?' suggested William Norgate.

'No,' interrupted Comphrey, 'let's do it ourselves. It'll give us something to do and take our minds off our troubles.'

'That's right,' said Sir Septimus. 'Start right away. Hate the sight of it.'

He savagely hauled a great branch of holly down from the mantelpiece and flung it, crackling, into the fire.

'That's the stuff,' said Richard Dennison. 'Make a good old blaze!' He leapt up from the table and snatched the mistletoe from the chandelier. 'Here goes! One more kiss for somebody before it's too late.'

'Isn't it unlucky to take it down before the New Year?' suggested Miss Tomkins.

'Unlucky be hanged. We'll have it all down. Off the stairs and out of the drawing-room too. Somebody go and collect it.'

'Isn't the drawing-room locked?' asked Oswald.

'No. Lord Peter says the pearls aren't there, wherever else they are, so it's unlocked. That's right, isn't it, Wimsey?'

'Quite right. The pearls were taken out of these rooms. I can't tell yet how, but I'm positive of it. In fact, I'll pledge my reputation that wherever they are, they're not up there.'

'Oh, well,' said Comphrey, 'in that case, have at it! Come along, Lavinia – you and Dennison do the drawing-room and I'll do the back room. We'll have a race.'

'But if the police are coming in,' said Dennison, 'oughtn't everything to be left just as it is?'

'Damn the police!' shouted Sir Septimus. 'They don't want evergreens.'

Oswald and Margharita were already pulling the holly and ivy from the staircase, amid peals of laughter. The party dispersed. Wimsey went quietly upstairs and into the drawing-room, where the work of demolition was taking place at a great rate, George having bet the other two ten shillings to a tanner that they would not finish their part of the job before he finished his.

'You mustn't help,' said Lavinia, laughing to Wimsey. 'It wouldn't be fair.'

Wimsey said nothing, but waited till the room was clear. Then he followed them down again to the hall, where the fire was sending up a great roaring and spluttering, suggestive of Guy Fawkes' night.

He whispered to Sir Septimus, who went forward and touched George Comphrey on the shoulder.

'Lord Peter wants to say something to you, my boy,' he said.

Comphrey started and went with him a little reluctantly, as it seemed. He was not looking very well.

'Mr Comphrey,' said Wimsey, 'I fancy these are some of your property.' He held out the palm of his hand, in which rested twenty-two fine, small-headed pins.

'Ingenious,' said Wimsey, 'but something less ingenious would have served his turn better. It was very unlucky, Sir Septimus, that you should have mentioned the pearls when you did. Of course, he hoped that the loss wouldn't be discovered till we'd chucked guessing games and taken to "Hide-and-Seek". Then the pearls might have been anywhere in the house, we shouldn't have locked the drawing-room door, and he could have recovered them at his leisure. He had had this possibility in his mind when he came here, obviously, and that was why he brought the pins, and Miss Shale's taking off the necklace to play "Dumb Crambo" gave him his opportunity.

'He had spent Christmas here before, and knew perfectly well that "Animal, Vegetable, and Mineral"

would form part of the entertainment. He had only
to gather up the necklace from the table when it
came to his turn to retire, and he knew he could
count on at least five minutes by himself while we
were all arguing about the choice of a word. He
had only to snip the pearls from the string with his
pocket-scissors, burn the string in the grate, and
fasten the pearls to the mistletoe with the fine pins.
The mistletoe was hung on the chandelier, pretty
high – it's a lofty room – but he could easily reach it
by standing on the glass table, which wouldn't show
footmarks, and it was almost certain that nobody
would think of examining the mistletoe for extra
berries. I shouldn't have thought of it myself if I
hadn't found that pin which he had dropped. That
gave me the idea that the pearls had been separated and the rest was easy. I took the pearls off the
mistletoe last night – the clasp was there, too, pinned
among the holly-leaves. Here they are. Comphrey
must have got a nasty shock this morning. I knew
he was our man when he suggested that the guests
should tackle the decorations themselves and that
he should do the back drawing-room – but I wish I
had seen his face when he came to the mistletoe and
found the pearls gone.'

'And you worked it all out when you found the
pin?' said Sir Septimus.

'Yes; I knew then where the pearls had gone to.'

'But you never even looked at the mistletoe.'

'I saw it reflected in the black glass floor, and it struck me then how much the mistletoe berries looked like pearls.'

ETHEL LINA WHITE

Waxworks

Sonia made her first entry in her notebook:

> Eleven o'clock. The lights are out. The porter has
> just locked the door. I can hear his footsteps echoing
> down the corridor. They grow fainter. Now there is
> silence. I am alone.

She stopped writing to glance at her company.
Seen in the light from the street-lamp, which
streamed in through the high window, the room
seemed to be full of people. Their faces were those
of men and women of character and intelligence.
They stood in groups, as though in conversation, or
sat apart, in solitary reverie.

But they neither moved nor spoke.

When Sonia had last seen them in the glare of
the electric globes, they had been a collection of
ordinary waxworks, some of which were the worse
for wear. The black velvet which lined the walls of
the Gallery was alike tawdry and filmed with dust.

The side opposite to the window was built into

alcoves, which held highly moral tableaux, depicting contrasting scenes in the career of Vice and Virtue. Sonia had slipped into one of these recesses, just before closing-time, in order to hide for her vigil.

It had been a simple affair. The porter had merely rung his bell, and the few courting-couples which represented the Public had taken his hint and hurried towards the exit.

No one was likely to risk being locked in, for the Waxwork Collection of Oldhampton, had lately acquired a sinister reputation. The foundation for this lay in the fate of a stranger to the town—a commercial traveller—who had cut his throat in the Hall of Horrors.

Since then, two persons had, separately, spent the night in the Gallery and, in the morning, each had been found dead.

In both cases the verdict had been 'Natural death, due to heart failure.' The first victim—a local alderman—had been addicted to alcoholism, and was in very bad shape. The second—his great friend—was a delicate little man, a martyr to asthma, and slightly unhinged through unwise absorption in spiritualism.

While the coincidence of the tragedies stirred up a considerable amount of local superstition, the general belief was that both deaths were due to the power of suggestion, in conjunction with macabre surroundings. The victims had let themselves be frightened to death by the Waxworks.

Sonia was there, in the Gallery, to test its truth.

She was the latest addition to the staff of the *Oldhampton Gazette*. Bubbling with enthusiasm, she made no secret of her literary ambitions, and it was difficult to feed her with enough work. Her colleagues listened to her with mingled amusement and boredom, but they liked her as a refreshing novelty. As for her fine future, they looked to young Wells—the Sporting Editor—to effect her speedy and painless removal from the sphere of journalism.

On Christmas Eve, Sonia took them all into her confidence over her intention to spend a night in the Waxworks, on the last night of the old year.

'Copy there,' she declared. 'I'm not timid and I have fairly sensitive perceptions, so I ought to be able to write up the effect of imagination on the nervous system. I mean to record my impressions, every hour, while they're piping-hot.'

Looking up suddenly, she had surprised a green glare in the eyes of Hubert Poke.

When Sonia came to work on the *Gazette*, she had a secret fear of unwelcome amorous attentions, since she was the only woman on the staff. But the first passion she awoke was hatred.

Poke hated her impersonally, as the representative of a Force, numerically superior to his own sex, which was on the opposing side in the battle for existence. He feared her, too, because she was the unknown element, and possessed the unfair weapon of charm.

Before she came, he had been the star turn on the *Gazette*. His own position on the staff gratified his vanity and entirely satisfied his narrow ambition. But Sonia had stolen some of his thunder. On more than one occasion she had written up a story he had failed to cover, and he had to admit that her success was due to a quicker wit.

For some time past he had been playing with the idea of spending a night in the Waxworks, but was deterred by the knowledge that his brain was not sufficiently temperate for the experiment. Lately he had been subject to sudden red rages, when he had felt a thick hot taste in his throat, as though of blood. He knew that his jealousy of Sonia was accountable. It had almost reached the stage of mania, and trembled on the brink of homicidal urge.

While his brain was still creaking with the idea of first-hand experience in the ill-omened Gallery, Sonia had nipped in with her ready-made plan.

Controlling himself with an effort, he listened while the sub-editor issued a warning to Sonia.

'Bon idea, young woman, but you will find the experience a bit raw. You've no notion how uncanny these big deserted buildings can be.'

'That's so,' nodded young Wells, 'I once spent a night in a haunted house.'

Sonia looked at him with her habitual interest. He was short and thick-set, with a three-cornered smile which appealed to her.

'Did you see anything?' she asked.

'No, I cleared out before the show came on. Windy. After a bit, one can imagine *anything*.'

It was then that Poke introduced a new note into the discussion by his own theory of the mystery deaths.

Sitting alone in the deserted Gallery, Sonia preferred to forget his words. She resolutely drove them from her mind while she began to settle down for the night.

Her first action was to cross to the figure of Cardinal Wolsey and unceremoniously raise his heavy scarlet robe. From under its voluminous folds, she drew out her cushion and attaché-case, which she had hidden earlier in the evening.

Mindful of the fact that it would grow chilly at dawn, she carried on her arm her thick white tennis-coat. Slipping it on, she placed her cushion in the angle of the wall, and sat down to await developments.

The Gallery was far more mysterious now that the lights were out. At either end, it seemed to stretch away into impenetrable black tunnels. But there was nothing uncanny about it, or about the figures, which were a tame and conventional collection of historical personages. Even the adjoining Hall of Horrors contained no horrors, only a selection of respectable-looking poisoners.

Sonia grinned cheerfully at the row of waxworks which were visible in the lamplight from the street.

'So you are the villains of the piece,' she murmured. 'Later on, if the office is right, you will assume unpleasant mannerisms to try to cheat me into believing you are alive. I warn you, old sports, you'll have your work cut out for you . . . And now I think I'll get better acquainted with you. Familiarity breeds contempt.'

She went the round of the figures, greeting each with flippancy or criticism. Presently she returned to her corner and opened her notebook ready to record her impressions.

Twelve o'clock. The first hour has passed almost too quickly. I've drawn a complete blank. Not a blessed thing to record. Not a vestige of reaction.

The waxworks seem a commonplace lot, without a scrap of hypnotic force. In fact, they're altogether too matey.

Sonia had left her corner, to write her entry in the light which streamed through the window. Smoking was prohibited in the building, and, lest she should yield to temptation, she had left both her cigarettes and matches behind her, on the office table.

At this stage she regretted the matches. A little extra light would be a boon. It was true she carried an electric torch, but she was saving it, in case of emergency.

It was a loan from young Wells. As they were leaving the office together, he spoke to her confidentially.

'Did you notice how Poke glared at you? Don't get up against him. He's a nasty piece of work. He's so mean he'd sell his mother's shroud for old rags. And he's a cruel little devil, too. He turned out his miserable pup, to starve in the streets, rather than cough up for the licence.'

Sonia grew hot with indignation.

'What he needs to cure his complaint is a strong dose of rat-poison,' she declared.

'What became of the poor little dog?'

'Oh, he's all right. He was a matey chap, and he soon chummed up with a mongrel of his own class.'

'You?' asked Sonia, her eyes suddenly soft.

'A mongrel, am I?' grinned Wells. 'Well, anyway, the pup will get a better Christmas than his first, when Poke went away and left him on the chain . . . We're both of us going to over-eat and over-drink. You're on your own, too. Won't you join us?'

'I'd love to.'

Although the evening was warm and muggy the invitation suffused Sonia with the spirit of Christmas. The shade of Dickens seemed to be hovering over the parade of the streets. A red-nosed Santa Claus presided over a spangled Christmas-tree outside a toy-shop. Windows were hung with tinseled balls and coloured paper festoons. Pedestrians, laden with parcels, called out seasonable greetings.

'Merry Christmas.'

Young Wells' three-cornered smile was his tribute to the joyous feeling of festival. His eyes were eager as he turned to Sonia.

'I've an idea. Don't wait until after the holidays to write up the Waxworks. Make it a Christmas stunt, and go there tonight.'

'I will,' declared Sonia.

It was then that he slipped the torch into her hand.

'I know you belong to the stronger sex,' he said.

'But even your nerve might crash. If it does, just flash this torch under the window. Stretch out your arm above your head, and the light will be seen from the street.'

'And what will happen then?' asked Sonia.

'I shall knock up the miserable porter and let you out.'

'But how will *you* see the light?'

'I shall be in the street.'

'All night?'

'Yes; I sleep there.' Young Wells grinned. 'Understand,' he added loftily, 'that this is a matter of principle. I could not let any woman—even one so aged and unattractive as yourself—feel beyond the reach of help.'

He cut into her thanks as he turned away with a parting warning.

'Don't use the torch for light, or the juice may give out. It's about due for a new battery.'

As Sonia looked at the torch, lying by her side, it seemed a link with young Wells. At this moment he was patrolling the street, a sturdy figure in old tweed overcoat, with his cap pulled down over his eyes.

As she tried to pick out his footsteps from among those of the other passers-by, it struck her that there was plenty of traffic, considering that it was past twelve o'clock.

'The witching hour of midnight is another lost illusion,' she reflected. 'Killed by night-clubs, I suppose.'

It was cheerful to know that so many citizens were abroad, to keep her company. Some optimists were still singing carols. She faintly heard the strains of 'Good King Wenceslas.' It was in a tranquil frame of mind that she unpacked her sandwiches and thermos.

'It's Christmas Day,' she thought, as she drank hot coffee. 'And I'm spending it with Don and the pup.'

At that moment her career grew misty, and the flame of her literary ambition dipped as the future glowed with the warm firelight of home. In sudden elation, she held up her flask and toasted the waxworks.

'Merry Christmas to you all! And many of them.'

The faces of the illuminated figures remained stolid, but she could almost swear that a low murmur of acknowledgment seemed to swell from the rest of her company—invisible in the darkness.

She spun out her meal to its limit, stifling her craving for a cigarette. Then, growing bored, she counted the visible waxworks, and tried to memorise them.

'Twenty-one, twenty-two . . . Wolsey. Queen Elizabeth, Guy Fawkes, Napoleon ought to go on a diet. Ever heard of eighteen days, Nap? Poor old Julius Caesar looks as though he'd been sun-bathing on the Lido. He's about due for the melting-pot.'

In her eyes they were a second-rate set of dummies. The local theory that they could terrorise a human being to death or madness seemed a fantastic notion.

'No,' concluded Sonia. 'There's really more in Poke's bright idea.'

Again she saw the sun-smitten office—for the big unshielded window faced south—with its blistered paint, faded wall-paper, ink-stained desks, typewriters, telephones, and a huge fire in the untidy grate. Young Wells smoked his big pipe, while the subeditor—a ginger, pig-headed young man—laid down the law about the mystery deaths.

And then she heard Poke's toneless dead-man's voice.

'You may be right about the spiritualist. He died of fright—but not of the waxworks. My belief is that he established contact with the spirit of his dead friend, the alderman, and so learned his real fate.'

'What fate?' snapped the sub-editor.

'I believe that the alderman was murdered,' replied Poke.

He clung to his point like a limpet in the face of all counter-arguments.

'The alderman had enemies,' he said. 'Nothing would be easier than for one of them to lie in wait for him. In the present circumstances, *I* could commit a murder in the Waxworks, and get away with it.'

'How?' demanded young Wells.

'How? To begin with, the Gallery is a one-man show and the porter's a bonehead. Anyone could enter, and leave, the Gallery without his being wise to it.'

'And the murder?' plugged young Wells.

With a shudder Sonia remembered how Poke had glanced at his long knotted fingers.

'If I could not achieve my object by fright, which is the foolproof way,' he replied, 'I should try a little artistic strangulation.'

'And leave your marks?'

'Not necessarily. Every expert knows that there are methods which show no trace.'

Sonia fumbled in her bag for the cigarettes which were not there.

'Why did I let myself think of that, just now?' she thought. 'Really too stupid.'

★

As she reproached herself for her morbidity, she broke off to stare at the door which led to the Hall of Horrors.

When she had last looked at it, she could have sworn that it was tightly closed . . . But now it gaped open by an inch.

She looked at the black cavity, recognizing the first test of her nerves. Later on, there would be others. She realized the fact that, within her cool, practical self, she carried a hysterical, neurotic passenger, who would doubtless give her a lot of trouble through officious suggestions and uncomfortable reminders.

She resolved to give her second self a taste of her quality, and so quell her at the start.

'That door was merely closed,' she remarked as, with a firm step, she crossed to the Hall of Horrors and shut the door.

One o'clock. I begin to realize that there is more in this than I thought. Perhaps I'm missing my sleep. But I'm keyed up and horribly expectant. Of what? I don't know. But I seem to be waiting for—something. I find myself listening—listening. The place is full of mysterious noises. I know they're my fancy . . . And things appear to move. I can distinguish footsteps and whispers, as though those waxworks which I cannot see in the darkness are beginning to stir to life.

Sonia dropped her pencil at the sound of a low chuckle. It seemed to come from the end of the Gallery which was blacked out by shadows.

As her imagination galloped away with her, she reproached herself sharply.

'Steady, don't be a fool. There must be a cloak-room here. That chuckle is the air escaping in a pipe—or something. I'm betrayed by my own ignorance of hydraulics.'

In spite of her brave words, she returned rather quickly to her corner.

With her back against the wall she felt less apprehensive. But she recognized her cowardice as an ominous sign.

She was desperately afraid of someone—or something—creeping up behind her and touching her.

'I've struck the bad patch,' she told herself. 'It will be worse at three o'clock and work up to a climax. But when I make my entry, at three, I shall have reached the peak. After that every minute will be bringing the dawn nearer.'

But of one fact she was ignorant. There would be no recorded impression at three o'clock.

Happily unconscious, she began to think of her copy. When she returned to the office—sunken-eyed, and looking like nothing on earth—she would then rejoice over every symptom of groundless fear.

'It's a story all right,' she gloated, looking at Hamlet. His gnarled, pallid features and dark smouldering eyes were strangely familiar to her.

Suddenly she realized that he reminded her of Hubert Poke.

Against her will, her thoughts again turned to him. She told herself that he was exactly like a waxwork. His yellow face—symptomatic of heart-trouble—had the same cheesy hue, and his eyes were like dull black glass. He wore a denture which was too large for him, and which forced his lips apart in a mirthless grin.

He always seemed to smile—even over the episode of the lift—which had been no joke.

It happened two days before. Sonia had rushed into the office in a state of molten excitement because she had extracted an interview from a Personage who had just received the Freedom of the City. This distinguished freeman had the reputation of shunning newspaper publicity, and Poke had tried his luck, only to be sent away with a flea in his ear.

At the back of her mind, Sonia knew that she had not fought level, for she was conscious of the effect of violet-blue eyes and a dimple upon a reserved but very human gentleman. But in her elation she had been rather blatant about her score.

She transcribed her notes, rattling away at her typewriter in a tremendous hurry, because she had a dinner-engagement. In the same breathless speed she had rushed towards the automatic lift.

She was just about to step into it when young Wells had leaped the length of the passage and dragged her back.

'Look, where you're going,' he shouted.

Sonia looked—and saw only the well of the shaft. The lift was not waiting in its accustomed place.

'Out of order,' explained Wells before he turned to blast Hubert Poke, who stood by.

'You almighty chump, why didn't you grab Miss Fraser, instead of standing by like a stuck pig?'

At the time Sonia had vaguely remarked how Poke had stammered and sweated, and she accepted the fact that he had been petrified by shock and had lost his head.

For the first time, she realized that his inaction had been deliberate. She remembered the flame of terrible excitement in his eyes and his stretched ghastly grin.

'He *hates* me,' she thought. 'It's my fault. I've been tactless and cocksure.'

Then a flood of horror swept over her.

'But he wanted to see me crash. It's almost *murder*.'

As she began to tremble, the jumpy passenger she carried reminded her of Poke's remark about the alderman.

'He had enemies.'

Sonia shook away the suggestion angrily.

'My memory's uncanny,' she thought. 'I'm stimulated and all strung up. It must be the atmosphere . . . Perhaps there's some gas in the air that accounts for these brainstorms. It's hopeless to be so utterly unscientific. Poke would have made a better job of this.'

She was back again to Hubert Poke. He had become an obsession.

Her head began to throb and a tiny gong started to beat in her temples. This time, she recognized the signs without any mental ferment.

'Atmospherics. A storm's coming up. It might make things rather thrilling. I must concentrate on my story. Really, my luck's in.'

She sat for some time, forcing herself to think of

pleasant subjects—of arguments with young Wells and the Tennis Tournament. But there was always a point when her thoughts gave a twist and led her back to Poke.

Presently she grew cramped and got up to pace the illuminated aisle in front of the window. She tried again to talk to the waxworks, but, this time, it was not a success.

They seemed to have grown remote and secretive, as though they were removed to another plane, where they possessed a hidden life.

Suddenly she gave a faint scream. Someone—or something—had crept up behind her, for she felt the touch of cold fingers upon her arm.

Two o'clock. They're only wax. They shall not frighten me. But they're trying to. One by one they're coming to life . . . Charles the Second no longer looks sour dough. He is beginning to leer at me. His eyes remind me of Hubert Poke.

Sonia stopped writing, to glance uneasily at the image of the Stuart monarch. His black velveteen suit appeared to have a richer pile. The swart curls which fell over his lace collar looked less like horse-hair. There really seemed a gleam of amorous interest lurking at the back of his glass optics.

Absurdly, Sonia spoke to him, in order to reassure herself.

'Did *you* touch me? At the first hint of a liberty, Charles Stuart, I'll smack your face. You'll learn a modern journalist has not the manners of an orange-girl.'

Instantly the satyr reverted to a dummy in a moth-eaten historical costume.

Sonia stood, listening for young Wells' footsteps. But she could not hear them, although the street now was perfectly still. She tried to picture him, propping up the opposite building, solid and immovable as the Rock of Gibraltar.

But it was no good. Doubts began to obtrude.

'I don't believe he's there. After all, why should he stay? He only pretended, just to give me confidence. He's gone.'

She shrank back to her corner, drawing her tennis-coat closer, for warmth. It was growing colder, causing her to think of tempting things—of a hot-water bottle and a steaming tea-pot.

Presently she realized that she was growing drowsy. Her lids felt as though weighted with lead, so that it required an effort to keep them open.

This was a complication which she had not

foreseen. Although she longed to drop off to sleep, she sternly resisted the temptation.

'No. It's not fair. I've set myself the job of recording a night spent in the Waxworks. It *must* be the genuine thing.'

She blinked more vigorously, staring across to where Byron drooped like a sooty flamingo.

'Mercy, how he yearns! He reminds me of—No, I won't think of *him* . . . I must keep awake . . . Bed . . . blankets, pillows . . . No.'

Her head fell forward, and for a minute she dozed. In that space of time, she had a vivid dream.

She thought that she was still in her corner in the Gallery, watching the dead alderman as he paced to and fro, before the window. She had never seen him, so he conformed to her own idea of an alderman—stout, pompous, and wearing the dark-blue, fur-trimmed robe of his office.

'He's got a face like a sleepy pear,' she decided. 'Nice old thing, but brainless.'

And then, suddenly, her tolerant derision turned to acute apprehension on his account, as she saw that he was being followed. A shape was stalking him as a cat stalks a bird.

Sonia tried to warn him of his peril, but, after the fashion of nightmares, she found herself voiceless. Even as she struggled to scream, a grotesquely long arm shot out and monstrous fingers gripped the alderman's throat.

In the same moment, she saw the face of the killer. It was Hubert Poke.

She awoke with a start, glad to find that it was but a dream. As she looked around her with dazed eyes, she saw a faint flicker of light. The mutter of very faint thunder, together with a patter of rain, told her that the storm had broken.

It was still a long way off, for Oldhampton seemed to be having merely a reflection and an echo.

'It'll clear the air,' thought Sonia.

Then her heart gave a violent leap. One of the waxworks had come to life. She distinctly saw it move, before it disappeared into the darkness at the end of the Gallery.

She kept her head, realizing that it was time to give up.

'My nerve's crashed,' she thought. 'That figure was only my fancy. I'm just like the others. Defeated by wax.'

Instinctively, she paid the figures her homage. It was the cumulative effect of their grim company, with their simulated life and sinister associations, that had rushed her defences.

Although it was bitter to fail, she comforted

herself with the reminder that she had enough copy for her article. She could even make capital out of her own capitulation to the force of suggestion.

With a slight grimace, she picked up her notebook. There would be no more on-the-spot impressions. But young Wells, if he was still there, would be grateful for the end of his vigil, whatever the state of mind of the porter.

She groped in the darkness for her signal-lamp. But her fingers only scraped bare polished boards.

The torch had disappeared.

In a panic, she dropped down on her knees, and searched for yards around the spot where she was positive it had lain.

It was the instinct of self-preservation which caused her to give up her vain search.

'I'm in danger,' she thought. 'And I've no one to help me now. I must see this through myself.'

She pushed back her hair from a brow which had grown damp.

'There's a brain working against mine. When I was asleep, someone—or something—stole my torch.'

Something? The waxworks became instinct with terrible possibility as she stared at them. Some were merely blurred shapes—their faces opaque oblongs or ovals. But others—illuminated from the street—were beginning to reveal themselves in a new guise.

Queen Elizabeth, with peaked chin and fiery hair, seemed to regard her with intelligent malice. The countenance of Napoleon was heavy with brooding power, as though he were willing her to submit. Cardinal Wolsey held her with a glittering eye.

Sonia realized that she was letting herself be hypnotized by creatures of wax—so many pounds of candles moulded to human form.

'This is what happened to those others,' she thought. '*Nothing happened.* But I'm afraid of them. I'm terribly afraid . . . There's only one thing to do. I must count them again.'

She knew that she must find out whether her torch had been stolen through human agency; but she shrank from the experiment, not knowing which she feared more—a tangible enemy or the unknown.

As she began to count, the chilly air inside the building seemed to throb with each thud of her heart.

'Seventeen, eighteen.' She was scarcely conscious of the numerals she murmured. 'Twenty-two, twenty-three.'

She stopped. Twenty-three? If her tally were correct, there was an extra waxwork in the Gallery.

On the shock of the discovery came a blinding flash of light, which veined the sky with fire. It seemed to run down the figure of Joan of Arc like a flaming torch. By a freak of atmospherics, the storm, which had been a starved, whimpering affair of flicker and murmur, culminated, and ended, in what was apparently a thunderbolt.

The explosion which followed was stunning; but Sonia scarcely noticed it, in her terror.

The unearthly violet glare had revealed to her a figure which she had previously overlooked.

It was seated in a chair, its hand supporting its peaked chin, and its pallid, clean-shaven features nearly hidden by a familiar broad-brimmed felt hat, which—together with the black cape—gave her the clue to its identity.

It was Hubert Poke.

Three o'clock.

Sonia heard it strike, as her memory began to reproduce, with horrible fidelity, every word of Poke's conversation on murder.

'Artistic strangulation.' She pictured the cruel agony of life leaking—bubble by bubble, gasp by gasp. It would be slow—for he had boasted of a method which left no tell-tale marks.

'Another death,' she thought dully. 'If it happens everyone will say that the Waxworks have killed me. What a story . . . Only, I shall not write it up.'

The tramp of feet rang out on the pavement below. It might have been the policeman on his beat; but Sonia wanted to feel that young Wells was still faithful to his post.

She looked up at the window, set high in the wall, and, for a moment, was tempted to shout. But the idea was too desperate. If she failed to attract outside attention, she would seal her own fate, for Poke would be prompted to hasten her extinction.

'Awful to feel he's so near, and yet I cannot reach him,' she thought. 'It makes it so much worse.'

She crouched there, starting and sweating at every faint sound in the darkness. The rain, which still pattered on the sky-light, mimicked footsteps and whispers. She remembered her dream and the nightmare spring and clutch.

It was an omen. At any moment it would come . . .

Her fear jolted her brain. For the first time she had a glimmer of hope.

'I didn't see him before the flash, because he looked exactly like one of the waxworks. Could I hide among them, too?' she wondered.

She knew that her white coat alone revealed her position to him. Holding her breath, she wriggled out of it, and hung it on the effigy of Charles II. In her black coat, with her handkerchief-scarf tied over her face, burglar fashion, she hoped that she was invisible against the sable-draped walls.

Her knees shook as she crept from her shelter. When she had stolen a few yards, she stopped to listen . . . In the darkness, someone was astir. She heard a soft padding of feet, moving with the certainty of one who sees his goal.

Her coat glimmered in her deserted corner.

In a sudden panic, she increased her pace, straining her ears for other sounds. She had reached the far end of the Gallery where no gleam from the window penetrated the gloom. Blindfolded and muffled, she groped her way towards the alcoves which held the tableaux.

Suddenly she stopped, every nerve in her body quivering. She had heard a thud, like rubbered soles alighting after a spring.

'He knows now.' Swift on the trail of her thought flashed another. 'He will look for me. Oh, *quick*!'

She tried to move, but her muscles were bound, and she stood as though rooted to the spot, listening. It was impossible to locate the footsteps. They seemed to come from every quarter of the Gallery.

Sometimes they sounded remote, but, whenever she drew a freer breath, a sudden creak of the boards close to where she stood made her heart leap.

At last she reached the limit of endurance. Unable to bear the suspense of waiting, she moved on.

Her pursuer followed her at a distance. He gained on her, but still withheld his spring. She had the feeling that he held her at the end of an invisible string.

'He's playing with me, like a cat with a mouse,' she thought.

If he had seen her, he let her creep forward until the darkness was no longer absolute. There were gradations in its density, so that she was able to recognize the first alcove. Straining her eyes, she could distinguish the outlines of the bed where the Virtuous Man made his triumphant exit from life, surrounded by a flock of his sorrowing family and their progeny.

Slipping inside the circle, she added one more mourner to the tableau.

The minutes passed, but nothing happened. There seemed no sound save the tiny gong beating inside her temples. Even the raindrops had ceased to patter on the sky-light.

Sonia began to find the silence more deadly than

noise. It was like the lull before the storm. Question after question came rolling into her mind.

'Where is he? What will he do next? Why doesn't he strike a light?'

As though someone were listening-in to her thoughts, she suddenly heard a faint splutter as of an ignited match. Or it might have been the click of an exhausted electric torch.

With her back turned to the room, she could see no light. She heard the half-hour strike, with a faint wonder that she was still alive.

'What will have happened before the next quarter?' she asked.

Presently she began to feel the strain of her pose, which she held as rigidly as any artist's model. For the time—if her presence were not already detected—her life depended on her immobility.

As an overpowering weariness began to steal over her a whisper stirred in her brain:

'The alderman was found dead on a bed.'

The newspaper account had not specified which especial tableau had been the scene of the tragedy, but she could not remember another alcove which held a bed. As she stared at the white dimness of the quilt she seemed to see it blotched with a dark, sprawling form, writhing under the grip of long fingers.

To shut out the suggestion of her fancy, she closed her eyes. The cold, dead air in the alcove was sapping her exhausted vitality, so that once again she began to nod. She dozed as she stood, rocking to and fro on her feet.

Her surroundings grew shadowy. Sometimes she knew that she was in the alcove, but at others she strayed momentarily over strange borders . . . She was back in the summer, walking in a garden with young Wells. Roses and sunshine . . .

She awoke with a start at the sound of heavy breathing. It sounded close to her—almost by her side. The figure of a mourner kneeling by the bed seemed to change its posture slightly.

Instantly maddened thoughts began to flock and flutter wildly inside her brain.

'Who was it? Was it Hubert Poke? Would history be repeated? Was she doomed also to be strangled inside the alcove? Had Fate led her there?'

She waited, but nothing happened. Again she had the sensation of being played with by a master mind—dangled at the end of his invisible string.

Presently she was emboldened to steal from the alcove, to seek another shelter. But though she held on to the last flicker of her will, she had reached the limit of endurance. Worn out with the violence of her emotions and physically spent from the strain of long periods of standing, she staggered as she walked.

She blundered round the Gallery, without any sense of direction, colliding blindly with the groups of waxwork figures. When she reached the window her knees shook under her and she sank to the ground—dropping immediately into a sleep of utter exhaustion.

She awoke with a start as the first grey gleam of dawn was stealing into the Gallery. It fell on the row of waxworks, imparting a sickly hue to their features, as though they were creatures stricken with plague.

It seemed to Sonia that they were waiting for her to wake. Their peaked faces were intelligent and their eyes held interest, as though they were keeping some secret.

She pushed back her hair, her brain still thick with clouded memories. Disconnected thoughts began to stir, to slide about . . . Then suddenly her mind cleared, and she sprang up—staring at a figure wearing a familiar black cape.

Hubert Poke was also waiting for her to wake.

He sat in the same chair, and in the same posture, as when she had first seen him, in the flash of lightning. He looked as though he had never moved from his place—as though he could not move. His face had not the appearance of flesh.

As Sonia stared at him, with the feeling of a bird hypnotised by a snake, a doubt began to gather in her mind. Growing bolder, she crept closer to the figure.

It was a waxwork—a libelous representation of the actor—Kean.

Her laugh rang joyously through the Gallery as she realized that she had passed a night of baseless terrors, cheated by the power of imagination. In her relief she turned impulsively to the waxworks.

'My congratulations,' she said. 'You are my masters.'

They did not seem entirely satisfied by her homage, for they continued to watch her with an expression half-benevolent and half-sinister.

'*Wait!*' they seemed to say.

Sonia turned from them and opened her bag to get out her mirror and comb. There, among a jumble of notes, letters, lipsticks and powder-compresses, she saw the electric torch.

'*Of course!*' she cried. 'I remember now, I put it there. I was too windy to think properly . . . Well, I have my story. I'd better get my coat.'

The Gallery seemed smaller in the returning light. As she approached Charles Stuart, who looked

like an umpire in her white coat, she glanced down
the far end of the room, where she had groped in its
shadows before the pursuit of imaginary footsteps.

A waxwork was lying prone on the floor. For
the second time she stood and gazed down upon a
familiar black cape—a broad-brimmed conspirator's
hat. Then she nerved herself to turn the figure so
that its face was visible.

She gave a scream. There was no mistaking the
glazed eyes and ghastly grin. She was looking down
on the face of a dead man.

It was Hubert Poke.

The shock was too much for Sonia. She heard
a singing in her ears, while a black mist gathered
before her eyes. For the first time in her life she
fainted.

When she recovered consciousness she forced
herself to kneel beside the body and cover it with
its black cape. The pallid face resembled a death-
mask, which revealed only too plainly the lines of
egotism and cruelty in which it had been moulded
by a gross spirit.

Yet Sonia felt no repulsion—only pity. It was
Christmas morning, and he was dead, while her
own portion was life triumphant. Closing her eyes,
she whispered a prayer of supplication for his
warped soul.

Presently, as she grew calmer, her mind began to work on the problem of his presence. His motive seemed obvious. Not knowing that she had changed her plan, he had concealed himself in the Gallery, in order to poach her story.

'He was in the Hall of Horrors at first,' she thought, remembering the opened door. 'When he came out he hid at this end. We never saw each other, because of the waxworks between us; but we heard each other.'

She realized that the sounds which had terrified her had not all been due to imagination, while it was her agency which had converted the room into a whispering gallery of strange murmurs and voices. The clue to the cause of death was revealed by his wrist-watch, which had smashed when he fell. Its hands had stopped at three minutes to three, proving that the flash and explosion of the thunderbolt had been too much for his diseased heart—already over-strained by superstitious fears.

Sonia shuddered at a mental vision of his face, distraught with terror and pulped by raw primal impulses, after a night spent in a madman's world of phantasy.

She turned to look at the waxworks. At last she understood what they seemed to say.

'*But for Us, you should have met—at dawn.*'

'Your share shall be acknowledged, I promise you,' she said, as she opened her notebook.

Eight o'clock. The Christmas bells are ringing and it is wonderful just to be alive. I'm through the night, and none the worse for the experience, although I cracked badly after three o'clock. A colleague who, unknown to me, was also concealed in the Gallery has met with a tragic fate, caused, I am sure, by the force of suggestion. Although his death is due to heart-failure, the superstitious will certainly claim it is another victory for the Waxworks.

JOSEPH SHEARING

The Chinese Apple

Marjorie Bowen's second contribution to this anthology first appeared, under her pseudonym 'Joseph Shearing', in the 1948 Christmas Number of *The Illustrated London News*. As 'Joseph Shearing' she wrote many bestselling novels of which the best known are *Moss Rose* and *Blanche Fury* (filmed in 1947 and 1948 respectively).

Isabelle Crosland felt very depressed when the boat train drew into the vast London station. The gas lamps set at intervals down the platform did little more than reveal filth, fog and figures huddled in wraps and shawls. It was a mistake to arrive on Christmas Eve, a matter of missed trains, of indecision and reluctance about the entire journey. The truth was she had not wanted to come to London at all. She had lived in Italy too long to be comfortable in England. In Florence she had friends, admirers; she had what is termed 'private means' and she was an expert in music. She performed a little on the harpsichord and she wrote a great deal about ancient musical instruments and ancient music. She had been married and widowed some years before and was a childless woman who had come to good terms with life. But with life in Florence, not London. Mrs Crosland really rather resented the fact that she was performing a duty. She liked things to be taken lightly, even with a touch of malice, of heartlessness, and here she was in this gloomy, cold station, having left the pleasant south behind, just because she ought to be there.

'How,' she thought, as she watched the porter sorting out her baggage, 'I dislike doing the right thing; it is never becoming, at least to me.'

A widowed sister she scarcely remembered had died: there was a child, quite alone. She, this Lucy Bayward, had written; so had her solicitors. Mrs Crosland was her only relation. Money was not needed, companionship was. At last it had been arranged, the child was coming up from Wiltshire, Mrs Crosland was to meet her in London and take her back to Florence.

It would really be, Isabelle Crosland reflected, a flat sort of Christmas. She wished that she could shift her responsibility, and, as the four-wheeled cab took her along the dingy streets, she wondered if it might not be possible for her to evade taking Lucy back to Italy.

London was oppressive. The gutters were full of dirty snow, overhead was a yellow fog.

'I was a fool,' thought Mrs Crosland, 'ever to have left Florence. The whole matter could have been settled by letter.'

She did not care for the meeting-place. It was the old house in Islington where she and her sister had been born and had passed their childhood. It was her own property and her tenant had lately left, so it was empty. Convenient, too, and suitable. Only Isabelle Crosland did not very much want to return to those somber rooms. She had not liked her own childhood, nor her own youth. Martha had married, though a poor sort of man, and got away early. Isabelle had stayed on, too long, then married desperately, only saving herself by Italy and music. The south had saved her in another way, too. Her husband, who was a dull, retired half-pay officer, had died of malaria.

Now she was going back. On Christmas Eve, nothing would be much altered; she had always let the house furnished. Why had she not sold, long ago, those heavy pieces of Jamaica mahogany? Probably out of cowardice, because she did not wish to face up to writing, or hearing anything about them. There it was, just as she remembered it, Roscoe Square, with the church and graveyard in the centre, and the houses, each like one another as peas in a pod, with the decorous areas and railings and the semicircular fanlights over the doors with heavy knockers.

The street lamps were lit. It was really quite late at night. 'No wonder,' Mrs Crosland thought, 'that I am feeling exhausted.' The sight of the Square chilled her: it was as if she had been lured back there by some malign power. A group of people were gathered round the house in the corner, directly facing her own that was number twelve. 'Carols,' she thought, 'or a large party.' But there seemed to be no children and the crowd was very silent.

There were lights in her own house. She noticed that bright façade with relief. Alike in the parlour and in the bedrooms above, the gas flared. Lucy had arrived then. That part of the arrangements had gone off well. The lawyers must have sent the keys, as Isabelle Crosland had instructed them to do, and the girl had had the good sense to get up to London before the arrival of the boat train.

Yet Mrs Crosland felt unreasonably depressed. She would, after all, have liked a few hours by herself in the hateful house.

Her own keys were ready in her purse. She opened the front door and shuddered. It was as if she had become a child again and dreaded the strong voice of a parent.

There should have been a maid. Careful in everything that concerned her comfort, Mrs Crosland
had written to a woman long since in her employ-
ment to be in attendance. The woman had replied,
promising compliance. But now she cried: 'Mrs
Jocelyn! Mrs Jocelyn!' in vain, through the gas-lit
house.

The cabby would not leave his horse and his
rugs, but her moment of hesitancy was soon filled.
One of the mongrel idlers who, more frequently
than formerly, lounged about the streets, came forward. Mrs Crosland's trunks and bags were placed
in the hall, and she had paid her dues with the English money carefully acquired at Dover.

The cab drove away, soon lost in the fog. But the
scrawny youth lingered. He pointed to the crowd
the other side of the Square, a deeper patch amid
the surrounding gloom.

'Something has happened there, Mum,' he
whispered.

'Something horrible, you mean?' Mrs Crosland
was annoyed she had said this, and added: 'No, of
course not; it is a gathering for Christmas.' With this
she closed her front door on the darkness and stood
in the lamp-lit passage.

She went into the parlour, so well remembered,
so justly hated.

The last tenant, selected prudently, had left everything in even too good a state of preservation. Save for some pale patches on the walls where pictures had been altered, everything was as it had been.

Glowering round, Mrs Crosland thought what a fool she had been to stay there so long.

A fire was burning and a dish of cakes and wine stood on the deep red mahogany table.

With a gesture of bravado, Mrs Crosland returned to the passage, trying to throw friendliness into her voice as she called out: 'Lucy, Lucy, my dear, it is I, your aunt Isabelle Crosland.'

She was vexed with herself that the words did not have a more genial sound. 'I am ruined,' she thought, 'for all family relationship.'

A tall girl appeared on the first landing.

'I have been waiting,' she said, 'quite a long time.'

In the same second Mrs Crosland was relieved that this was no insipid bore, and resentful of the other's self-contained demeanour.

'Well,' she said, turning it off with a smile. 'It doesn't look as if I need have hurried to your assistance.'

Lucy Bayward descended the stairs.

'Indeed, I assure you, I am extremely glad to see you,' she said gravely.

The two women seated themselves in the parlour.

Mrs Crosland found Lucy looked older than her eighteen years and was also, in her dark, rather flashing way, beautiful. Was she what one might have expected Martha's girl to be? Well, why not?

'I was expecting Mrs Jocelyn, Lucy.'

'Oh, she was here; she got everything ready, as you see – then I sent her home because it is Christmas Eve.'

Mrs Crosland regretted this; she was used to ample service. 'We shall not be able to travel until after Christmas,' she complained.

'But we can be very comfortable here,' said Lucy, smiling.

'No,' replied Mrs Crosland, the words almost forced out of her. 'I don't think I can – be comfortable here – I think we had better go to an hotel.'

'But you arranged this meeting.'

'I was careless. You can have no idea – you have not travelled?'

'No.'

'Well, then, you can have no idea how different things seem in Florence, with the sun and one's friends about—'

'I hope we shall be friends.'

'Oh, I hope so. I did not mean that, only the Square and the house. You see, I spent my childhood here.'

Lucy slightly shrugged her shoulders. She poured herself out a glass of wine. What a false impression those school-girlish letters had given! Mrs Crosland was vexed, mostly at herself.

'You – since we have used the word – have friends of your own?' she asked.

Lucy bowed her dark head.

'Really,' added Mrs Crosland, 'I fussed too much. I need not have undertaken all that tiresome travelling at Christmas, too.'

'I am sorry that you did – on my account; but please believe that you are being of the greatest help to me.'

Mrs Crosland apologised at once.

'I am overtired. I should not be talking like this. I, too, will have a glass of wine. We ought to get to know each other.'

They drank, considering one another carefully.

Lucy was a continuing surprise to Mrs Crosland. She was not even in mourning, but wore a rather ill-fitting stone-coloured satin, her sleek hair had recently been twisted into ringlets, and there was no doubt that she was slightly rouged.

'Do you want to come to Italy? Have you any plans for yourself?'

'Yes – and they include a trip abroad. Don't be afraid that I shall be a burden on you.'

'This independence could have been expressed by letter,' smiled Mrs Crosland. 'I have my own interests – that Martha's death interrupted—'

'Death always interrupts – some one or some thing, does it not?'

'Yes, and my way of putting it was harsh. I mean you do not seem a rustic miss, eager for sympathy.'

'It must be agreeable in Florence,' said Lucy. 'I dislike London very much.'

'But you have not been here more than a few hours—'

'Long enough to dislike it—'

'And your own home, also?'

'You did not like your own youth, either, did you?' asked Lucy, staring.

'No, no, I understand. Poor Martha would be dull, and it is long since your father died. I see, a narrow existence.'

'You might call it that. I was denied everything. I had not the liberty, the pocket-money given to the kitchenmaid.'

'It was true of me also,' said Mrs Crosland, shocked at her own admission.

'One is left alone, to struggle with dark things,' smiled Lucy. 'It is not a place that I dislike, but a condition – that of being young, vulnerable, defenceless.'

'As I was,' agreed Mrs Crosland. 'I got away and now I have music.'

'I shall have other things.' Lucy sipped her wine.

'Well, one must talk of it: you are not what I expected to find. You are younger than I was when I got away,' remarked Mrs Crosland.

'Still too old to endure what I endured.'

Mrs Crosland shivered. 'I never expected to hear this,' she declared. 'I thought you would be a rather flimsy little creature.'

'And I am not?'

'No, indeed, you seem to me quite determined.'

'Well, I shall take your small cases upstairs. Mrs Jocelyn will be here in the morning.'

'There's a good child.' Mrs Crosland tried to sound friendly. She felt that she ought to manage the situation better. It was one that she had ordained herself, and now it was getting out of hand.

'Be careful with the smallest case in red leather: it has some English gold in it, and a necklace of Roman pearls that I bought as a Christmas present for you—'

Mrs Crosland felt that the last part of this sentence fell flat. '. . . pearl beads, they are really very pretty.'

'So are these.' Lucy put her hand to her ill-fitting tucker and pulled out a string of pearls.

'The real thing,' said Mrs Crosland soberly. 'I did not know that Martha—'

Lucy unclasped the necklace and laid it on the table; the sight of this treasure loosened Mrs Crosland's constant habit of control. She thought of beauty, of sea-water, of tears, and of her own youth, spilled and wasted away, like water running into sand.

'I wish I had never come back to this house,' she said passionately.

Lucy went upstairs. Mrs Crosland heard her moving about overhead. How well she knew that room. The best bedroom, where her parents had slept, the huge wardrobe, the huge dressing-table, the line engravings, the solemn air of tedium, the hours that seemed to have no end. What had gone wrong with life anyway? Mrs Crosland asked herself this question fiercely, daunted, almost frightened by the house.

The fire was sinking down and with cold hands she piled on the logs.

How stupid to return. Even though it was such a reasonable thing to do. One must be careful of these reasonable things. She ought to have done the unreasonable, the reckless thing, forgotten this old house in Islington, and taken Lucy to some cheerful hotel.

The steps were advancing, retreating, overhead.

Mrs Crosland recalled old stories of haunted houses. How footsteps would sound in an upper storey and then, on investigation, the room be found empty.

Supposing she were to go upstairs now and find the great bedroom forlorn and Lucy vanished! Instead, Lucy entered the parlour.

'I have had the warming-pan in the bed for over two hours, the fire burns briskly and your things are set out—'

Mrs Crosland was grateful in rather, she felt, an apathetic manner.

This journey had upset a painfully acquired serenity. She was really fatigued, the motion of the ship, the clatter of the train still made her senses swim.

'Thank you, Lucy, dear,' she said, in quite a humble way, then leaning her head in her hand and her elbow on the table, she began to weep.

Lucy regarded her quietly and drank another glass of wine.

'It is the house,' whimpered Mrs Crosland, 'coming back to it – and those pearls – I never had a necklace like that—'

She thought of her friends, of her so-called successful life, and of how little she had really had.

She envied this young woman who had escaped in time.

'Perhaps you had an accomplice?' she asked cunningly.

'Oh, yes, I could have done nothing without that.'

Mrs Crosland was interested, slightly confused by the wine and the fatigue. Probably, she thought, Lucy meant that she was engaged to some young man who had not been approved by Martha. But what did either of them mean by the word 'accomplice'?

'I suppose Charles Crosland helped me,' admitted his widow. 'He married me and we went to Italy. I should never have had the courage to do that alone. And by the time he died, I had found out about music, and how I understood it and could make money out of it—' 'Perhaps,' she thought to herself, 'Lucy will not want, after all, to come with me to Italy – what a relief if she marries someone. I don't really care if she has found a ruffian, for I don't like her – no, nor the duty, the strain and drag of it.'

She was sure that it was the house making her feel like that. Because in this house she had done what she ought to have done so often. Such wretched meals, such miserable silences, such violences of speech. Such suppression of all one liked or wanted. Lucy said:

'I see that you must have suffered, Mrs Crosland. I don't feel I can be less formal than that – we are strangers. I will tell you in the morning what my plans are—'

'I hardly came from Italy in the Christmas season to hear your plans,' replied Mrs Crosland with a petulance of which she was ashamed. 'I imagined you as quite dependent and needing my care.'

'I have told you that you are the greatest possible service to me,' Lucy assured her, at the same time taking up the pearls and hiding them in her bosom. 'I wear mourning when I go abroad, but in the house I feel it to be a farce,' she added.

'I never wore black for my parents,' explained Mrs Crosland. 'They died quite soon, one after the other; with nothing to torment, their existence became insupportable.'

Lucy sat with her profile towards the fire. She was thin, with slanting eyebrows and a hollow at the base of her throat.

'I wish you would have that dress altered to fit you,' remarked Mrs Crosland. 'You could never travel in it, either, a grey satin—'

'Oh, no, I have some furs and a warm pelisse of a dark rose colour.'

'Then certainly you were never kept down as I was—'

'Perhaps I helped myself, afterwards – is not that the sensible thing to do?'

'You mean you bought these clothes since Martha's death? I don't see how you had the time or the money.' And Mrs Crosland made a mental note to consult the lawyers as to just how Lucy's affairs stood.

'Perhaps you have greater means than I thought,' she remarked. 'I always thought Martha had very little.'

'I have not very much,' said Lucy. 'But I shall know how to spend it. And how to make more.'

Mrs Crosland rose. The massive pieces of furniture seemed closing in on her, as if they challenged her very right to exist.

Indeed, in this house she had no existence, she was merely the wraith of the child, of the girl who had suffered so much in this place, in this house, in this Square with the church and the graveyard in the centre, and from which she had escaped only just in time. Lucy also got to her feet.

'It is surprising,' she sighed, 'the amount of tedium there is in life. When I think of all the dull Christmases—'

'I also,' said Mrs Crosland, almost in terror. 'It was always so much worse when other people seemed to be rejoicing.' She glanced round her with apprehension.

'When I think of all the affectations of good will, of pleasure—'

'Don't think of it,' urged the younger woman. 'Go upstairs, where I have put everything in readiness for you.'

'I dread the bedroom.'

The iron bell clanged in the empty kitchen below.

'The waits,' added Mrs Crosland. 'I remember when we used to give them sixpence, nothing more. But I heard no singing.'

'There was no singing. I am afraid those people at the corner house have returned.'

Mrs Crosland remembered vaguely the crowd she had seen from the cab window, a blot of dark in the darkness. 'You mean someone has been here before?' she asked. 'What about?'

'There has been an accident, I think. Someone was hurt—'

'But what could that have to do with us?'

'Nothing, of course. But they said they might return—'

'Who is "they"?'

Mrs Crosland spoke confusedly and the bell rang again.

'Oh, do go, like a good child,' she added. She was rather glad of the distraction. She tried to think of the name of the people who had lived in the house on the opposite corner. Inglis – was not that it? And one of the family had been a nun, a very cheerful, smiling nun, or had she recalled it all wrongly?

She sat shivering over the fire, thinking of those past musty Christmas Days, when the beauty and magic of the season had seemed far away, as if behind a dense wall of small bricks. That had always been the worst of it, that somewhere, probably close at hand, people had really been enjoying themselves.

She heard Lucy talking with a man in the passage. The accomplice, perhaps? She was inclined to be jealous, hostile.

But the middle-aged and sober-looking person who followed Lucy into the parlour could not have any romantic complications.

He wore a pepper-and-salt-pattern suit and carried a bowler hat. He seemed quite sure of himself, yet not to expect any friendliness.

'I am sorry to disturb you again,' he said.

'I am sorry that you should,' agreed Mrs Crosland. 'But on the other hand, my memories of this house are by no means pleasant.'

'Name of Teale, Henry Teale,' said the stranger.

'Pray be seated,' said Mrs Crosland.

The stranger, this Mr Teale, took the edge of the seat, as if very diffident. Mrs Crosland was soon fascinated by what he had to say.

He was a policeman in private clothes. Mrs Crosland meditated on the word 'private' – 'private life,' 'private means.' He had come about the Inglis affair, at the corner house.

'Oh, yes, I recall that was the name, but we never knew anyone – who are they now – the Inglis family?'

'I've already told Miss Bayward here – it was an old lady, for several years just an old lady living with a companion—'

'And found dead, you told me, Mr Teale,' remarked Lucy.

'Murdered, is what the surgeon says and what was suspected from the first.'

'I forgot that you said that, Mr Teale. At her age it does not seem to matter very much – you said she was over eighty years of age, did you not?' asked Lucy, pouring the detective a glass of wine.

'Very old, nearly ninety years of age, I understand, Miss Bayward. But murder is murder.'

Mrs Crosland felt this affair to be an added weariness. Murder in Roscoe Square on Christmas Eve. She felt that she ought to apologise to Lucy. 'I suppose that was what the crowd had gathered for,' she remarked.

'Yes, such news soon gets about, Ma'am. A nephew called to tea and found her – gone.'

Mr Teale went over, as if it were a duty, the circumstances of the crime. The house had been ransacked and suspicion had fallen on the companion, who had disappeared. Old Mrs Inglis had lived so much like a recluse that no one knew what she possessed. There had been a good deal of loose money in the house, the nephew, Mr Clinton, thought. A good deal of cash had been drawn every month from the Inglis bank account, and very little of it spent. The companion was a stranger to Islington. Veiled and modest, she had flitted about doing the meagre shopping for the old eccentric, only for the last few weeks.

The woman she had replaced had left in tears and temper some months ago. No one knew where this creature had come from – probably an orphanage; she must have been quite friendless and forlorn to have taken such a post.

'You told me all this,' protested Lucy.

'Yes, Miss, but I did say that I would have to see Mrs Crosland when she arrived—'

'Well, you are seeing her,' remarked that lady. 'And I cannot help you at all. One is even disinterested. I lived, Mr Teale, so cloistered a life when I was here, that I knew nothing of what was going on – even in the Square.'

'So I heard from Miss Bayward here, but I

thought you might have seen someone; I'm not speaking of the past, but of the present—'

'Seen someone here – on Christmas Eve—?'

Mr Teale sighed, as if, indeed, he had been expecting too much. 'We've combed the neighbourhood, but can't find any trace of her—'

'Why should you? Of course, she has fled a long way off—'

'Difficult, with the railway stations and then the ports all watched.'

'You may search again through the cellars if you wish,' said Lucy. 'I am sure that my aunt won't object—'

Mrs Crosland put no difficulties in the way of the detective, but she felt the whole situation was grotesque.

'I hope she escapes,' Mrs Crosland, increasingly tired and confused by the wine she had drunk without eating, spoke without her own volition. 'Poor thing – shut up – caged—'

'It was a very brutal murder,' said Mr Teale indifferently.

'Was it? An over-draught of some sleeping potion, I suppose?'

'No, Ma'am, David and Goliath, the surgeon said. A rare kind of murder. A great round stone in a sling, as it might be a lady's scarf, and pretty easy to get in the dusk round the river ways.'

Mrs Crosland laughed. The picture of this miserable companion, at the end of a dismal day lurking round the dubious dockland streets to find a target of her skill with sling and stone, seemed absurd.

'I know what you are laughing at,' said Mr Teale without feeling. 'But she found her target – it was the shining skull of Mrs Inglis, nodding in her chair—'

'One might understand the temptation,' agreed Mrs Crosland. 'But I doubt the skill.'

'There is a lovely walled garden,' suggested the detective. 'And, as I said, these little by-way streets. Anyway, there was her head smashed in, neatly; no suffering, you understand.'

'Oh, very great suffering, for such a thing to be possible,' broke out Mrs Crosland. 'On the part of the murderess, I mean—'

'I think so, too,' said Lucy soberly.

'That is not for me to say,' remarked the detective. 'I am to find her if I can. There is a fog and all the confusion of Christmas Eve parties, and waits, and late services at all the churches.'

Mrs Crosland impulsively drew back the curtains. Yes, there was the church, lit up, exactly as she recalled it, light streaming from the windows over the graveyard, altar tombs and headstones, sliding into oblivion.

'Where would a woman like that go?' asked Lucy, glancing over Mrs Crosland's shoulder at the churchyard.

'That is what we have to find out,' said Mr Teale cautiously. 'I'll be on my way again, ladies, just cautioning you against any stranger who might come here, on some pretext. One never knows.'

'What was David's stone? A polished pebble? I have forgotten.' Mrs Crosland dropped the curtains over the view of the church and the dull fog twilight of evening in the gas-lit Square.

'The surgeon says it must have been a heavy stone, well aimed, and such is missing. Mr Clinton, the nephew, her only visitor and not in her confidence, remarked on such a weapon, always on each of his visits on the old lady's table.'

'How is that possible?' asked Mrs Crosland.

Mr Teale said that the object was known as the Chinese apple. It was of white jade, dented like the fruit, with a leaf attached, all carved in one and beautifully polished. The old lady was very fond of it, and it was a most suitable weapon.

'But this dreadful companion,' said Mrs Crosland, now perversely revolted by the crime, 'could not have had time to practise with this – suitable weapon – she had not been with Mrs Inglis long enough.'

'Ah,' smiled Mr Teale. 'We don't know where she was before, Ma'am. She might have had a deal of practice in some lonely place – birds, Ma'am, and rabbits. Watching in the woods, like boys do.'

Mrs Crosland did not like this picture of a woman lurking in coverts with a sling. She bade the detective 'Good-evening' and Lucy showed him to the door.

In the moment that she was alone, Mrs Crosland poured herself another glass of wine. When Lucy returned, she spoke impulsively.

'Oh, Lucy, that is what results when people are driven too far – they kill and escape with the spoils, greedily. I do wish this had not happened. What sort of woman do you suppose this may have been? Harsh, of course, and elderly—'

'Mr Teale, when he came before, said she might be in almost any disguise.'

'Almost any disguise,' repeated Mrs Crosland, thinking of the many disguises she had herself worn until she had found herself in the lovely blue of Italy, still disguised, but pleasantly enough. She hoped that this mask was not now about to be torn from her; the old house was very oppressive, it had been foolish to return. A relief, of course, that Lucy seemed to have her own plans. But the house was what really mattered: the returning here and finding everything the same, and the memories of that dreadful childhood.

Lucy had suffered also, it seemed. Odd that she did not like Lucy, did not feel any sympathy with her or her schemes.

At last she found her way upstairs and faced the too-familiar bedroom. Her own was at the back of the house; that is, it had been. She must not think like this: her own room was in the charming house of the villa in Fiesole, this place had nothing to do with her at all.

But it had, and the knowledge was like a lead cloak over her. Of course it had. She had returned to meet not Lucy, but her own childhood.

Old Mrs Inglis – how did she fit in?

Probably she had always been there, even when the woman who was now Isabelle Crosland had been a child. Always there, obscure, eccentric, wearing out a succession of companions until one of them brained her with the Chinese apple, the jade fruit, slung from a lady's scarf.

'Oh, dear,' murmured Mrs Crosland, 'what has that old, that very old woman got to do with me?'

Her cases were by her bedside. She was too tired to examine them. Lucy had been scrupulous in putting out her toilet articles. She began to undress. There was nothing to do but to rest; what was it to her that a murderess was being hunted round Islington – what had Mr Teale said? The stations, the docks . . . She was half-undressed and had pulled out her wrapper when the front-door bell rang.

Hastily covering herself up, she was out on the landing. At least this was an excuse not to get into the big, formal bed where her parents had died, even if this was only Mr Teale returned. Lucy was already in the hall, speaking to someone. The gas-light in the passage illuminated the girl in the stone-coloured satin and the man on the threshold to whom she spoke.

It was not Mr Teale.

Isabelle Crosland, half-way down the stairs, had a glance of a sharp face, vividly lit. A young man, with his collar turned up and a look of expectation in his brilliant eyes. He said something that Isabelle Crosland could not hear, and then Lucy closed the heavy front door.

Glancing up at her aunt, she said:

'Now we are shut in for the night.'

'Who was that?' asked Mrs Crosland, vexed that Lucy had discerned her presence.

'Only a neighbour; only a curiosity-monger.'

Lucy's tone was reassuring. She advised her aunt to go to bed.

'Really, it is getting very late. The church is dark again. All the people have gone home.'

'Which room have you, Lucy, dear?'

'That which you had, I suppose; the large room at the back of the house.'

'Oh, yes – that—'

'Well, do not concern yourself – it has been rather a disagreeable evening, but it is over now.'

Lucy, dark and pale, stood in the doorway, hesitant for a second. Mrs Crosland decided, unreasonably, not to kiss her and bade her a quick good-night of a forced cheerfulness.

Alone, she pulled the chain of the gas-ring and was at once in darkness. Only wheels of light across the ceiling showed the passing of a lonely hansom cab.

Perhaps Mr Teale going home.

Mrs Inglis, too, would have gone home by now; the corner house opposite would be empty.

Isabelle Crosland could not bring herself to sleep on the bed after all. Wrapped in travelling rugs, snatched up in the dark, she huddled on the couch. Presently she slept, but with no agreeable dreams. Oppressive fancies lay heavily on her and several times she woke, crying out.

It was with a dismal sense of disappointment that she realised each time that she was not in Florence.

With the dawn she was downstairs. Christmas morning; how ridiculous!

No sign of Lucy, and the cold, dismal house was like a trap, a prison.

Almost crying with vexation, Mrs Crosland was forced to look into the room that once had been her own. The bed had not been slept in. On the white honeycomb coverlet was a package and a note.

This, a single sheet of paper, covered an opened letter. Mrs Crosland stared at this that was signed 'Lucy Bayward.' It was a childish sort of scrawl, the writer excused herself from reaching London until after the holidays.

The note was in a different hand:

I promised to let you know my plans. I am away down the river with my accomplice. Taking refuge in your empty house I found this note. The whole arrangement was entirely useful to me. I left the Roman pearls for Lucy, as I had those of my late employer, but I took the gold. No one will ever find us. I leave you a Christmas present.

Mrs Crosland's cold fingers undid the package. In the ghastly half-light she saw the Chinese apple.

G. K. CHESTERTON

The Hole in the Wall

Two men, the one an architect and the other an
archæologist, met on the steps of the great house
at Prior's Park; and their host, Lord Bulmer, in his
breezy way, thought it natural to introduce them. It
must be confessed that he was hazy as well as breezy,
and had no very clear connection in his mind,
beyond the sense that an architect and an archæologist begin with the same series of letters. The world
must remain in a reverent doubt as to whether he
would, on the same principles, have presented a diplomatist to a dipsomaniac or a ratiocinator to a rat
catcher. He was a big, fair, bull-necked young man,
abounding in outward gestures, unconsciously flap-
ping his gloves and flourishing his stick.

"You two ought to have something to talk
about," he said, cheerfully. "Old buildings and all
that sort of thing; this is rather an old building, by
the way, though I say it who shouldn't. I must ask
you to excuse me a moment; I've got to go and see
about the cards for this Christmas romp my sister's
arranging. We hope to see you all there, of course.

Juliet wants it to be a fancy-dress affair—abbots and crusaders and all that. My ancestors, I suppose, after all."

"I trust the abbot was not an ancestor," said the archæological gentleman, with a smile.

"Only a sort of great-uncle, I imagine," answered the other, laughing; then his rather rambling eye rolled round the ordered landscape in front of the house; an artificial sheet of water ornamented with an antiquated nymph in the center and surrounded by a park of tall trees now gray and black and frosty, for it was in the depth of a severe winter.

"It's getting jolly cold," his lordship continued. "My sister hopes we shall have some skating as well as dancing."

"If the crusaders come in full armor," said the other, "you must be careful not to drown your ancestors."

"Oh, there's no fear of that," answered Bulmer; "this precious lake of ours is not two feet deep anywhere." And with one of his flourishing gestures he stuck his stick into the water to demonstrate its shallowness. They could see the short end bent in the water, so that he seemed for a moment to lean his large weight on a breaking staff.

"The worst you can expect is to see an abbot

sit down rather suddenly," he added, turning away. "Well, *au revoir*; I'll let you know about it later."

The archæologist and the architect were left on the great stone steps smiling at each other; but whatever their common interests, they presented a considerable personal contrast, and the fanciful might even have found some contradiction in each considered individually. The former, a Mr. James Haddow, came from a drowsy den in the Inns of Court, full of leather and parchment, for the law was his profession and history only his hobby; he was indeed, among other things, the solicitor and agent of the Prior's Park estate. But he himself was far from drowsy and seemed remarkably wide awake, with shrewd and prominent blue eyes, and red hair brushed as neatly as his very neat costume. The latter, whose name was Leonard Crane, came straight from a crude and almost cockney office of builders and house agents in the neighboring suburb, sunning itself at the end of a new row of jerry-built houses with plans in very bright colors and notices in very large letters. But a serious observer, at a second glance, might have seen in his eyes something of that shining sleep that is called vision; and his yellow hair, while not affectedly long, was unaffectedly untidy. It was a manifest if melancholy truth that the architect was an artist. But the artistic temperament was far from explaining him; there was something else about him that was not definable, but which some even felt to be dangerous. Despite his dreaminess, he would sometimes surprise his friends with arts and even sports apart from his ordinary life, like memories of some previous existence. On this occasion, nevertheless, he hastened to disclaim any authority on the other man's hobby.

"I mustn't appear on false pretences," he said, with a smile. "I hardly even know what an archæologist is, except that a rather rusty remnant of Greek suggests that he is a man who studies old things."

"Yes," replied Haddow, grimly. "An archæologist is a man who studies old things and finds they are new."

Crane looked at him steadily for a moment and then smiled again.

"Dare one suggest," he said, "that some of the things we have been talking about are among the old things that turn out not to be old?"

His companion also was silent for a moment, and the smile on his rugged face was fainter as he replied, quietly:

"The wall round the park is really old. The one gate in it is Gothic, and I cannot find any trace of destruction or restoration. But the house and the estate generally—well the romantic ideas read into these things are often rather recent romances, things almost like fashionable novels. For instance, the very name of this place, Prior's Park, makes everybody think of it as a moonlit mediæval abbey; I dare say the spiritualists by this time have discovered the ghost of a monk there. But, according to the only authoritative study of the matter I can find, the place was simply called Prior's as any rural place is called Podger's. It was the house of a Mr. Prior, a farmhouse, probably, that stood here at some time or other and was a local landmark. Oh, there are a great many examples of the same thing, here and everywhere else. This suburb of ours used to be a village, and because some of the people slurred the name and pronounced it Holliwell, many a minor poet indulged in fancies about a Holy Well, with spells and fairies and all the rest of it, filling the suburban drawing-rooms with the Celtic twilight. Whereas anyone acquainted with the facts knows that 'Hollinwall' simply means 'the hole in the wall,' and probably referred to some quite trivial accident. That's what I mean when I say that we don't so much find old things as we find new ones."

Crane seemed to have grown somewhat inattentive to the little lecture on antiquities and novelties, and the cause of his restlessness was soon apparent, and indeed approaching. Lord Bulmer's sister, Juliet

Bray, was coming slowly across the lawn, accompanied by one gentleman and followed by two others. The young architect was in the illogical condition of mind in which he preferred three to one.

The man walking with the lady was no other than the eminent Prince Borodino, who was at least as famous as a distinguished diplomatist ought to be, in the interests of what is called secret diplomacy. He had been paying a round of visits at various English country houses, and exactly what he was doing for diplomacy at Prior's Park was as much a secret as any diplomatist could desire. The obvious thing to say of his appearance was that he would have been extremely handsome if he had not been entirely bald. But, indeed, that would itself be a rather bald way of putting it. Fantastic as it sounds, it would fit the case better to say that people would have been surprised to see hair growing on him; as surprised as if they had found hair growing on the bust of a Roman emperor. His tall figure was buttoned up in a tight-waisted fashion that rather accentuated his potential bulk, and he wore a red flower in his buttonhole. Of the two men walking behind one was also bald, but in a more partial and also a more premature fashion, for his drooping mustache was still yellow, and if his eyes were somewhat heavy it was with languor and not with age. It was Horne

Fisher, and he was talking as easily and idly about everything as he always did. His companion was a more striking, and even more sinister, figure, and he had the added importance of being Lord Bulmer's oldest and most intimate friend. He was generally known with a severe simplicity as Mr. Brain; but it was understood that he had been a judge and police official in India, and that he had enemies, who had represented his measures against crime as themselves almost criminal. He was a brown skeleton of a man with dark, deep, sunken eyes and a black mustache that hid the meaning of his mouth. Though he had the look of one wasted by some tropical disease, his movements were much more alert than those of his lounging companion.

"It's all settled," announced the lady, with great animation, when they came within hailing distance. "You've all got to put on masquerade things and very likely skates as well, though the prince says they don't go with it; but we don't care about that. It's freezing already, and we don't care about that. It's freezing already, and we don't often get such a chance in England."

"Even in India we don't exactly skate all the year round," observed Mr. Brain.

"And even Italy is not primarily associated with ice," said the Italian.

"Italy is primarily associated with ices," remarked Mr. Horne Fisher. "I mean with ice cream men. Most people in this country imagine that Italy is entirely populated with ice cream men and organ grinders. There certainly are a lot of them; perhaps they're an invading army in disguise."

"How do you know they are not the secret emissaries of our diplomacy?" asked the prince, with a slightly scornful smile. "An army of organ grinders might pick up hints, and their monkeys might pick up all sort of things."

"The organs are organized in fact," said the flippant Mr. Fisher. "Well, I've known it pretty cold before now in Italy and even in India, up on the Himalayan slopes. The ice on our own little round pond will be quite cozy by comparison."

Juliet Bray was an attractive lady with dark hair and eyebrows and dancing eyes, and there was a geniality and even generosity in her rather imperious ways. In most matters she could command her brother, though that nobleman, like many other men of vague ideas, was not without a touch of the bully when he was at bay. She could certainly command her guests, even to the extent of decking out the most respectable and reluctant of them with her mediæval masquerade. And it really seemed as if she could command the elements also, like a witch. For the weather steadily hardened and sharpened; that night the ice of the lake, glimmering in the moonlight, was like a marble floor, and they had begun to dance and skate on it before it was dark.

Prior's Park, or, more properly, the surrounding district of Holinwall, was a country seat that had become a suburb; having once had only a dependent village at its doors, it now found outside all its doors the signals of the expansion of London. Mr. Haddow, who was engaged in historical researches both in the library and the locality, could find little assistance in the latter. He had already realized, from the documents, that Prior's Park had originally been something like Prior's Farm, named after some local figure, but the new social conditions were all against his tracing the story by its traditions. Had any of the real rustics remained, he would probably have found some lingering legend of Mr. Prior, however remote he might be. But the new nomadic population of clerks and artisans, constantly shifting their homes from one suburb to another, or their children from one school to another, could have no corporate continuity. They had all that forgetfulness of history that goes everywhere with the extension of education.

Nevertheless, when he came out of the library next morning and saw the wintry trees standing round the frozen pond like a black forest, he felt he might well have been far in the depths of the country. The old wall running round the park kept that inclosure itself still entirely rural and romantic, and one could easily imagine that the depths of that dark forest faded away indefinitely into distant vales and hills. The gray and black and silver of the wintry wood were all the more severe or somber as a contrast to the colored carnival groups that already stood on and around the frozen pool. For the house party had already flung themselves impatiently into fancy dress, and the lawyer, with his neat black suit and red hair, was the only modern figure among them.

"Aren't you going to dress up?" asked Juliet, indignantly shaking at him a horned and towering blue headdress of the fourteenth century which framed her face very becomingly, fantastic as it was. "Everybody here has to be in the Middle Ages. Even Mr. Brain has put on a sort of brown dressing gown and says he's a monk; and Mr. Fisher got hold of some old potato sacks in the kitchen and sewed them together; he's supposed to be a monk, too. As to the prince, he's perfectly glorious, in great crimson robes as a cardinal. He looks as if he could poison everybody. You simply must be something."

"I will be something later in the day," he replied.

THE HOLE IN THE WALL

"At present I am nothing but an antiquary and an attorney. I have to see your brother presently, about some legal business and also some local investigations he asked me to make. I must look a little like a steward when I give an account of my stewardship."

"Oh, but my brother has dressed up!" cried the girl. "Very much so. No end, if I may say so. Why he's bearing down on you now in all his glory."

The noble lord was indeed marching toward them in a magnificent sixteenth-century costume of purple and gold, with a gold-hilted sword and a plumed cap, and manners to match. Indeed, there was something more than his usual expansiveness of bodily action in his appearance at that moment. It almost seemed, so to speak, that the plumes on his hat had gone to his head. He flapped his great, gold-lined cloak like the wings of a fairy king in a pantomime; he even drew his sword with a flourish and waved it about as he did his walking stick. In the light of after events there seemed to be something monstrous and ominous about that exuberance, something of the spirit that is called *fey*. At the time it merely crossed a few people's minds that he might possibly be drunk.

As he strode toward his sister the first figure he passed was that of Leonard Crane, clad in Lincoln green, with the horn and baldrick and sword appropriate to Robin Hood; for he was standing nearest to the lady, where, indeed, he might have been found during a disproportionate part of the time. He had displayed one of his buried talents in the matter of skating, and now that the skating was over seemed disposed to prolong the partnership. The boisterous Bulmer playfully made a pass at him with his drawn sword, going forward with the lunge in the proper fencing fashion, and making a somewhat too familiar Shakespearean quotation about a rodent and a Venetian coin.

Probably in Crane also there was a subdued excitement just then; anyhow, in one flash he had drawn his own sword and parried; and then suddenly, to the surprise of everyone, Bulmer's weapon seemed to spring out of his hand into the air and rolled away on the ringing ice.

"Well, I never!" said the lady, as if with justifiable indignation. "You never told me you could fence, too."

Bulmer put up his sword with an air rather bewildered than annoyed, which increased the impression of something irresponsible in his mood at the moment; then he turned rather abruptly to his lawyer, saying:

"We can settle up about the estate after dinner; I've missed nearly all the skating as it is, and I doubt if the ice will hold till to-morrow night. I think I shall get up early and have a spin by myself."

"You won't be disturbed with my company," said Horne Fisher, in his weary fashion. "If I have to begin the day with ice, in the American fashion, I prefer it in smaller quantities. But no early hours for me in December. The early bird catches the cold."

"Oh, I shan't die of catching a cold," answered Bulmer, and laughed.

A considerable group of the skating party had consisted of the guests staying at the house, and the rest had tailed off in twos and threes some time before most of the guests began to retire for the night. Neighbors, always invited to Prior's Park on such occasions, went back to their own houses in motors or on foot; the legal and archæological gentleman had returned to the Inns of Court by a late train, to get a paper called for during his consultation with his client; and most of the other guests were drifting and lingering at various stages on their way up to bed. Horne Fisher, as if to deprive himself of any excuse for his refusal of early rising, had been the first to retire to his room; but, sleepy as he looked, he could not sleep. He had picked up from a table the book of antiquarian topography, in which Haddow had found his first hints about the origin of the local name, and, being a man with a quiet and quaint capacity for being interested in anything, he began to read it steadily, making notes now and then of details on which his previous reading left him with a certain doubt about his present conclusions. His room was the one nearest to the lake in the center of the woods, and was therefore the quietest, and none of the last echoes of the evening's festivity could reach him He had followed carefully the argument which established the derivation from Mr. Prior's farm and the hole in the wall, and disposed of any fashionable fancy about monks and magic wells, when he began to be conscious of a noise audible in the frozen silence of the night. It was not a particularly loud noise, but it seemed to consist of a series of thuds or heavy blows, such as might be struck on a wooden door by a man seeking to enter. They were followed by something like a faint creak or crack, as if the obstacle had either been opened or had given way. He opened his own bedroom door and listened, but as he heard talk and laughter all over the lower floors, he had no reason to fear that a summons would be neglected or the house left without protection. He went to his open window, looking out over the frozen pond and the moonlit statue in the middle of their circle of darkling woods, and listened again. But silence had returned to that silent place, and, after straining his ears for a considerable time, he could hear nothing but the solitary hoot of a distant departing train. Then he reminded himself how many nameless noises can be heard by the wakeful during the most ordinary night, and shrugging his shoulders, went wearily to bed.

He awoke suddenly and sat up in bed with his ears filled, as with thunder, with the throbbing echoes of a rending cry. He remained rigid for a moment, and then sprang out of bed, throwing on the loose gown of sacking he had worn all day. He went first to the window, which was open, but covered with a thick curtain, so that his room was still completely dark; but when he tossed the curtain aside and put his head out, he saw that a gray and silver daybreak had already appeared behind the black woods that surrounded the little lake, and that was all that he did see. Though the sound had certainly come in through the open window from this direction, the whole scene was still and empty under the morning light as under the moonlight. Then the long, rather lackadaisical hand he had laid on a window sill gripped it tighter, as if to master a tremor, and his peering blue eyes grew bleak with fear. It may seem that his emotion was exaggerated and needless, considering the effort of common sense by which he had conquered his nervousness about the noise on the previous night. But that had been a very different sort of noise. It might have been made by half a hundred things, from the chopping of wood to the breaking of bottles. There was only one thing in nature from which could come the sound that echoed through the dark house at daybreak. It was the awful articulate voice of man; and it was something worse, for he knew what man.

He knew also that it had been a shout for help. It seemed to him that he had heard the very word; but the word, short as it was, had been swallowed up, as if the man had been stifled or snatched away even as he spoke. Only the mocking reverberations of it remained even in his memory, but he had no doubt of the original voice. He had no doubt that the great bull's voice of Francis Bray, Baron Bulmer, had been heard for the last time between the darkness and the lifting dawn.

How long he stood there he never knew, but he was startled into life by the first living thing that he saw stirring in that half-frozen landscape. Along the path beside the lake, and immediately under his window, a figure was walking slowly and softly, but with great composure—a stately figure in robes of a splendid scarlet; it was the Italian prince, still in his cardinal's costume. Most of the company had indeed lived in their costumes for the last day or two, and Fisher himself had assumed his frock of sacking as a convenient dressing gown; but there seemed, nevertheless, something unusually finished and formal, in the way of an early bird, about this magnificent red cockatoo. It was as if the early bird had been up all night.

"What is the matter?" he called, sharply, leaning out of the window, and the Italian turned up his great yellow face like a mask of brass.

"We had better discuss it downstairs," said Prince Borodino.

Fisher ran downstairs, and encountered the great, red-robed figure entering the doorway and blocking the entrance with his bulk.

"Did you hear that cry?" demanded Fisher.

"I heard a noise and I came out," answered the diplomatist, and his face was too dark in the shadow for its expression to be read.

"It was Bulmer's voice," insisted Fisher. "I'll swear it was Bulmer's voice."

"Did you know him well?" asked the other.

The question seemed irrelevant, though it was not illogical, and Fisher could only answer in a random fashion that he knew Lord Bulmer only slightly.

"Nobody seems to have known him well," continued the Italian, in level tones. "Nobody except that man Brain. Brain is rather older than Bulmer, but I fancy they shared a good many secrets."

Fisher moved abruptly, as if waking from a momentary trance, and said, in a new and more vigorous voice, "But look here, hadn't we better get outside and see if anything has happened."

"The ice seems to be thawing," said the other, almost with indifference.

When they emerged from the house, dark stains and stars in the gray field of ice did indeed indicate that the frost was breaking up, as their host had prophesied the day before, and the very memory of yesterday brought back the mystery of to-day.

"He knew there would be a thaw," observed the prince. "He went out skating quite early on purpose. Did he call out because he landed in the water, do you think?"

Fisher looked puzzled. "Bulmer was the last man to bellow like that because he got his boots wet. And that's all he could do here; the water would hardly come up to the calf of a man of his size. You can see the flat weeds on the floor of the lake, as if it were through a thin pane of glass. No, if Bulmer had only broken the ice he wouldn't have said much at the moment, though possibly a good deal afterward. We should have found him stamping and damning up and down this path, and calling for clean boots."

"Let us hope we shall find him as happily employed," remarked the diplomatist. "In that case the voice must have come out of the wood."

"I'll swear it didn't come out of the house," said Fisher; and the two disappeared together into the twilight of wintry trees.

The plantation stood dark against the fiery colors of sunrise, a black fringe having that feathery appearance which makes trees when they are bare the very reverse of rugged. Hours and hours afterward, when the same dense, but delicate, margin was dark against the greenish colors opposite the sunset, the search thus begun at sunrise had not come to an end. By successive stages, and to slowly gathering groups of the company, it became apparent that the most extraordinary of all gaps had appeared in the party; the guests could find no trace of their host anywhere. The servants reported that his bed had been slept in and his skates and his fancy costume were gone, as if he had risen early for the purpose he had himself avowed. But from the top of the house to the bottom, from the walls round the park to the pond in the center, there was no trace of Lord Bulmer, dead or alive. Horne Fisher realized that a chilling premonition had already prevented him from expecting to find the man alive. But his bald brow was wrinkled over an entirely new and unnatural problem, in not finding the man at all.

He considered the possibility of Bulmer having gone off of his own accord, for some reason; but after fully weighing it he finally dismissed it. It was inconsistent with the unmistakable voice heard at daybreak, and with many other practical obstacles. There was only one gateway in the ancient and lofty wall round the small park; the lodge keeper kept it locked till late in the morning, and the lodge keeper had seen no one pass. Fisher was fairly sure that he had before him a mathematical problem in an inclosed space. His instinct had been from the first so attuned to the tragedy that it would have been almost a relief to him to find the corpse. He would have been grieved, but not horrified, to come on the nobleman's body dangling from one of his own trees as from a gibbet, or floating in his own pool like a pallid weed. What horrified him was to find nothing.

He soon became conscious that he was not alone even in his most individual and isolated experiments. He often found a figure following him like his shadow, in silent and almost secret clearings in the plantation or outlying nooks and corners of the old wall. The dark-mustached mouth was as mute as the deep eyes were mobile, darting incessantly hither and thither, but it was clear that Brain of the Indian police had taken up the trail like an old hunter after a tiger. Seeing that he was the only personal friend of the vanished man, this seemed natural enough, and Fisher resolved to deal frankly with him.

"This silence is rather a social strain," he said. "May I break the ice by talking about the weather?—which, by the way, has already broken the ice. I know that breaking the ice might be a rather melancholy metaphor in this case."

"I don't think so," replied Brain, shortly. "I don't fancy the ice had much to do with it. I don't see how it could."

"What would you propose doing?" asked Fisher.

"Well, we've sent for the authorities, of course, but I hope to find something out before they come," replied the Anglo-Indian. "I can't say I have much hope from police methods in this country. Too much red tape, habeas corpus and that sort of thing. What we want is to see that nobody bolts; the nearest we could get to it would be to collect the company and count them, so to speak. Nobody's left lately, except that lawyer who was poking about for antiquities."

"Oh, he's out of it; he left last night," answered the other. "Eight hours after Bulmer's chauffeur saw his lawyer off by the train I heard Bulmer's own voice as plain as I hear yours now."

"I suppose you don't believe in spirits?" said the

man from India. After a pause he added: "There's somebody else I should like to find, before we go after a fellow with an alibi in the Inner Temple. What's become of that fellow in green—the architect dressed up as a forester? I haven't seem him about."

Mr. Brain managed to secure his assembly of all the distracted company before the arrival of the police. But when he first began to comment once more on the young architect's delay in putting in an appearance, he found himself in the presence of a minor mystery, and a psychological development of an entirely unexpected kind.

Juliet Bray had confronted the catastrophe of her brother's disappearance with a somber stoicism in which there was, perhaps, more paralysis than pain; but when the other question came to the surface she was both agitated and angry.

"We don't want to jump to any conclusions about anybody," Brain was saying in his staccato style. "But we should like to know a little more about Mr. Crane. Nobody seems to know much about him, or where he comes from. And it seems a sort of coincidence that yesterday he actually crossed swords with poor Bulmer, and could have stuck him, too, since he showed himself the better swordsman. Of course, that may be an accident and couldn't possibly be called a case against anybody; but then we haven't the means to make a real case against anybody. Till the police come we are only a pack of very amateur sleuthhounds."

"And I think you're a pack of snobs," said Juliet. "Because Mr. Crane is a genius who's made his own way, you try to suggest he's a murderer without daring to say so. Because he wore a toy sword and happened to know how to use it, you want us to believe he used it like a bloodthirsty maniac for no reason in the world. And because he could have hit my brother and didn't, you deduce that he did. That's the sort of way you argue. And as for his having disappeared, you're wrong in that as you are in everything else, for here he comes."

And, indeed, the green figure of the fictitious Robin Hood slowly detached itself from the gray background of the trees, and came toward them as she spoke.

He approached the group slowly, but with composure; but he was decidedly pale, and the eyes of Brain and Fisher had already taken in one detail of the green-clad figure more clearly than all the rest. The horn still swung from his baldrick, but the sword was gone.

Rather to the surprise of the company, Brain did not follow up the question thus suggested; but, while

G. K. CHESTERTON

retaining an air of leading the inquiry, had also an appearance of changing the subject.

"Now we're all assembled," he observed, quietly, "there is a question I want to ask to begin with. Did anybody here actually see Lord Bulmer this morning?"

Leonard Crane turned his pale face round the circle of faces till he came to Juliet's; then he compressed his lips a little and said:

"Yes, I saw him."

"Was he alive and well?" asked Brain, quickly. "How was he dressed?"

"He appeared exceedingly well," replied Crane, with a curious intonation. "He was dressed as he was yesterday, in that purple costume copied from the portrait of his ancestor in the sixteenth century. He had his skates in his hand."

"And his sword at his side, I suppose," added the questioner. "Where is your own sword, Mr. Crane?"

"I threw it away."

In the singular silence that ensued, the train of thought in many minds became involuntarily a series of colored pictures.

They had grown used to their fanciful garments looking more gay and gorgeous against the dark gray and streaky silver of the forest, so that the moving figures glowed like stained-glass saints walking.

262

The effect had been more fitting because so many of them had idly parodied pontifical or monastic dress. But the most arresting attitude that remained in their memories had been anything but merely monastic; that of the moment when the figure in bright green and the other in vivid violet had for a moment made a silver cross of their crossing swords. Even when it was a jest it had been something of a drama; and it was a strange and sinister thought that in the gray daybreak the same figures in the same posture might have been repeated as a tragedy.

"Did you quarrel with him?" asked Brain, suddenly.

"Yes," replied the immovable man in green. "Or he quarreled with me."

"Why did he quarrel with you?" asked the investigator; and Leonard Crane made no reply.

Horne Fisher, curiously enough, had only given half his attention to this crucial cross-examination. His heavy-lidded eyes had languidly followed the figure of Prince Borodino, who at this stage had strolled away toward the fringe of the wood; and, after a pause, as of meditation, had disappeared into the darkness of the trees.

He was recalled from his irrelevance by the voice of Juliet Bray, which rang out with an altogether new note of decision:

G. K. CHESTERTON

"If that is the difficulty, it had best be cleared up. I am engaged to Mr. Crane, and when we told my brother he did not approve of it; that is all."

Neither Brain nor Fisher exhibited any surprise, but the former added, quietly:

"Except, I suppose, that he and your brother went off into the wood to discuss it, where Mr. Crane mislaid his sword, not to mention his companion."

"And may I ask," inquired Crane, with a certain flicker of mockery passing over his pallid features, "what I am supposed to have done with either of them? Let us adopt the cheerful thesis that I am a murderer; it has yet to be shown that I am a magician. If I ran your unfortunate friend through the body, what did I do with the body? Did I have it carried away by seven flying dragons, or was it merely a trifling matter of turning it into a milk-white hind?"

"It is no occasion for sneering," said the Anglo-Indian judge, with abrupt authority. "It doesn't make it look better for you that you can joke about the loss."

Fisher's dreamy, and even dreary, eye was still on the edge of the wood behind, and he became conscious of masses of dark red, like a stormy sunset cloud, glowing through the gray network of the thin trees, and the prince in his cardinal's robes re-emerged on to the pathway. Brain had had half a notion that the prince might have gone to look for the lost rapier. But when he reappeared he was carrying in his hand, not a sword, but an ax.

The incongruity between the masquerade and the mystery had created a curious psychological atmosphere. At first they had all felt horribly ashamed at being caught in the foolish disguises of a festival, by an event that had only too much the character of a funeral. Many of them would have already gone back and dressed in clothes that were more funereal or at least more formal. But somehow at the moment this seemed like a second masquerade, more artificial and frivolous than the first. And as they reconciled themselves to their ridiculous trappings, a curious sensation had come over some of them, notably over the more sensitive, like Crane and Fisher and Juliet, but in some degree over everybody except the practical Mr. Brain. It was almost as if they were the ghosts of their own ancestors haunting that dark wood and dismal lake, and playing some old part that they only half remembered. The movements of those colored figures seemed to mean something that had been settled long before, like a silent heraldry. Acts, attitudes, external objects, were accepted as an allegory even without the key; and they knew when a crisis had come, when they did not know what it was. And somehow they knew subconsciously that the whole tale had taken a new and terrible turn, when they saw the prince stand in the gap of the gaunt trees, in his robes of angry crimson and with his lowering face of bronze, bearing in his hand a new shape of death. They could not have named a reason, but the two swords seemed indeed to have become toy swords and the whole tale of them broken and tossed away like a toy. Borodino looked like the Old World headsman, clad in terrible red, and carrying the ax for the execution of the criminal. And the criminal was not Crane.

Mr. Brain of the Indian police was glaring at the new object, and it was a moment or two before he spoke, harshly and almost hoarsely.

"What are you doing with that?" he asked. "Seems to be a woodman's chopper."

"A natural association of ideas," observed Horne Fisher. "If you meet a cat in a wood you think it's a wildcat, though it may have just strolled from the drawing-room sofa. As a matter of fact, I happen to know that is not the woodman's chopper. It's the kitchen chopper, or meat ax, or something like that, that somebody has thrown away in the wood. I saw it in the kitchen myself when I was getting the potato sacks with which I reconstructed a mediæval hermit."

"All the same, it is not without interest,"

remarked the prince, holding out the instrument to Fisher, who took it and examined it carefully. "A butcher's cleaver that done butcher's work."

"It was certainly the instrument of the crime," assented Fisher, in a low voice.

Brain was staring at the dull blue gleam of the ax head with fierce and fascinated eyes. "I don't understand you," he said. "There is no—there are no marks on it."

"It has shed no blood," answered Fisher, "but for all that it has committed a crime. This is as near as the criminal came to the crime when he committed it."

"What do you mean?"

"He was not there when he did it," explained Fisher. "It's a poor sort of murderer who can't murder people when he isn't there."

"You seem to be talking merely for the sake of mystification," said Brain. "If you have any practical advice to give you might as well make it intelligible."

"The only practical advice I can suggest," said Fisher, thoughtfully, "is a little research into local topography and nomenclature. They say there used to be a Mr. Prior, who had a farm in this neighborhood. I think some details about the domestic life of the late Mr. Prior would throw a light on this terrible business."

"And you have nothing more immediate than your topography to offer," said Brain, with a sneer, "to help me avenge my friend?"

"Well," said Fisher, "I should find out the truth about the Hole in the Wall."

That night, at the close of a stormy twilight and under a strong west wind that followed the breaking of the frost, Leonard Crane was wending his way in a wild rotatory walk round and round the high, continuous wall that inclosed the little wood. He was driven by a desperate idea of solving for himself the riddle that had clouded his reputation and already even threatened his liberty. The police authorities, now in charge of the inquiry, had not arrested him, but he knew well enough that if he tried to move far afield he would be instantly arrested. Horne Fisher's fragmentary hints, though he had refused to expand them as yet, had stirred the artistic temperament of the architect to a sort of wild analysis, and he was resolved to read the hieroglyph upside down and every way until it made sense. If it was something connected with a hole in the wall he would find the hole in the wall; but, as a matter of fact, he was unable to find the faintest crack in the wall. His professional knowledge told him that the masonry was all of one workmanship and one date,

and, except for the regular entrance, which threw
no light on the mystery, he found nothing suggest-
ing any sort of hiding place or means of escape.
Walking a narrow path between the winding wall
and the wild eastward bend and sweep of the gray
and feathery trees, seeing shifting gleams of a lost
sunset winking almost like lightning as the clouds of
tempest scudded across the sky and mingling with
the first faint blue light from a slowly strengthened
moon behind him, he began to feel his head going
round as his heels were going round and round the
blind recurrent barrier. He had thoughts on the
border of thought; fancies about a fourth dimen-
sion which was itself a hole to hide anything, of
seeing everything from a new angle out of a new
window in the senses; or of some mystical light
and transparency, like the new rays of chemistry,
in which he could see Bulmer's body, horrible and
glaring, floating in a lurid halo over the woods and
the wall. He was haunted also with the hint, which
somehow seemed to be equally horrifying, that it all
had something to do with Mr. Prior. There seemed
even to be something creepy in the fact that he was
always respectfully referred to as Mr. Prior, and that
it was in the domestic life of the dead farmer that he
had been bidden to seek the seed of these dreadful
things. As a matter of fact, he had found that no

local inquiries had revealed anything at all about the Prior family.

The moonlight had broadened and brightened, the wind had driven off the clouds and itself died fitfully away, when he came round again to the artificial lake in front of the house. For some reason it looked a very artificial lake; indeed, the whole scene was like a classical landscape with a touch of Watteau; the Palladian façade of the house pale in the moon, and the same silver touching the very pagan and naked marble nymph in the middle of the pond. Rather to his surprise, he found another figure there beside the statue, sitting almost equally motionless; and the same silver pencil traced the wrinkled brow and patient face of Horne Fisher, still dressed as a hermit and apparently practicing something of the solitude of a hermit. Nevertheless, he looked up at Leonard Crane and smiled, almost as if he had expected him.

"Look here," said Crane, planting himself in front of him, "can you tell me anything about this business?"

"I shall soon have to tell everybody everything about it," replied Fisher, "but I've no objection to telling you something first. But, to begin with, will you tell me something? What really happened when you met Bulmer this morning? You did throw away your sword, but you didn't kill him."

"I didn't kill him because I threw away my sword," said the other. "I did it on purpose—or I'm not sure what might have happened."

After a pause he went on, quietly: "The late Lord Bulmer was a very breezy gentleman, extremely breezy. He was very genial with his inferiors, and would have his lawyer and his architect staying in his house for all sorts of holidays and amusements. But there was another side to him, which they found out when they tried to be his equals. When I told him that his sister and I were engaged, something happened which I simply can't and won't describe. It seemed to me like some monstrous upheaval of madness. But I suppose the truth is painfully simple. There is such a thing as the coarseness of a gentleman. And it is the most horrible thing in humanity."

"I know," said Fisher. "The Renaissance nobles of the Tudor time were like that."

"It is odd that you should say that," Crane went on. "For while we were talking there came on me a curious feeling that we were repeating some scene of the past, and that I was really some outlaw, found in the woods like Robin Hood, and that he had really stepped in all his plumes and purple out of the picture frame of the ancestral portrait. Anyhow, he was the man in possession, and he neither feared God nor regarded man. I defied him, of course, and walked away. I might really have killed him if I had not walked away."

"Yes," said Fisher, nodding, "his ancestor was in possession and he was in possession, and this is the end of the story. It all fits in."

"Fits in with what?" cried his companion, with sudden impatience. "I can't make head or tail of it. You tell me to look for the secret in the hole in the wall, but I can't find any hole in the wall."

"There isn't any," said Fisher. "That's the secret." After reflecting a moment, he added: "Unless you call it a hole in the wall of the world. Look here; I'll tell you if you like, but I'm afraid it involves an introduction. You've got to understand one of the tricks of the modern mind, a tendency that most people obey without noticing it. In the village or suburb outside there's an inn with the sign of St. George and the Dragon. Now suppose I went about telling everybody that this was only a corruption of King George and the Dragoon. Scores of people would believe it, without any inquiry, from a vague feeling that it's probable because it's prosaic. It turns something romantic and legendary into something recent and ordinary. And that somehow makes it sound rational, though it is unsupported by reason. Of course some people would have the sense to remember having seen St. George in old Italian pictures and French romances, but a good many wouldn't think about it at all. They would just swallow the skepticism because it was skepticism. Modern intelligence won't accept anything on authority. But it will accept anything without authority. That's exactly what has happened here.

"When some critic or other chose to say that Prior's Park was not a priory, but was named after some quite modern man named Prior, nobody really tested the theory at all. It never occurred to anybody repeating the story to ask if there *was* any Mr. Prior, if anybody had ever seen him or heard of him. As a matter of fact, it was a priory, and shared the fate of most priories—that is, the Tudor gentleman with the plumes simply stole it by brute force and turned it into his own private house; he did worse things, as you shall hear. But the point here is that this is how the trick works, and the trick works in the same way in the other part of the tale. The name of this district is printed Holinwall in all the best maps produced by the scholars; and they allude lightly, not without a smile, to the fact that it was pronounced Holiwell by the most ignorant and old-fashioned of the poor. But it is spelled wrong and pronounced right."

"Do you mean to say," asked Crane, quickly, "that there really was a well?"

"There is a well," said Fisher, "and the truth lies at the bottom of it."

As he spoke he stretched out his hand and pointed toward the sheet of water in front of him.

"The well is under that water somewhere," he said, "and this is not the first tragedy connected with it. The founder of this house did something which his fellow ruffians very seldom did; something that had to be hushed up even in the anarchy of the pillage of the monasteries. The well was connected with the miracles of some saint, and the last prior that guarded it was something like a saint himself; certainly he was something very like a martyr. He defied the new owner and dared him to pollute the place, till the noble, in a fury, stabbed him and flung his body into the well, whither, after four hundred years, it has been followed by an heir of the usurper, clad in the same purple and walking the world with the same pride."

"But how did it happen," demanded Crane, "that for the first time Bulmer fell in at that particular spot?"

"Because the ice was only loosened at that particular spot, by the only man who knew it," answered Horne Fisher. "It was cracked deliberately, with the kitchen chopper, at that special place; and I myself heard the hammering and did not understand it. The place had been covered with an artificial lake, if only because the whole truth had to be covered with an artificial legend. But don't you see that it is exactly what those pagan nobles would have done, to desecrate it with a sort of heathen goddess, as the Roman Emperor built a temple to Venus on the Holy Sepulchre. But the truth could still be traced out, by any scholarly man determined to trace it. And this man was determined to trace it."

"What man?" asked the other, with a shadow of the answer in his mind.

"The only man who has an alibi," replied Fisher. "James Haddow, the antiquarian lawyer, left the night before the fatality, but he left that black star of death on the ice. He left abruptly, having previously proposed to stay; probably, I think, after an ugly scene with Bulmer, at their legal interview. As you know yourself, Bulmer could make a man feel pretty murderous, and I rather fancy the lawyer had himself irregularities to confess, and was in danger of exposure by his client. But it's my reading of human nature that a man will cheat in his trade, but not in his hobby. Haddow may have been a dishonest lawyer, but he couldn't help being an honest antiquary. When he got on the track of the truth about the Holy Well he had to follow it up; he was not to be bamboozled with newspaper anecdotes about Mr. Prior and a hole in the wall; he found out everything, even to the exact location of the well, and he was rewarded, if being a successful assassin can be regarded as a reward."

"And how did you get on the track of all this hidden history?" asked the young architect.

A cloud came across the brow of Horne Fisher. "I knew only too much about it already," he said, "and, after all, it's shameful for me to be speaking lightly of poor Bulmer, who has paid his penalty; but the rest of us haven't. I dare say every cigar I smoke and every liqueur I drink comes directly or indirectly from the harrying of the holy places and the persecution of the poor. After all, it needs very little poking about in the past to find that hole in the wall, that great breach in the defenses of English history. It lies just under the surface of a thin sheet of sham information and instruction, just as the black and blood-stained well lies just under that floor of shallow water and flat weeds. Oh, the ice is thin, but it bears; it is strong enough to support us when we dress up as monks and dance on it, in mockery of the dear, quaint old Middle Ages. They told me I must put on fancy dress; so I did put on fancy dress, according to my own taste and fancy. I put on the only costume I think fit for a man who has inherited the position of a gentleman, and yet has not entirely lost the feelings of one."

In answer to a look of inquiry, he rose with a sweeping and downward gesture.

"Sackcloth," he said; "and I would wear the ashes as well if they would stay on my bald head."

J. Jefferson Farjeon

Secrets in the Snow

The Christmas Eve motor-coach stopped in the middle of nowhere. Rubbing the steam from her window, Janet looked out into a whirling white wilderness. She could not see any sign of town or village, and nobody got in and nobody got out saving the conductor, who had vanished the moment the coach had come to a halt.

"Is anything wrong?" she asked the untalkative man next to her.

For two hours this man had taken no advantage of the fact that, at a season of easy comradeship, he had been sitting beside an exceptionally pretty girl.

"Don't know, can't say," he answered, shortly.

"*I'm* betting it's a jolly old snowdrift!" exclaimed the more loquacious young man in the seat behind. He had been doing his best to cheer a woman with a toothache, and had failed signally. "Any takers?"

The bet was not accepted, which was a misfortune for him since his guess proved accurate. In a short while the conductor returned with a gloomy face to report that the road was blocked. "There's snowdrifts as big as St. Paul's," he added. "We've got to go back for help"

The untalkative man jumped up. "That doesn't suit me!" he grunted. "I was getting out at the next stop, anyway."

"So was I," said Janet. "You're not going to West Mallerton, by any chance?"

He hesitated, then murmured, "That direction," and the next moment was outside.

"Whoa, wait a minute!" exclaimed Janet, seizing her suit-case. "That's my direction, too!"

To her surprise, the loquacious passenger interposed.

"I say! I wouldn't, really!" he urged, thrusting out his foot.

"Why not?" she demanded, frowning at him.

"Why not? Well—just look at the weather!" he replied. "You'd better wait here. You'd never do it."

"Thanks, but I've got a house-party on," she retorted, "and I *mean* to do it! Do you mind moving your foot, or I'll lose my guide!"

She stepped over the impeding boot, and a couple of seconds later was out in the blinding snow.

For an instant, as the cold caught her and the flakes flung themselves into her face, she wondered whether the loquacious young man's advice had not been sound. Still, sound or not, she was not going back, and she plunged forward after a dim figure that was rapidly becoming obliterated. The figure moved as quickly as she, and it was not until she had increased her pace that she caught it up in a narrow lane.

"You *are* in a hurry!" she cried, breathlessly.

The pursued one turned, and his expression, a mixture of surprise and annoyance, was not complimentary.

"You said you were going to West Mallerton," Janet explained, "so I thought we might walk together. I don't know the way."

"I said I was going in that direction," the man corrected her.

"But you didn't mention that you loathed company!" she shot back, incensed by his rudeness. "Don't worry—I'll keep behind!"

He regarded her fixedly for a few seconds, as though sizing her up. Then he said, in a slightly changed tone,

"Let me advise you, young lady, to keep well behind—otherwise you may walk into more trouble than you've just come from."

"Really?"

"Really."

"What sort of trouble?"

"Curiosity killed a cat."

"Only I don't happen to be one."

He smiled rather grimly, and responded after a moment's consideration.

"Very well. I'm on a Scotland Yard job—and there *may* be some rough stuff coming along."

He patted a side-pocket suggestively.

The weather chose this moment to create a diversion. A sudden wind drove a flurry of snow viciously into her eyes, and her suit-case slipped from her cold fingers. She stopped to regain it, stumbled, and took a soft fall. When she had picked herself up, she found herself alone.

"And policemen are supposed to be polite!" she thought. "Well, if I've lost my guide, I've still got his footprints!"

They ran down the virgin carpet of the lane till they were lost in the white kaleidoscopic mist. She began to follow them, but stopped almost at once.

"That's funny!" she murmured. "*Two* sets of prints! Whose are the others?"

Both sets of prints were very recent; of that there was no doubt. With fresh snow falling all the while, old marks soon ceased to be, and new marks had but a short life. Moreover, before she had overtaken the Scotland Yard man, she had been following only one set . . . Yes, but if that were so . . . ?

She gave it up, and hastened down the lane.

The lane turned and twisted. The footprints became less and less distinct. That meant that those ahead of her were outpacing her, and that the length of time between the reaching and the making of the marks was increasing. "They must be in a hurry!" she reflected, as she accelerated.

Presently, near a snow-covered barn, one set faded out completely. She had met nobody and there were no sign-posts, so all she could do was to follow the remaining set and hope Heaven would be kind to her. The joy of Christmas was fast oozing away, and she was wet and shivery. Already she regretted that she had not taken the advice of the idiotic young man.

Yes, he *had* been idiotic. The scraps of conversation she had overheard behind her in the coach had, in Shakespearean terms, written him down an ass. Yet, as he had tried to dissuade her, and had impudently stuck out his boot, there had been something not unpleasant in his ingenuous blue eyes. Perhaps, if a man were born a fool, he could not help it!

She found herself walking mechanically. She had a sensation that if she stopped she would stop for good. She was growing colder and colder, her feet had become two lumps of squelching numbness, and tiny streams of chilly moisture were running down her neck. Then the worst happened. The last footprints faded out, and she reached a fork where the lane divided into two.

"*Now* what?" she asked herself.

She tossed up in her mind. Heads right, tails left. The imaginary coin came down heads, and she took the right-hand fork.

Walking became increasingly difficult. The lane narrowed to a snow-clothed track. Once, avoiding a big white mound, she trod deeply and sprawled into a ditch. She rose spluttering, rescued her suit-case, and wondered whether to turn back.

But now the blessed miracle for which she had prayed occurred. A little way ahead, its roof just visible behind a high hedge, was a cottage. She staggered towards it, as a spent man staggers towards the oasis in the desert.

The small gate in the hedge was closed, but the door of the house was open. Without hesitation, when her knock failed to produce any response, she walked in.

The sight that met her gaze was as welcome as it was unexpected. On a small table by a smaller fire was a pot of tea. A saucerless cup was half-filled with milkless fluid. A chair near the table was at an untidy angle, and on the floor was a large spade, its metal moist; but if the last items were less welcome than the first, in that quick initial glance the tea towered above everything.

But for these frugal signs of a meal, and the open front-door, the house seemed unoccupied. It had a musty, closed-in smell, and dust was everywhere.

"Anybody at home?" she called.

Only her echo answered her.

She walked to the table. The tea in the cup was still hot. The spade on the floor was still wet. She glanced towards a door at the back of the room. It was ajar.

About to call again, she paused. Her ears, grown acute through tension, had caught a sound on the other side of the door. At first she could not decipher it; then, as it was repeated with a sort of jerky regularity, she guessed what it was. It resembled the breathing of a short-winded ghost, but she did not believe in ghosts.

"Are you coming in, or shall I come out?" she asked, adopting bold tactics.

In a moment or two the door moved, and a head peered in cautiously.

It was not a prepossessing head. Small, pale, with straw-coloured hair, a flat nose, and eyes that did not agree, it came round the door like a bad joke. For a few seconds, beauty and ugliness stared at each other. Then the head inquired, in a husky voice,

"'Oo are you?"

"My name won't interest you," answered Janet, "but my condition may—if you've a heart. I'm cold and sopping, and I've lost my way."

"Oh! 'Ave yer," blinked the head. "Yus, I've got a 'eart, but it ain't a strong 'un. Yer give me a proper scare."

"I'm sorry. May I know who you are?"

"Me? Oh, Caretaker!" Now he entered completely. From the look of his shabby suit, he did not earn a high salary for his job. "I was just 'avin' a cup o' tea." His eyes fixed themselves on the spade. "Arter doin' a bit o' snow-shovellin'. Mikes yer 'ot. See, I dropped the spade when I 'eard yer comin'."

"Did you think I was a ghost?"

He smiled queerly. He was a horrid little fellow, but Janet found herself feeling rather sorry for him.

"Tha's right, miss. Bein' alone in a hempy 'ouse gives yer the creeps, speshully at Chrismus, tha's right, ain't it?" He looked at her earnestly. "This 'ouse is 'aunted. I wouldn't reckermend nobody ter stay 'ere!"

"At the present moment, I'm not in a mood to be particular," she pointed out.

"Oh, I see. Where yer tryin' ter git ter?"

"West Mallerton."

"Never 'eard of it." He saw the astonishment in

hcr eyes, and added hastily, "See, I on'y bin caretaker 'ere cupple o' days. Yer better arsk some'un
helse."

"Thank you! Who?" He scratched his head.
"Listen," she went on to her unsatisfactory host, "I
don't want to trouble you, but I'm really in a frightful mess. If I can sit by your fire and dry myself for
ten minutes, and if you could let me have just one
cup of tea from that pot, I'll give you a jolly good
Christmas present."

She produced from her sopping bag a dry ten
shilling note, and the caretaker's eyes gleamed.

"And if you could add a towel," she said, with
sudden inspiration, "and could give me those ten
minutes to myself, I might turn this note into a
pound one!"

"It's a go!" exclaimed the caretaker, and dived
back to the kitchen.

In a few moments he reappeared with an empty
cup and a roller-towel.

"I fahnd this 'angin' up, I 'ope it'll do," he said
hoarsely. "The cup's clean, any'ow."

"Any chance of a drop of milk?" she asked.

He shook his head.

"Sugar?"

"Sorry, miss. See, I ain't started orderin' things
proper yet," he explained, "and the bloke wot

engaged me didn't leave no stores, on'y the tea. But there's plenty o' that in the pot, so 'elp yerself, miss—and yer can 'ave 'arf-a-hour, if yer like, while I goes on with me diggin'."

He seized the spade and ran out of the room again. She heard his hurried footsteps fading away across a floor. She gazed after him with a little frown, trying to quell disturbing thoughts.

"Of course, it hasn't really been shopping weather lately," she reflected, "but if you've been here for two days, Mr. Caretaker, have you been living *entirely* on tea-leaves? And whose ghost did you expect to walk in on you?"

Well, these things were nothing to do with her. Her own concern was to make good use of this half-hour, and she proceeded to do so very thoroughly.

Her first action was to lock the doors of the parlour, to ensure privacy. Then she drew a blue check curtain across the window. The pale, subdued light gave her a comforting sense of peace, and the little fire, coming into its own, added to her pleasure. Secure against interruption, she took off her wet coat and slipped out of her dress, almost purring with pleasure as the warmth of the fire caressed her bare arms.

"This is the moment for that tea!" she thought.

She filled the empty cup, then sipped gingerly.

Minus milk, the tea was still too hot to gulp. Somewhere outside she believed she heard the sound of shoveling, but she could not be sure. Where was he? At the back or front? Drawn by idle curiosity she began to move towards the window, but retreated quickly as her shadow fell upon the blue check curtain. She heard soft steps outside. He was in the front.

"Well, I hope he's enjoying himself," she murmured, "but it isn't *my* idea of fun!"

In her retreat she had nearly stumbled over her suit-case on the floor, and the incident gave her a new idea, or elaborated a previous one. She opened the case and, after removing a top layer of gifts destined for sundry folk at West Mallerton, if she ever reached them, she unpacked a complete change of lingerie. Then she stripped, life growing better and better as she shed each damp garment.

Naked, she laughed. The outrageous absurdity of her position swept over her, and she wondered what the absent house-owner would have thought had he known of the use that was being made of his parlour! Would he have been amused or indignant? Pleased or annoyed? Well, he would never know, so why worry? She laughed again. Then, suddenly, stood rigid.

A sound she could not—or would not—interpret

had broken the velvet silence outside, and frozen her laughter. She remained motionless, waiting for its repetition. When it was not repeated, and the only sound she could hear was the beating of her heart, she began diving into her clothes with desperate speed, striving to comfort herself as she dressed.

"Of *course* it wasn't!" she thought. "It was an owl hooting! Or some animal or other. Or—yes—the whistle of a distant train! That silly idiot talking about his precious ghost—he's given me the jim-jams!"

Redressed, she unlocked the back door with definite distaste, and called into the dim kitchen.

"Are you in there?"

As once before, her echo answered her, but this time it was a particularly unpleasant echo, repeating her question with ironic derision.

Then she unlocked the front door, and looked out into the gloaming. Dusk had come abruptly. It was a dusk choked with thick flakes. For a short space she could see nothing but the snow, falling as relentlessly as ever, and drowning the world beneath its dull white monotone. But presently, as she stared, shapes and outlines grew, and she made out the laden trees, the muffled bushes, and the boundary hedge.

What she did not see was the little, flat-nosed, pale-faced caretaker.

Her mind fretted nervily, swinging inconsistently from one decision to another.

"I must find him," it ran; then recanted. "Why should I find him? I can just go. I expect I'll come across somebody somewhere who'll direct me. And of *course* it was an owl! No, Janet, you don't think that! Stop playing tricks with yourself! You know you can't go yet. Why, you haven't even paid him . . . I could leave the note on the table, couldn't I? Yes, why not? . . . You know very well why not!"

She had just decided to brave the elements, this time not on her own behalf, when a figure came round the angle of the wall. At first she thought it was the caretaker, and she breathed a sigh of relief, but then she realized that even the illusions of the snow could not have increased him to this size, and as the newcomer stopped abruptly and stared at her, she stared back in equal astonishment. It was the Scotland Yard detective.

"Get back!" he ordered, sharply.

To ensure her obedience, he advanced and thrust her back unceremoniously into the room. Then he entered after her, glanced quickly around, and closed the door behind him.

"How did *you* get here?" he demanded.

Her nerves on edge, she was not in a mood for cross-examination and she retorted,

"How did *you*?"

"You seem to be a very disobedient young lady," he frowned. "I think I advised you not to follow me?"

"Since I seem to have got here first," she returned, "I suppose you're quite sure you haven't followed me? And what right have you to call me disobedient? I'm not under your orders!"

He apologized impatiently.

"Forgive me, but you'll recall I told you I was on a job, and—

"Perhaps, if you're more polite, I can help you with the job!"

"I beg your pardon?"

"You heard me. Let's start fresh. A few minutes ago somebody gave a cry out there."

"Are you sure?" he asked.

"Sufficiently. Didn't you hear it?"

"We'll have your story first, if you don't mind. When did you hear the cry?"

"Four or five minutes ago. I can't say exactly."

"But you didn't go out?"

She flushed slightly as she recalled the reason, but she did not give the reason. She answered simply, "No".

"Are you alone in here?"

"Don't you think", she suggested, "it would be quicker if I told you my story in my own words?

Unless it would be an even better idea to go out first and look for the trouble? There was a caretaker here when I arrived. He went out while I was trying to get dry. He hasn't come back."

The detective hesitated, then nodded.

"You're right. Will you wait here?"

"If you don't want me to come with you."

"It wouldn't help, and there's no need to put you into unnecessary danger. Where did the cry seem to come from? Which direction?"

"The back."

"Thank you. Stay in this parlour. Don't move out of it." He added, with a faint smile, "You don't mind being obedient this time?"

"I don't mind being sensible," she replied. "I don't call that obedience."

He turned to the door, but paused with his hand on the knob.

"For a couple of hours, you and I sat side by side without saying a word," he remarked. "Since then, we've got to know each other quite well!"

Then he left her.

She returned to the fire and finished her tea, but the comfort had gone out of it, and she found herself starting at shadows and eyeing the doors apprehensively. It would have helped if the detective had had a more appealing personality. She wanted the fiction

brand. Apparently there was nothing appealing in
the real thing. Romance, sentiment, even common
politeness, were lacking. She almost preferred the
quaint little horror who had gone out into the snow
with his spade and not come back again!

The minutes dragged by. A grandfather clock
on the wall should have ticked them away, but it
had stopped. Like everything else but the snow. She
had stopped herself. She ought to be travelling to
West Mallerton, or moving about the gay and bust-
ling house there—unpacking, chatting, laughing, or
drinking tea, with milk and sugar in it, out of a delicate, expensive cup!

Instead . . . She glanced round the musty, dusty
parlour, now transferred from a sanctuary to a sort
of prison.

"I've had enough of this!" she exclaimed, jumping
up suddenly. "I'm going to have a look for myself!"

The front-door opened, and the detective
returned.

"Still here?" he observed, superfluously.

"Just," she answered. "Did you find anything?"

He shook his head.

"Then what's your solution?" she asked.

"Quite a simple one, I imagine," he said, "but let
me have the rest of your story."

She gave it to him briefly. He listened without

interruption. When she had finished, she recalled one point she had forgotten to mention.

"Oh, there's just one more thing," she added, "if it's important. You remember, you left me rather hurriedly after I'd caught you up from the motor-coach?"

"I recall it," he admitted.

"After you left me, I found two sets of footprints. I'm practically sure that, before then, there had only been one set. Your own."

"What about yours?"

"Excluding mine, of course."

He stared at the fire for a few moments, then said,

"Yes, you're right. And the whole thing fits. So here is my side of the story. I told you I was on a job. Your so-called caretaker was the job. I came to this neighbourhood to track him—he broke prison a few days ago, and had been reported in this locality. Just as you and I were talking in that lane, I spotted the fellow dashing by. In effect, I've been chasing him ever since."

"You mean—he came here?" she exclaimed.

"Obviously. Thinking himself safe, he lit a fire and made himself some tea. Then you came in, and gave him the shock of his life. Probably he thought you were me. He posed as a caretaker, played his cards carefully, and as soon as he got a chance, hopped it. Naturally, he extended those ten minutes to half-an-hour! It gave him longer for his get-away."

"I—see," replied Janet, slowly. "Yes, of course. Only—"

"What?"

"That cry?"

"He probably tripped and banged his nose."

"You don't bang your nose in soft snow. I've tried it myself."

"You may bang it against something else, or imagine you're going to."

"And—if he was making his get-away, why didn't he do it at once?"

"I've told you. He had to pose as the caretaker first and make quite sure you weren't suspicious. He didn't want you following him."

"You haven't got me," she corrected him. "What I meant was, why didn't he make his get-away as soon as he left me the last time?"

"How do you know he didn't?"

"Because that cry didn't come till quite a while afterwards. I'd—begun to get dry—had some tea—gone to the front door to listen to those steps outside—returned—unpacked some things from my case—I'm sure it was quite seven or eight minutes."

"I see your point," answered the detective. "It's a good one."

"Then how do you get over it?"

"He may have been delayed through some cause unknown to us, or—the cry may not have come from him at all."

"Who from, then?"

"An owl."

"I thought of that."

"Well, think of it again."

"Yes, but now I'm thinking of something else," she said.

"For a modern young lady," smiled the detective, "you seem to do an unusual amount of thinking. What is your thought this time."

"His spade."

"What about the spade?"

"If he'd just dived in here to get away from you—if he wasn't a caretaker—why was he digging the snow away?"

"Perhaps he was trying to make a funk-hole."

"Did you find the spade?"

"Not a sign of it. And the next?"

She stared at the tip of her toe before putting her last question.

"Can you tell me the way to West Mallerton?"

He laughed. "This time our thoughts match,"

he said, "for I was just about to suggest myself that you continued your journey. I'm afraid I have a little disappointment for you, though."

"What is it?"

"The direction of West Mallerton. A detective on the job doesn't care to give his own direction away in public, so—when you made your enquiry in the coach, I implied I was going towards West Mallerton when actually I was going precisely the opposite way. You'll remember, I tried to dissuade you from following me, but you were somewhat pig-headed. Return to the high-road, and take the lane on the other side."

"Thank you for not very much," she answered. "What will you do?"

"Light a pipe, take five minutes off by this fire, and then catch my man. Good afternoon."

He opened the front door and gave a stiff little bow.

She took up her suit-case, but paused in the door-way.

"He looked a misery," she said. "What had he done?"

"Eighteen months for housebreaking," replied the detective, "and he has another eighteen to come."

Then she passed out into the snow, and heard the front door close behind her.

She walked towards the gate, slowly and dissatisfied. Before she reached it, something caught her eye. It was a long object on the ground on her right. The falling flakes had almost covered it.

Quickly she glanced back at the cottage. The blue curtain glowed faintly in the firelight behind it. It was in position, and if the detective had drawn it aside to watch her go, he had replaced it. Darting to the object, she bent and examined it. It was a spade.

The detective had said that, for a modern girl, Janet did an unusual amount of thinking. In the next few seconds she justified the assertion, and she acted while she thought. She was back at the gate in a flash. In another she had opened and closed it with a loud click, though whether the click was heard inside the parlour she had no means of knowing. In another, she had slipped behind the cold, snow-laden foliage of a big clump of bushes.

A second assertion of the detective's proved less accurate. He had promised himself five minutes respite in the parlour. He came out in less than two. From her white bower she watched him emerge; watched the smudge of his form, a grim blot in the gloaming, pause in a listening attitude, move swiftly to the gate, peer over, and then slip in front of the bushes towards the spade. He had said he had not found the spade, but he knew where it was! A third assertion tested; and, like the second, disproved.

Risking whatever might be coming to her, Janet crept from her concealment, and was just in time to see the detective pick up the spade and make for the back of the cottage.

She left her suit-case under the bushes and followed him. He walked slowly and cautiously, and once he stopped dead and looked round. If she had not anticipated the movement and dodged behind a large water-butt he would have seen her, with what results she could not guess. Proceeding, the stalker and the stalked reached a back-yard, and what seemed, as far as Janet could make out from the irregular white surface, an untidy kitchen garden or neglected, half-worked field beyond. Here the man suddenly stopped.

He stared at the ground. From where she stood she could not see what he was staring at, but it appeared to be a small mound of snow. She waited breathlessly. Would he never move again? But presently he stopped staring, and began shovelling. He was shovelling snow on to the mound with the spade. After working for three minutes or thereabouts, he ceased the shovelling and again stared at the mound. Then he moved on again.

But Janet did not move. She dreaded to. Through

the blinding snow she could just discern the shape of the mound, and it terrified her; yet, mixed with the terror was a queer, compelling anger.

It was not until she feared his slowly-moving form would fade out beyond the mound that she advanced. As she neared the spot the man stopped once more, and began digging in the snow ten yards away. Reaching the mound, she bent over it, and failed to stifle her exclamation at what she saw. The man turned swiftly. The next moment he was confronting her.

"What the hell are you doing here!"

His expression was livid.

"What are *you* doing here?" she answered, astonished at the steadiness of her voice. "And how do you explain—that?"

She did not have to point to the snow-covered shape on the ground. His gaze followed hers.

"I didn't tell you—I didn't want to frighten you," he rasped. "He was digging, and he fell on his spade, cracking his skull."

"And why are you digging?"

"To find out why he was! What silly ideas have you got into your head?"

She faced his challenging eyes.

"Shall I tell you?"

"Do you dare?"

He seized her wrist and held it cruelly.

"I suppose you're trying to impress me with your strength," she said, with scorn in her voice, "but isn't that a bit superfluous? You've got a heavy spade— and evidently know how to use it!"

She regretted her remark immediately afterwards, for in a sudden mad frenzy he raised the spade, and she knew it was not the first time he had raised it so that afternoon. But the next moment the implement dropped harmlessly to the ground, and the man himself dropped, too, with a shout of pain.

"Put your hands up, Benson," said a quiet voice behind them, "or the next one won't be in your foot."

Janet turned, weakly. It was the loquacious young man from the coach.

The man on the ground glared helplessly, then obeyed the order as the newcomer advanced. A pair of handcuffs clicked. After that the young man stooped to the mound, brushed aside some of the snow, and stared for a long while at what lay beneath.

"I see—you got Smith," he murmured.

"The damned double-crosser!" muttered Benson.

"You talked too much, eh, before he was let out?"

"Smart, aren't you?"

"And so you broke prison to try and race him to the spot."

"And you were the also ran!" sneered Benson.

"Who nevertheless appears to have won the race," the young man pointed out. "Well, Benson, let's have it. Which of you dug up the necklace you buried before you were caught for the West Maller-ton robbery? You or Smith?"

Benson moistened his dry lips.

"I didn't talk then," he growled, "and I'm not talking now!"

"No? Well, I don't expect it matters. The reason I didn't settle you in the coach was because I wanted you first to lead me all the way—and the only mistake I made," he added, turning to Janet for a moment, "was to show myself too soon in that lane when *you* were talking to him. You'll remember, I tried to dissuade you from following him, didn't I?"

"You did," she answered. "I suppose it was you who caused him to vanish so suddenly—and who made that second set of footprints."

"Yes—when I vanished after him," smiled the young man. "But he was too quick for me that time—I lost him for half-an-hour." Addressing Benson again, now without the smile, he went on, "Come along. I gather you've been busy a little way off. Let's see what you've been up to—or got down to!"

Picking up the spade, he forced the unwilling

Benson to the spot where he had been digging.
Janet followed them slowly, reaching them just as
the young man gave an exclamation. He stooped,
and picked a long string of pearls from the snow-
cleared earth.

"May I have it, please?" she asked.

The young man turned and stared at her. Even
the handcuffed thief forgot for a moment the injured
foot he was nursing.

"I'm spending Christmas at the house where that
robbery occurred," she explained, "and I'd rather
like to give my hostess her necklace as a present!"

But the young man, after looking at her oddly,
shook his head, and became unprofessionally
human.

"For two hours", he said, "I have had the tan-
talizing experience of sitting behind the back of
your head. If you don't mind, I think I'll give your
hostess her necklace myself to-morrow morning—
using it as a means to a frontal introduction!" The
unprofessional moment passed. He added, gravely,
"Meanwhile, since the snow is stopping, perhaps
you'd better continue with your pleasure—while I
continue with my business?"

As Janet resumed her way, this time in the right
direction, by all the laws of logic she should have
been thinking of an extremely interesting young

man with whom, on the morrow, she was to renew her acquaintance. Instead she found herself dwelling on a mound of snow, and a miserable, pathetic little fellow with a squint, for whom no morrow would dawn.

EDMUND CRISPIN

The Name on the Window

Boxing Day; snow and ice; road-surface like glass under a cold fog. In the North Oxford home of the University Professor of English Language and Literature, at three minutes past seven in the evening, the front door bell rang.

The current festive season had taken heavy toll of Fen's vitality and patience; it had culminated, that afternoon, in a quite exceptionally tiring children's party, amid whose ruins he was now recouping his energies with whisky; and on hearing the bell he jumped inevitably to the conclusion that one of the infants he had bundled out of the door half an hour previously had left behind it some such prized inessential as a false nose or a bachelor's button, and was returning to claim this. In the event, however, and despite his premonitory groans, this assumption proved to be incorrect: his doorstep was occupied, he found, not by a dyspeptic, over-heated child with an unintelligible query, but by a neatly-dressed greying man with a red tip to his nose and woebegone eyes.

"I can't get back," said this apparition. "I really can't get back to London tonight. The roads are impassable and such trains as there are are running hours late. Could you possibly let me have a bed?"

The tones were familiar; and by peering more attentively at the face, Fen discovered that that was familiar too. "My dear Humbleby," he said cordially, "do come in. Of course you can have a bed. What are you doing in this part of the world, anyway?"

"Ghost-hunting." Detective-Inspector Humbleby, of New Scotland Yard, divested himself of his coat and hat and hung them on a hook inside the door. "Seasonable but not convenient." He stamped his feet violently, thereby producing, to judge from his expression, sensations of pain rather than of warmth; and stared about him. "*Children*," he said with sudden gloom. "I dare say that one of the Oxford hotels—"

"The children have left," Fen explained, "and will not be coming back."

"Ah. Well, in that case—" And Humbleby followed Fen into the drawing-room, where a huge fire was burning and a slightly lop-sided Christmas tree, stripped of its treasures, wore tinsel and miniature witch-balls and a superincumbent fairy with a raffish air. "My word, this is better. Is there a drink, perhaps? I could do with some advice, too."

Fen was already pouring whisky. "Sit down and be comfortable," he said. "As a matter of interest, do you believe in ghosts?"

"The evidence for *poltergeists*," Humbleby answered warily as he stretched out his hands to the blaze, "seems very convincing to me . . . The Wesleys, you know, and Harry Price and so forth. Other sorts of ghosts I'm not so sure about—though I must say I *hope* they exist, if only for the purpose of taking that silly grin off the faces of the newspapers." He picked up a battered tin locomotive from beside him on the sofa. "I say, Gervase, I was under the impression that your own children were all too old for—"

"Orphans," said Fen, jabbing at the siphon. "I've been entertaining orphans from a nearby Home . . . But as regards this particular ghost you were speaking of—"

"Oh, I don't believe in *that*." Humbleby shook his head decisively. "There's an obscure sort of nastiness about the place it's supposed to haunt—like a very sickly cake gone stale—and a man *was* killed there once, by a girl he was trying to persuade to certain practices she didn't relish at all; but the haunting part of it is just silly gossip for the benefit of visitors." Humbleby accepted the glass which Fen held out to him and brooded over it for a moment before drinking. ". . . Damned Chief-Inspector," he muttered aggrievedly, "dragging me away from my Christmas lunch because—"

"Really, Humbleby"—Fen was severe—"you're very inconsequent this evening. Where is this place you're speaking of?"

"Rydalls."

"Rydalls?"

"Rydalls," said Humbleby. "The residence," he elucidated laboriously, "of Sir Charles Moberley, the architect. It's about fifteen miles from here, Abingdon way."

"Yes, I remember it now. Restoration."

"I dare say. Old, in any case. And there are big grounds, with an eighteenth-century pavilion about a quarter of a mile away from the house, in a park. That's where it happened—the murder, I mean."

"The murder of the man who tried to induce the girl—"

"No, no. I mean, yes. *That* murder took place in the pavilion, certainly. But then, so did the other one—the one the day before yesterday, that's to say."

Fen stared. "Sir Charles Moberley has been murdered?"

"No, no, no. Not *him*. Another architect, another knight—Sir Lucas Welsh. There's been quite a large house-party going on at Rydalls, with Sir Lucas Welsh and his daughter Jane among the guests, and it was on Christmas Eve, you see, that Sir Lucas decided he wanted to investigate the ghost."

"This is all clear enough to you, no doubt, but—"

"Do *listen* . . . It seems that Sir Lucas is—was—credulous about ghosts, so on Christmas Eve he arranged to keep vigil alone in the pavilion and—"

"And was murdered, and you don't know who did it."

"Oh yes, I do. Sir Lucas didn't die at once, you see: he had time to write up his murderer's name in the grime of the window-pane, and the gentleman concerned, a young German named Otto Mörike, is now safely under arrest. But what I can't decide is how Mörike got in and out of the pavilion."

"A locked-room mystery."

"In the wider sense, just that. The pavilion wasn't actually locked, but—"

Fen collected his glass from the mantelpiece, where he had put it on rising to answer the door-bell. "Begin," he suggested, "at the beginning."

"Very well." Settling back in the sofa, Humbleby sipped his whisky gratefully. "Here, then, is this Christmas house-party at Rydalls. Host, Sir Charles Moberley, the eminent architect . . . Have you ever come across him?"

Fen shook his head.

"A big man, going grey: in some ways rather

boisterous and silly, like a rugger-playing medical student in a state of arrested development. Unmarried; private means—quite a lot of them, to judge from the sort of hospitality he dispenses; did the Wandsworth power-station and Beckford Abbey, among other things; athlete; a simple mind, and generous, I should judge, in that jealous sort of way which resents generosity in anyone else. Probably tricky, in some respects—he's not the kind of person *I* could ever feel completely at ease with.

"A celebrity, however: unquestionably that. And Sir Lucas Welsh, whom among others he invited to this house-party, was equally a celebrity, in the same line of business. Never having seen Sir Lucas alive, I can't say much about his character, but—"

"I think," Fen interrupted, "that I may have met him once, at the time when he was designing the fourth quadrangle for my college. A small dark person, wasn't he?"

"Yes, that's right."

"And with a tendency to be nervy and obstinate."

"The obstinacy there's evidence for, certainly. And I gather he was also a good deal of a faddist— Yogi, I mean, and the Baconian hypothesis, and a lot of other intellectual—um—detritus of the same dull, obvious kind: that's where the ghost-vigil comes in. Jane, his daughter and heiress (and Sir Lucas was if anything even better off than Sir Charles) is a pretty little thing of eighteen of whom all you can really say is that she's a pretty little thing of eighteen. Then there's Mörike, the man I've arrested: thin, thirty-ish, a Luftwaffe pilot during the war, and at present an architecture-student working over here under one of these exchange schemes the Universities are always getting up—which accounts for Sir Charles's knowing him and inviting him to the house-party. Last of the important guests—important from the point of view of the crime, that is—is a C.I.D. man (not Metropolitan, Sussex County) called James Wilburn. He's important because the evidence he provides is quite certainly reliable—there has to be a *point d'appui* in these affairs, and Wilburn is it, so you mustn't exhaust yourself doubting his word about anything."

"I won't," Fen promised. "I'll believe him."

"Good. At dinner on Christmas Eve, then, the conversation turns to the subject of the Rydalls ghost—and I've ascertained that the person respon-sible for bringing this topic up was Otto Mörike. So far, so good: the Rydalls ghost was a bait Sir Lucas could be relied on to rise to, and rise to it he did, arranging eventually with his rather reluctant host to go down to the pavilion after dinner and keep watch there for an hour or two. The time arriving, he was accompanied to the place of trial by Sir Charles and by Wilburn—neither of whom actually *entered* the pavilion. Wilburn strolled back to the house alone, leaving Sir Charles and Sir Lucas talking shop. And presently Sir Charles, having seen Sir Lucas go into the pavilion, retraced his steps likewise, arriving at the house just in time to hear the alarm-bell ringing."

"Alarm-bell?"

"People had watched for the ghost before, and there was a bell installed in the pavilion for them to ring if for any reason they wanted help . . . This bell sounded, then, at shortly after ten o'clock, and a whole party of people, including Sir Charles, Jane Welsh and Wilburn, hastened to the rescue.

"Now, you must know that this pavilion is quite small. There's just one circular room to it, having two windows (both very firmly nailed up); and you get into this room by way of a longish, narrow hall projecting from the perimeter of the circle, the one and only door being at the outer end of this hall."

"Like a key-hole," Fen suggested. "If you saw it from the air it'd look like a key-hole, I mean; with the round part representing the room, and the part where the wards go in representing the entrance-hall, and the door right down at the bottom."

"That's it. It stands in a clearing among the trees

of the park, on a very slight rise—inferior Palladian in style, with pilasters or whatever you call them: something like a decayed miniature classical temple. No one's bothered about it for decades, not since that earlier murder put an end to its career as a love-nest for a succession of squires. What is it Eliot says?—something about lusts and dead limbs? Well, anyway, that's the impression it gives. A *house* is all right, because a house has been used for other things as well—eating and reading and births and deaths and so on. But this place has been used for one purpose and one purpose only, and that's exactly what it feels like . . .

"There's no furniture in it, by the way. And until the wretched Sir Lucas unlocked its door, no one had been inside it for two or three years.

"To get back to the story, then.

"The weather was all right: you'll remember that on Christmas Eve none of this snow and foulness had started. And the rescue-party, so to call them, seem to have regarded their expedition as more or less in the nature of a jaunt; I mean that they weren't seriously alarmed at the ringing of the bell, with the exception of Jane, who knew her father well enough to suspect that he'd never have interrupted his vigil, almost as soon as it had begun, for the sake of a rather futile practical joke; and even she seems to have allowed herself to be half convinced by the reassurances of the others. On arrival at the pavilion, they found the door shut but not locked; and when they opened it, and shone their torches inside, they saw a single set of footprints in the dust on the hall floor, leading to the entrance to the circular room. Acting on instinct or training or both, Wilburn kept his crowd clear of these footprints; and so it was that they came—joined now by Otto Mörike, who according to his subsequent statement had been taking a solitary stroll in the grounds—to the scene of the crime.

"Fireplace, two windows, a crudely painted ceiling—crude in subject as well as in execution—a canvas chair, an unlit electric torch, festoons of cobwebs, and on everything except the chair and the torch *dust*, layers of it. Sir Lucas was lying on the floor beneath one of the windows, quite close to the bell-push; and an old stiletto, later discovered to have been stolen from the house, had been stuck into him under the left shoulder-blade (no damning fingerprints on it, by the way; or on anything else in the vicinity). Sir Lucas was still alive, and just conscious. Wilburn bent over him to ask who was responsible. And a queer smile crossed Sir Lucas's face, and he was just able to whisper"—here Humbleby produced and consulted a notebook—"to whisper: '*Wrote it—on the window. Very first thing I did when I came round. Did it before I rang the bell or anything else, in case you didn't get here in time—in time for me to tell you who—*'

"His voice faded out then. But with a final effort he moved his head, glanced up at the window, nodded and smiled again. That was how he died.

"They had all heard him, and they all looked. There was bright moonlight outside, and the letters traced on the grimy pane stood out clearly.

"Otto.

"Well, it seems that then Otto started edging away, and Sir Charles made a grab at him, and they fought, and presently a wallop from Sir Charles sent Otto clean through the tell-tale window, and Sir Charles scrambled after him, and they went on fighting outside, trampling the glass to smithereens, until Wilburn and company joined in and put a stop to it. Incidentally, Wilburn says that Otto's going through the window looked *contrived* to him—a deliberate attempt to destroy evidence; though of course, so many people *saw* the name written there that it remains perfectly good evidence in spite of having been destroyed."

"Motive?" Fen asked.

"Good enough. Jane Welsh was wanting to marry Otto—had fallen quite dementedly in love with him, in fact—and her father didn't approve; partly on the grounds that Otto was a German, and partly because he thought the boy wanted Jane's prospective inheritance rather than Jane herself. To clinch it, moreover, there was the fact that Otto had been in the Luftwaffe and that Jane's mother had been killed in 1941 in an air-raid. Jane being only eighteen years of age—and the attitude of magistrates, if appealed to, being in the circumstances at best problematical—it looked as if that was one marriage that would definitely not take place. So the killing of Sir Lucas had, from Otto's point of view, a double advantage: it made Jane rich, and it removed the obstacle to the marriage."

"Jane's prospective guardian not being against it."

"Jane's prospective guardian being an uncle she could twist round her little finger . . . But here's the point." Humbleby leaned forward earnestly. "Here is the point: windows nailed shut; no secret doors—emphatically none; chimney too narrow to admit a baby; and in the dust on the hall floor, only one set of footprints, made unquestionably by Sir Lucas himself . . . If you're thinking that Otto might have walked in and out on top of those prints, as that page-boy we've been hearing so much about recently did with King Wenceslaus, then you're wrong. Otto's feet are much too large, for one thing, and the prints hadn't been disturbed, for another: so that's out. But then, how on earth did he manage it? There's no furniture in that hall whatever—nothing he could have used to crawl across, nothing he could have swung himself from. It's a long, bare box, that's all; and the distance between the door and the circular room (in which room, by the way, the dust on the floor was all messed up by the rescue-party) is miles too far for anyone to have jumped it. Nor was the weapon the sort of thing that could possibly have been fired from a bow or an air-gun or a blowpipe, or any nonsense of that sort; nor was it sharp enough or heavy enough to have penetrated as deeply as it did if it had been *thrown*. So ghosts apart, what *is* the explanation? Can you see one?"

Fen made no immediate reply. Throughout this narrative he had remained standing, draped against the mantelpiece. Now he moved, collecting Humbleby's empty glass and his own and carrying them across to the decanter; and it was only after they were refilled that he spoke.

"Supposing," he said, "that Otto had crossed the entrance hall on a tricycle—"

"A tricycle!" Humbleby was dumbfounded. "A—"

"A tricycle, yes," Fen reiterated firmly. "Or supposing, again, that he had laid down a carpet, unrolling it in front of him as he entered and rolling it up again after him when he left . . ."

"But the dust!" wailed Humbleby. "Have I really not made it clear to you that apart from the footprints the dust on the floor was undisturbed? Tricycles, carpets . . ."

"A section of the floor at least," Fen pointed out, "was trampled on by the rescue-party."

"Oh, that . . . Yes, but that didn't happen until after Wilburn had examined the floor."

"Examined it in detail?"

"Yes. At that stage they still didn't realise anything was wrong; and when Wilburn led them in they were giggling behind him while he did a sort of parody of detective work, throwing the beam of his torch over every inch of the floor in a pretended search for bloodstains."

"It doesn't," said Fen puritanically, "sound the sort of performance which would amuse me very much."

"I dare say not. Anyway, the point about it is that Wilburn's ready to swear that the dust was completely unmarked and undisturbed except for the footprints . . . I wish he weren't ready to swear that," Humbleby added dolefully, "because that's what's holding me up. But I can't budge him."

"You oughtn't to be trying to budge him,

anyway," retorted Fen, whose mood of self-righteousness appeared to be growing on him. "It's unethical. What about blood, now?"

"Blood? There was practically none of it. You don't get any bleeding to speak of from that narrow type of wound."

"Ah. Just one more question, then; and if the answer's what I expect, I shall be able to tell you how Otto worked it."

"If by any remote chance," said Humbleby suspiciously, "it's *stilts* that you have in mind—"

"My dear Humbleby, don't be so puerile."

Humbleby contained himself with an effort. "Well?" he said.

"The name on the window." Fen spoke almost dreamily. "Was it written in *capital* letters?"

Whatever Humbleby had been expecting, it was clearly not this. "Yes," he answered. "But—"

"Wait." Fen drained his glass. "Wait while I make a telephone call."

He went. All at once restless, Humbleby got to his feet, lit a cheroot, and began pacing the room. Presently he discovered an elastic-driven aeroplane abandoned behind an armchair, wound it up and launched it. It caught Fen a glancing blow on the temple as he reappeared in the doorway, and thence flew on into the hall, where it struck and smashed a vase. "Oh, I say, I'm sorry," said Humbleby feebly. Fen said nothing.

But after about half a minute, when he had simmered down a bit: "Locked rooms," he remarked sourly. "Locked rooms . . . I'll tell you what it is, Humbleby: you've been reading too much fiction; you've got locked rooms on the brain."

Humbleby thought it politic to be meek. "Yes," he said.

"Gideon Fell once gave a very brilliant lecture on The Locked-Room Problem, in connection with that business of the Hollow Man; but there was one category he didn't include."

"Well?"

Fen massaged his forehead resentfully. "He didn't include the locked-room mystery which *isn't* a locked-room mystery: like this one. So that the explanation of how Otto got into and out of that circular room is simple: he didn't get into or out of it at all."

Humbleby gaped. "But Sir Lucas can't have been knifed before he *entered* the circular room. Sir Charles said—"

"Ah yes. Sir Charles saw him go in—or so he asserts. And—"

"Stop a bit." Humbleby was much perturbed. "I

can see what you're getting at, but there are serious objections to it."

"Such as?"

"Well, for one thing, Sir Lucas *named* his murderer."

"A murderer who struck at him *from behind* . . . Oh, I've no doubt Sir Lucas acted in good faith: Otto, you see, would be the only member of the house-party whom Sir Lucas *knew* to have a *motive*. In actual fact, Sir Charles had one too—as I've just discovered. But Sir Lucas wasn't aware of that; and in any case, he very particularly didn't want Otto to marry his daughter after his death, so that the risk of doing an ex-Luftwaffe man an injustice was a risk he was prepared to take . . . Next objection?"

"The name on the window. If, as Sir Lucas said, his *very first* action on recovering consciousness was to denounce his attacker, then he'd surely, since he was capable of entering the pavilion after being knifed, have been capable of writing the name on the *outside* of the window, which would be nearest, and which was just as grimy as the inside. That objection's based, of course, on your assumption that he was struck before he ever entered the pavilion."

"I expect he did just that—wrote the name on the outside of the window, I mean."

"But the people who saw it were on the *inside*.

Inside a bank, for instance, haven't you ever noticed how the bank's name—"

"The name Otto," Fen interposed, "is a palindrome. That's to say, it reads the same backwards as forwards. What's more, the capital letters used in it are symmetrical—not like B or P or R or S, but like A or H or M. So write it on the outside of a window, and it will look exactly the same from the inside."

"My God, yes." Humbleby was sobered. "I never thought of that. And the fact that the name was on the *outside* would be fatal to Sir Charles, after his assertion that he'd seen Sir Lucas enter the pavilion unharmed, so I suppose that the 'contriving' Wilburn noticed in the fight was Sir Charles's, not Otto's: he'd realise that the name *must* be on the outside—Sir Lucas having said that the writing of it was the very first thing he did—and he'd see the need to destroy the window before anyone could investigate closely . . . Wait, though: couldn't Sir Lucas have entered the pavilion as Sir Charles said, and later emerged again, and—"

"One set of footprints," Fen pointed out, "on the hall floor. Not three."

Humbleby nodded. "I've been a fool about this. Locked rooms, as you said, on the brain. But what *was* Sir Charles's motive—the motive Sir Lucas didn't know about?"

"Belchester," said Fen. "Belchester Cathedral. As you know, it was bombed during the war, and a new one's going to be built. Well, I've just rung up the Dean, who's an acquaintance of mine, to ask about the choice of architect; and he says that it was a toss-up between Sir Charles's design and Sir Lucas's, and that Sir Lucas's won. The two men were notified by post, and it seems likely that Sir Charles's notification arrived on the morning of Christmas Eve. Sir Lucas's did too, in all probability; but Sir Lucas's was sent to his home, and even forwarded it can't, in the rush of Christmas postal traffic, have reached him at Rydalls before he was killed. So only Sir Charles *knew*; and since with Sir Lucas dead Sir Charles's design would have been accepted . . ." Fen shrugged. "Was it money, I wonder? Or was it just the blow to his professional pride? Well, well. Let's have another drink before you telephone. In the hangman's shed it will all come to the same thing."

Permissions Acknowledgements

'Secrets in the Snow' by J. Jefferson Farjeon reproduced by permission of David Higham Associates

'Blind Man's Hood' from *The Department of Queer Complaints* by Carter Dickson (Pan Books), reproduced by permission of David Higham Associates

'The Necklace of Pearls' from *Hangman's Holiday* by Dorothy L. Sayers, reproduced by permission of David Higham Associates

'The Chinese Apple' by Joseph Shearing reproduced by kind permission of Sharon Eden

'The Name on the Window' reprinted by permission of HarperCollins Publishers Ltd © 1951 Edmund Crispin; 'The Name on the Window' by Edmund Crispin reprinted by permission of Peters Fraser & Dunlop (www.petersfraserdunlop.com) on behalf of Worldwrites Holdings Limited